"My kis

Lucien ground out, annoyed as much with his own show of weakness as with her perfidy.

"You know they do not," she answered coolly.

"I think you are lying. Do not disappoint me, Alayna. You have always been brutally honest." He forced himself to relax his grip, sending her stumbling back. "So tell me, what may I do to please you?"

Her lip curled as she tilted her head to its familiar angle. "Why do you keep taunting me in this cruel game? I cannot wait to be rid of you! You will regret it when my mother arrives."

"And what do you imagine will happen then, my lady love?" Derision dripped from every word.

Alayna did not flinch. She leveled her emerald gaze at him and said, "Then I will see your head served to me upon a silver platter for what you have done...!"

Dear Reader,

March is the time of spring, of growth, and the budding of things to come. Like these four never-before-published authors that we selected for our annual March Madness Promotion. These fresh new voices in historical romance are bound to be tomorrow's stars!

Among this year's choices for the month is *The Maiden and the Warrior* by Jacqueline Navin, a heartrending medieval tale about a fierce warrior who is saved from the demons that haunt him when he marries the widow of the man who sold him into slavery. Goodness also prevails in *Gabriel's Heart* by Madeline George. In this flirty Western, an ex-sheriff uses a feisty socialite to exact revenge, but ends up falling in love with her first!

Last Chance Bride by Jillian Hart is a touching portrayal of a lonely spinster-turned-mail-order-bride who shows an embittered widower the true meaning of love on the rugged Montana frontier. And don't miss *A Duke Deceived* by Cheryl Bolen, a Regency story about a handsome duke whose hasty marriage to a penniless noblewoman is tested by her secret deeds.

Whatever your tastes in reading, you'll be sure to find a romantic journey back to the past between the covers of a Harlequin Historical.

Sincerely,

Tracy Farrell, Senior Editor

Please address questions and book requests to:
Silhouette Reader Service
U.S.: 3010 Walden Ave., P.O. Box 1325, Buffalo, NY 14269
Canadian: P.O. Box 609, Fort Erie, Ont. L2A 5X3

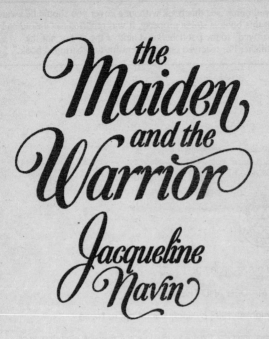

the
Maiden
and the
Warrior

Jacqueline Navin

Harlequin Books

TORONTO • NEW YORK • LONDON
AMSTERDAM • PARIS • SYDNEY • HAMBURG
STOCKHOLM • ATHENS • TOKYO • MILAN
MADRID • WARSAW • BUDAPEST • AUCKLAND

ISBN 0-373-29003-9

THE MAIDEN AND THE WARRIOR

Copyright © 1998 by Jacqueline Lepore Navin

Printed in U.S.A.

JACQUELINE NAVIN

lives in Maryland with her husband and three small children, where she works in private practice as a psychologist. Writing has been her hobby since the sixth grade, and she has boxes full of incomplete manuscripts to prove it. She decided to take writing seriously five years ago. *The Maiden and the Warrior* is the result.

When asked, as she often is, how she finds time in her busy schedule to write, she replies that it is not a problem—thanks to the staunch support of her husband, who is not unused to doing the dinner dishes and tucking the kids into bed. However, finding time to do the laundry—that's a problem.

Jacqueline would love to hear from readers. Please write to her at this address: c/o P.O. Box 1611, Bel Air, MD 21014.

To my parents, John and Patricia Lepore, for their unequivocal support and for teaching me an important lesson in real-life love.

To my children, Kelly, Lindsey and Lucas, whom I adore beyond imagining.

And to Mick, without whom I could never have done it. For your faith and strength and unfailing belief in me, I thank you. YOU are one in a thousand.

Chapter One

England, 1180

Lucien de Montregnier stood over his opponent, his sword pressed against the tender flesh of the other's neck so that the wicked edge raised a thin line of blood. Every fiber in his body was alive, humming with emotion, his mind exploding with a heady mixture of bitterness and joy. This moment, the one for which he had waited an eternity, was at last here. He had dreamed of it for so very long that the intensity filled him with exquisite, almost painful, rapture. His breath came in great gulps and a thunderous pulse pounded in his ears, but his hand was steady.

His captive said, "I will pay any ransom you demand."

De Montregnier grinned, feeling a surge of victory that left him trembling. "I have enough riches," he replied.

He could see by Edgar du Berg's sly expression that his mind was racing over possibilities. Patiently Lucien waited, watching every nuance of the other man's face, savoring the intoxicating knowledge that he had this man, his long-despised enemy, at his mercy.

Apparently du Berg decided on his tactic, saying, "Let

us bargain, like reasonable men. I have no quarrel with you. I do not even know who you are. You have attacked me without cause, and have fought for two days. You were very clever to strike the day after my wedding, when my men and I are the worse for the night's revelries. I can tell you, that is why it was so easy for you to breach the outer walls.''

"You are lazy, du Berg, and too sure of your tyranny. That is why I defeated you."

Edgar spread his hands out before him. "What I do not understand is your challenge to settle the matter between us. You had already won. Why did you wish to fight me alone?"

"Alone?" Lucien drawled, jerking his head to the tree line to his left. Beyond the clearing, Edgar had his men in hiding.

Du Berg tried to laugh. "You did not truly think I would come unescorted. What if it were a trap?"

"You excel at deceit, du Berg, but your men do not bother me as long as they do not interfere. In fact, I have made certain that they will not. You see, behind them, a bit farther into the woods, I have a few men of my own. Have you not wondered why they have not come to rescue you?"

The widened eyes and dropped jaw of his adversary were satisfying. Until this moment, Lucien realized, the bastard had not really thought himself in danger.

"You do not fight fair!" du Berg cried. He was losing the thin veneer of control that had fed his bravado thus far.

"I have merely evened the game. It is just you and I, as it should be, for the matter we have to settle is personal."

"Who the devil are you?" du Berg shouted. His voice cracked with strain.

Lucien held his gaze for an interminable period. Taking a deep, uneven breath, he said, "Do you recall the name de Montregnier?"

Du Berg's face registered puzzlement, realization and, finally, naked fear. "You are the boy. Raoul's son. I thought you dead."

"You should have gone with more reputable murderers," Lucien rasped. "They saw a second purse in selling me as a slave. They sent me to hell, du Berg, and like the demon I have been called, I have returned."

Du Berg tried to scrabble backward, but an increase in the pressure of Lucien's blade stopped him. Pinned, the man froze, his Adam's apple bobbing precariously as he swallowed. "Do you want Thalsbury back? I can give it to you."

"I will have it in any case."

"De Montregnier, listen to me," du Berg rushed, "I will restore your lands. Think on it—'tis a good offer. The days of anarchy are gone. King Henry will not appreciate his nobles killing themselves in revenge wars. You may do better to deal with me."

"I would just as soon deal with the devil," de Montregnier answered.

"Be reasonable, man! I can give you more alive than dead. You will never succeed—we have common law now in England."

Lucien's voice was very quiet, almost soft, as if he were imparting an endearment. "For my father's life, I will take revenge. And for my own losses, I shall take everything that was yours for my own."

Du Berg's mouth worked mutely, sweat pouring in riv-

ulets from his temples. De Montregnier saw the intent on
Edgar's face even before a single muscle twitched. In a
sudden move, he knocked aside de Montregnier's weapon
and lunged forward, reaching for a concealed dagger and
bringing it to bear with a flash of reflected light as bright
as a torch in the night.

Lucien stepped aside at the last moment and the deadly
thrust slashed harmlessly through the air. Du Berg staggered back, still brandishing his blade. He shouted, "What
do you want?"

"Your death," Lucien answered, and in one swift motion brought his sword up and then down again in a controlled arc. The blow landed with a satisfying *whack!* and
a spray of blood, nesting the blade deep into Edgar's side.

Eyes wide, he stared at Lucien. Not angry or afraid,
simply surprised. Then, slowly, pain flooded his features
and his eyes rolled up into his head as he collapsed.

Dispassionately de Montregnier yanked out his sword.
He stood very still for a moment, staring down at Edgar's
crumpled form. It was a long time before he turned away.

Edgar's men ran forward. Without a glance, Lucien
mounted, calling over his shoulder, "See that he is buried.
Have the grave blessed if you can find a priest that will
do it, but do not bring the body back to Gastonbury. The
barony is mine now, and I'll not have his rotting flesh
despoiling the land any longer."

Alayna of Avenford stood among the crowd gathered in
the bailey of Gastonbury Castle. It had been a long day,
one she had spent tending the wounded in the makeshift
infirmary set up in the chapel. After two days of war—
and that coming so quick on the heels of her disastrous
wedding—she was numb, but with fatigue or relief, she

was not sure. The news had come hours ago that the Lord of Gastonbury had been defeated by the leader of the attacking army, and, God have mercy on her, she was glad.

Edgar was dead, yes, and a blessing it was, but she had only to look at the faces of those around her to realize that her providence was their tragedy. These were the families of the wounded and the dead, facing an uncertain future at the hands of their conqueror.

A hand fumbled for hers, and she looked to see her nurse, Eurice. The older woman's face was lined with worry. "Sweetling," she whispered.

Alayna shook her head. "Rest easy. I am well."

Eurice's sharp eyes were troubled and searching. It was not difficult to surmise what was worrying her. "He did not harm me, Eurice. In fact, Edgar could not even remove his clothing, he was so far gone with drink. By the time he came up to the chamber, he was barely standing." It was true she was still a maid. Wed only a pair of days ago, already a widow, she had been spared the revolting ordeal of submitting her body to her despised husband. On their wedding night he had been too drunk, and the call to arms the following morn had saved her from Edgar putting the matter to rights. "Whatever this war brings to these poor folk, it has won me my freedom."

Eurice was not reassured. "I do not think it will be that simple, child. War rarely benefits the defeated."

Alayna shook her head, releasing dark tendrils of hair from its loose knot. "We are not of the defeated. I was forced into this marriage, and now God has provided an end to it. I do not belong to Gastonbury, but once again to myself. As soon as I can get a message to Mother, she will send her men to see me home."

"You are impetuous, child," Eurice scolded. "You

were Edgar's bride, and his enemy shall not overlook that.''

"But I was not!" Alayna insisted. "I am a virgin, still, and so no widow in truth, for I was never a wife." She narrowed her eyes as the faraway sound of hoofbeats began as a low, distant rumble. The victorious army was arriving. "And I *will* go home," she vowed.

The gates had been flung wide to admit the invading forces. Despite her brave words, Alayna clutched Eurice's arm and squinted in the glare of the late afternoon sun, surprised to note that her heart was racing and she was holding her breath as the soldiers appeared, seeming to be a solid mass silhouetted against the light. They moved forward as one, the sound of their approach rising to a steady thunder.

The amorphous form took on the shapes of individual men. Their leader rode on point ahead of the others, flanked by the mounted knights, then followed by footed soldiers who fanned out behind. They spilled into the courtyard, filling it and pressing the crowd back. When the last of the soldiers had come to a stop, the leader kicked his destrier forward so that he stood alone. All was silent as the people of Gastonbury and their conqueror regarded each other.

Alayna heard someone behind her hiss, "He looks like a devil!"

Indeed, his dark countenance and grim expression did put one to mind of a demon. He had a long mane of unruly black hair, matched by brows that hovered in a scowl over eyes of piercing black. They glowed like coals as he stared unwaveringly into the crowd. A close-cropped beard, cut so short it looked like only a few day's growth, ran along his jawline and chin, connecting to a thin mustache. His nose was strong, his cheekbones sharply defined. Upon his left cheek, high up next to his temple, a jagged scar showed starkly against his sun-darkened skin. It did not detract from his looks, only enhanced the sinister attractiveness he wore with ease. He was large, broad shouldered and hard muscled in the manner of a man taught well in the arts of war.

Alayna felt something curl tightly in the pit of her stomach, something within that reacted to the power of him, the unaffected handsomeness, the commanding presence and arrogant air that would make the most stouthearted tremble. Even if he had not ridden in front as was his due, she would have recognized him as the leader from the effortless mantle of authority he wore.

"I am Lucien de Montregnier," he announced without inflection.

There was a reaction to that name. A few people gasped and a low murmur echoed among the throng, but it died quickly. Alayna looked about, curious.

"Lord Edgar is dead," he said. "His defeat gives me this castle and all holdings tied to it." His voice held neither apology nor brag, merely stated fact. "As the victor in this challenge, I declare that I am your new lord until the justice of these events can be determined by a representative of King Henry, which is what the law commands."

Alayna watched his eyes scan the crowd, then settle on her. There was something there in that dark gaze that held her captive, even while she did not comprehend it. He frightened her in a different way than Edgar had. Of Edgar, she had feared his brute strength and unbridled cruelty, both of which she had sampled during their brief acquaintance. Yet, there was something far more dangerous in this man's look. She was unable to turn away.

"I will require an oath from each of you to be sworn to me, one by one. Those of you who will not do this will be held until the king's justiciar arrives. If justice does find me rightful lord of this burh, you will be given another opportunity at that time to make your choice but you will be fined. If you still do not wish to serve me, your properties will be assigned to one who will.

"However, if the king's man should disavow my claim and declare that I have no right to these lands, I will personally recompense any man who was unjustly imprisoned."

A chorus of incredulous murmurs rippled through the crowd. Lucien held up his hand to quiet them. "I do this to assure you that while I will tolerate no disloyalty, I will deal fairly with you. But I will not allow dissension to reign free, so I counsel you to think carefully before making your choice."

This said, he swung down from his saddle and moved through the crowd with a long stride. The populace hurriedly parted a path for him. Heading straight for the keep, he bounded up the steps, flung open the tall studded door and disappeared into the hall.

One of the other men, a handsome knight with shining blond hair, outfitted splendidly in a vest of well-kept chain mail and silver armor, called from his seat on his horse, "Your new baron awaits each of you in yonder hall." He grinned. His good looks were incongruous with the stained weapons he bore and the gore smeared over the fine silver plate.

From behind the knight who had just spoken, a large man loped into view. His long hair, of a shade so light it was almost white, fell past his massive shoulders. A Viking, that was plain to see by both his size and his coloring, but even that race of giants must take notice of this one.

"Agravar!" the other man called, laughing. "Lord Lucien will be most displeased if you frighten half of his new villeins to death!"

The Viking tossed his head in wordless response before he disappeared into the castle. The fair-haired knight cast a conspiratorial look to one of his fellows, apparently pleased with his jest.

"Dear Lord," Eurice breathed in Alayna's ear. "They look evil. That fair one has the handsome face of an angel, but 'tis Lucifer I am thinking he resembles! And what in the name of all that is holy does he find so funny? He mocks us, I think."

"Who among you is the Lady of Gastonbury?" that same knight called.

Faces turned toward Alayna. Stunned, she answered in a small voice, "I am."

The man dismounted. As he strode toward her, he smiled. "I am Sir Will, a mercenary of Lord Lucien's. He has asked me to bring you to him."

"Why me?" Alayna asked, casting an anxious look about her as if someone would step forward and protect her from this dreadful duty.

Sir Will shrugged. "You are the lady of the castle, are you not? You are to be the first to make your pledge to him."

Alayna wanted to refuse, feeling a strange premonition. How odd. She usually teased Eurice unmercifully for all of that one's belief in such notions. Yet, there it was—a fear inside her. She did not wish to confront this dark warrior all by herself. Looking to Eurice, the old nurse just shook her head.

Premonition or not, Alayna had no choice but to nod her acquiescence.

Chapter Two

Inside the keep, Alayna had to blink to adjust to the dimness of the hall. Other than the man pacing at the far wall, the vaulted chamber was empty. Being the social focal point of every castle, Alayna had never seen a hall without at least a dozen people about, engaged in various activities. It gave her an eerie feeling, this vast, barren place.

Or perhaps it was the way this Lucien de Montregnier moved, with a leonine grace that reminded Alayna of a caged animal, or a prowling beast searching for prey.

He stopped when he saw her, swinging around to arch an expectant brow. When she hesitated, he called, "Hurry up, then, come forward!"

She jumped at the sound of his voice echoing among the pointed cornices and hastened forward before she even realized she had obeyed. Catching herself, she slowed her steps, squared her shoulders and told herself to, above all, remain calm.

"Lady Alayna of Gastonbury," he said. His gaze flickered over her, and Alayna was at once taken aback at his bold, assessing glance.

Up close, he was more forbidding than he had been on

horseback. And more handsome. Even with the offensive proof of his day's chores staining the black chain mail— or because of it—he was an awe-inspiring sight. The chiseled features she had first noticed in the bailey were more appealing upon closer inspection—the straight, proud nose, the planes of his face, the firm set of his broad, sensuous mouth. Blood and grime streaked his face, and his hair was matted in some places, wild in others, giving him an untamed, almost feral look.

His face was unreadable, dark and scowling, while his eyes seemed to bore into her with black regard. It was perfectly reasonable, she told herself, that her knees seemed to suddenly go weak. After all, he was the warrior victorious, and she stood before him awaiting his pleasure. Anyone would be daunted in these circumstances, yet it was not like her. Even against Edgar she had stood in contempt, but this man…it gave her some disquiet to acknowledge he affected her like no other.

Seized with a sudden self-consciousness, she smoothed a stray lock into place, an unsuccessful venture as the tendril promptly sprang back into its original position. She forced her hand to her side, not wanting him to see her discomfort.

"Aye, I am," she answered, annoyed that her voice sounded meek. It took every ounce of courage to stand unflinching under the steady glare.

"As Edgar du Berg's widow, I will hear your pledge of fealty first."

A wild hope leaped to life. Was that all he wished? "Sir," she began, her voice stronger now, "I will gladly recognize any claim you make to this castle and its lands, or call you by any title you covet. It is nothing to me." She hesitated, gauging his reaction. He still regarded her with that uncanny calm. "I care nothing for Gastonbury, it is not my home."

"You are mistress of the castle," he said evenly. "How can you say that you do not belong here?"

Alayna swallowed hard. Her sharp eyes caught the whitening around the scar on his cheek, the only visible sign of his annoyance. "I was wed only two days, and I have been at Gastonbury for little over a month. My home is in London, where my mother is one of Eleanor's ladies."

He studied her for a moment. "And?" he rumbled.

"Since Edgar—my husband—is dead, then I wish to return to my family." He was so hard. Did he do it apurpose, she wondered, leveling that murderous glare to make her quake?

"You are not going anywhere," he said with finality. Again the easy mien of command took over as his irritation receded.

"But—" she began, hardly knowing what it was she would have said in objection. But his hand stayed her.

"It is not that I do not sympathize with your wish, my lady." A sardonic smile twisted his mouth, making him appear the scoundrel for a moment. "I do, in fact, understand the wish for freedom, perhaps more than you know. It simply does not serve my purpose to let you return to your former life, not just yet. You will indulge me in this, I trust, and when matters have been settled here to my satisfaction, we shall see about you."

He leaned against the hearth, striking an insolent pose that matched his manner. Pinned by his hard stare, she found herself wishing incongruously that she had taken the time to freshen her appearance.

Shaking off the thought, she ventured, "What matters?"

"I am most anxious that my work today has not been

in vain," he explained. A faraway look came to his eye that was chilling. "I have been waiting a long time for this day, and have come far to see it through. Defeating du Berg is only the beginning. I will take *everything* of his as my own."

Though unsaid, the implication that she was to be counted among his booty made Alayna stiffen her spine. She certainly had no quarrel with the man desiring revenge against Edgar du Berg. No doubt Edgar was deserving of it. But to include her was not fair.

"I do not understand," she said. "What does any of that have to do with me?"

"Are you unaware of your position, or merely think me daft?"

He was growing irate again, and the thought of his wrath directed at her nearly made her retreat. But Alayna was not without a temper of her own, and it rose now in her defense. "I have not called you daft. I only wish to leave."

"And go to Henry and plead your rights as widow of this burh? No doubt you are much put out by the loss of your husband. It would be advantageous for you if you could manage to win back what you have lost."

"I have no intentions of doing anything of the sort!" she objected. "I want nothing to do with this place. And make no mistake, my lord, I do not mourn *any* of my losses, least of all my husband!" With everything she had endured at Edgar's hands, this suggestion stung most. "I hated him, perhaps more than you did, de Montregnier. He tricked me into coming here and forced marriage upon me."

An insolent look lifted his brow in vague interest. "Trickery was du Berg's specialty. How is it you were duped?"

Taking a deep breath, Alayna steadied herself. She would have to explain it. "He sent a message telling my mother that he was a cousin of my father's and inviting us for a visit. My mother was anxious to get me away from court, for the intrigue and debauchery there troubled her, so she accepted. My father is dead these six years, you see, so she did not suspect Edgar's claim to be a relation was a lie. Once here, he set a trap with that vile creature who has the audacity to call himself a bishop, claiming my reputation had been compromised." She drew a breath, noting that he had the grace not to look bored with her explanation. "My choices were marriage or the stake."

"Now, is that not a bit dramatic?" he asked.

"Yes, I thought so, but the suggestion was bandied about just the same. You know, they can burn an adulteress. Edgar would have done it."

"Why did your family not intervene?"

"I was forbidden to write to my mother. She never knew."

His eyes narrowed to slits of black. "And what was the late Lord of Gastonbury's motivation for this great scheme?"

"My lands, you dolt!" she snapped, then immediately regretted it. This man was not someone to goad. He was not, however, perturbed by her insult; he didn't flinch. She continued in a calmer vein. "He sought me out because I was an heiress."

"A terrible tale," de Montregnier tsked insincerely, "but quite irrelevant, even if it is true. You *will* remain. At least until I can see what is to be done."

"You cannot do this!"

He smiled with audacious smugness, spreading his hands out before him. "Demoiselle, I have just killed your husband and defeated his army. I assure you I can do anything I wish.''

When she opened her mouth to protest again, he held up his hand, forbidding her entreaty even before it was made. "My lady, I have allowed you much freedom in expressing your displeasure. But I warn you not to try me." Again that superior grin appeared. "I have had a difficult day."

A slow burn of rage claimed her, banishing her previous fear and propelling her headlong into open rebellion. "You have no right—"

"But I do, lady, for all of Edgar's possessions revert to me."

"I am not a possession!"

"A modern opinion, but not one shared by our law," he drawled, watching her reaction through hooded eyes. "You were Edgar's property, and now you are mine. And since you will be here, where I can watch you, you can spread no mischief for me."

Alayna was speechless. So there it was. He thought her some kind of threat to him, to his hard-won prize. Hastening to reassure him, she said, "There is nothing I want here. I give you my word that I will do nothing to interfere with you."

The twitch of his eyes warned her of his displeasure and of a depth of rage she dared not tap. "I have no use for a woman's promises. They are not worth the breath required to speak them."

Her mouth worked in mute indignation as she struggled to find her argument. Then, a thought struck her suddenly, and she relaxed, returning his bitter smile.

"You have no need to worry. I am not Edgar's widow!"

Lucien gave a long sigh. "What nonsense is this now?

I am in no mood for your games. Now, will you pledge fealty to me, or will it be the dungeons?''

"You would not dare!"

"You do not know what I would dare, demoiselle," he threatened. He stood before her, legs spread, arms crossed before him with easy arrogance. He seemed to loom gigantic, impossibly immense and threatening. "And let me further warn you that I am not tolerant of the female sport of coyness and pointless intrigue. If you have something of import to say to me, speak it outright. My patience, what little I have for your sex, is wearing thin."

"The marriage contract is invalid," she stated, "for there was no consummation."

His brows shot up. "What lie is this? You say Edgar did not take you?"

Blushing deeply, Alayna forced herself to meet his incredulous stare. "That is what I said."

"I do not believe you," he challenged.

"'Tis true," she countered stubbornly.

Lucien raked a hand through his tousled hair. "Who knows of this?" he demanded, "Were not the linens displayed?"

"There was no time. Indeed, all assumed the marriage fulfilled, if they gave it any thought in the midst of being besieged."

"I returned to Gastonbury for one purpose only—to possess all which belonged to Edgar du Berg as payment for his crimes against my family. I intend to do just that. You were his beloved wife, so too shall you belong to me."

"But I told you, I am *not* the lady of the castle."

He gave no answer, but made a swift move toward her. She cringed, thinking he meant to strike her. Instead, his hand shot out and long, steellike fingers closed around her wrist.

"Wh—?" she began, but the objection was cut off by the hard jerk he gave, bringing her full against him. Stunned, she stared up at him, his face only inches from hers. For some strange reason, her gaze fastened on the clean, pale line marring his cheek, just under the eye. Unable to move, she was dimly aware of some distant part of herself urging her to protest this rough treatment. "Let go," she said softly, but it was without conviction.

His eyes flitted over her face for a moment before he turned away and pulled her behind without a word.

"Let go!" she said, this time more emphatically, when she saw which direction he was headed. Dragging her up the stairs, he was bringing her to the corridor that led only to the master's bedchamber.

My God, she thought with alarm, the knave meant to bed her!

Chapter Three

Lucien had no such intentions.

Hauling her along behind him, he went directly to Edgar's chamber. His chamber now. He knew the way well. He had played in this castle in his youth. His mother and he had come here every year when his father's service was due to his overlord.

It was here that he had made the tragic discovery, all that time ago.

Such an innocent mistake, his was. He had heard his mother's laughter, an unaccustomed sound to his young ears, and had been unable to resist. She had always been so cool, so removed, so indifferent to him. Yet he had adored her, thinking her the most beautiful of women and he had hungered for her love.

That was why he had been drawn to the laughter. It was so rare to hear it. Curiosity it had been. Deadly curiosity.

If not for that curiosity, his father would be alive. He himself would not have spent eleven years in hell. It was a guilt he had lived with for a long time. All because of curiosity and a spurned son's longing for a mother who was nothing but a spiteful and vain betrayer. It had taught him a painful, valuable lesson about life, and about women. That knowledge he had accepted, nay, embraced, as one of the truths that ruled his life: trust nothing which comes from a woman.

Flinging open the portal, he swept Alayna inside the chamber with him and slammed the door shut.

It did not look much different than it had that night. There was the glut of furnishings, the heavy tapestries, the lavish pile of furs on the bed...the bed, the same one in which he had seen them, entwined in a way that had shocked and embarassed him. A strange feeling constricted in his chest, but he pushed the rush of memory aside.

"Now, Lady Gastonbury," he said tightly, "you tell me Edgar, who is well-known in these parts for his taking of other men's wives, sadly neglected his own on the eve of their wedding? Is it possible that you did not suit? I doubt it, for though your tongue is waspish, your form is pretty enough. Pray tell, lady, how is it Edgar forgot you?"

"Hardly forgotten," Alayna snapped bitterly. "I am quite certain Edgar had every intention of taking advantage."

"Taking advantage? You were not wed?"

"Of course we were, but I told you it was trickery."

"One only has to consider Edgar's wealth to think perhaps you found your marriage advantageous, at least on some accounts."

She shrugged, doing a bad job of trying to appear unperturbed. "If it suits you to think me the eager bride, then I cannot dissuade you of the notion."

"Aye, I do indeed find it hard to believe Edgar did not avail himself of your...charms at his first opportunity."

"He passed out from the wine before he could..." Her face flooded with color. A pretty effect, Lucien thought sourly, meant to dissuade him from inquiring further. Oh, yes, his mother had been an excellent tutor on the cunning ways of women. This one would find her wiles wasted on him.

"What you are telling me is completely unbelievable."

"Do you think I care what you believe?" she flung. "You stand there and insist on what you want to be true, as if you can command it to be so because you say it. Well, you cannot command this, no matter how much it displeases you. I was not Edgar's wife! I am no part of this place and I demand that you release me at once."

Lucien regarded her coldly for a moment, trying to decide if she was lying. Her demands he ignored.

He went to the bed, standing between her and it so she could not see how his hand trembled as he lifted the covering of furs, throwing them aside as if scalded and forcing himself to look at the linen.

There were no signs of virginal stains there. When he turned back to her, his face was once again unreadable.

"'Tis most humorous to me that this bed, which has witnessed the taking of so many woman, goes unused on the night its master is to take the one woman to whom he has a right."

She was watching him carefully, not able to keep the faint gleam of victory from her eyes. She was waiting for him to concede. He was all at once struck by how incredibly beautiful she was. He had noticed before, of course. Even among the crowd in the bailey, she had shone like a jewel amongst cinders. Her eyes were a strange green, as deep and mysterious as the pine forests he had seen in the Northlands. They were almost luminescent, fringed with thick dark lashes and delicately arched brows. There was something about the shape of those eyes that made her look innocent and sensual at the same time. Her skin was flawless, smooth and the color of cream with a blush. Around the oval of her face, her hair was mussed, but the soft luster of sable was not subdued. Her mouth was pursed in anger now, but it was lovely despite her expression, full and lush, the kind that turned a man's thoughts away from the business at hand and prompted other, less worthy thoughts.

Suddenly he thought of how odd it was for him to be noticing all of this, and he scowled. "I am not troubled by the lack of proof of your virtue," he said softly, deliberately. "For all I know you were not a maiden on that night." He ignored her deep flush of rage. He was certain, of course, that she was indeed still a virgin. She was too obviously embarrassed by the whole matter to be lying on that account. "It makes no difference to me what these linens show, for I say you are the widow of my defeated enemy, and your disposition is mine."

Aghast at his words, Alayna snapped back at him, "How dare you, when you know the truth! I will tell the king's man about this, and others will back me, for there is no proof on those linens to credit your false claim."

Ignoring her, he drew a short dagger from his belt. She shrank away with a small cry. *Good Lord, she thought he meant to threaten her with it!* Deliberately he held the blade up as if to show it to her, then grasped the naked steel with his other hand and drew it across his palm. He did not flinch at the sting as the cut opened, welling up blood in a vivid crimson line. The wound was nothing. As she watched, horrified and stunned, he reached for the bedclothes and grasped them in his fist.

He waited for the moment of comprehension. With a

cry she leaped forward, snatching the cloth from his hand. Lucien released it, letting her see the bright red stain.

"Learn this, lady, for it will serve you well. I have waited upon my vengeance and planned carefully for it. No one, least of all a woman, will thwart me."

"You are an evil liar," she whispered vehemently.

"Perhaps. I have been called worse," Lucien replied. "Take care not to aggravate me, for I have no wish to punish you. Simply mind your place, and we will get along sufficiently."

She curled her lips in a derisive sneer. "You are more despicable than Edgar. If you think you will hold me here in disgrace and—"

"Be at ease," he drawled. "I intend no such thing. Your reputation will be safeguarded, for I have no nefarious intentions." A wicked impulse made him add, "Unless you so wish it."

She sputtered a moment or two, unable to give voice to the rage that choked her. God's teeth, she was magnificent! Finally she shouted, "I will see you pay for this. You are a liar and a brute, a cad of the first rank, a fiendish—"

"And you are a mere woman with nothing else but to accept that you have been bested. Why not concede gracefully? I have assured you I intend you no harm. Take heart, my fiery vixen, for I promise when the matter of the barony is settled with the king, we will see then what there is to be done with you. But until that time, you are far too valuable a player in the game to set free."

"I shall make you regret this," she promised hotly.

He laughed, a cold, sharp sound. Unable to resist, he pushed her a bit further. "'Tis regrettable to me that you insist on this senseless opposition." He took a step closer, lifting his unwounded hand to touch an errant lock curling gently at her ear. It was thick, the color of chestnut burnished to a high sheen and incredibly silky. He let the strand sift through his fingers.

Standing frozen, like an animal caught in a snare, she stared back at him with wide eyes. Her gaze flitted to his hand entwined in her hair, so close to her cheek. He had meant only a jest, a simple maneuver to intimidate her, but suddenly there was between them an enigmatic tension. She felt it, too—he could see it in her startled expression, in the stiff posture. And she was as taken aback by it as he was himself. He pressed on. "There is more worth in an alliance between us. Methinks it would bring much greater reward than this sparring."

Green eyes slid back to him. They seemed to glow with a light of their own, looking as clear and bright as a tiger's. She smacked his hand away. "You must be mad!" she snapped.

He genuinely laughed then, surprising her and even himself, for he was a man who did not laugh often.

She stepped away, anxious to put some distance between them. "That is something which will never be, for the choice to be enemies was yours. However, I will oblige you on that regard, and so I vow I will do my best not to disappoint. I shall be a worthy adversary."

With that, she whirled, presenting her back to him in an angry dismissal. Lucien couldn't keep his eyes from drifting down to notice the shapely curve of her hips.

"I know you mean every word of your promise to vex me. I have no concern about these threats, for I am hard-pressed to imagine any damage you would be able to inflict." He thought for a moment. "Still, many a woman has sewed trouble for a man for whom she harbored ill."

"And well do I know the selfish destruction of men!" she flung over her shoulder.

He smiled tightly. "You show yourself to be a credit to womankind, with your threats and foolish pouts. Do your best, demoiselle, for I am eager to meet your contest. But let me, in all fairness, issue a warning of my own. Know that there is little I will tolerate from you without punishment."

Alayna turned to face him again, her eyes narrowed to bits of emerald ice.

He cut off her brewing tirade. "As long as you behave rightly, I will not trouble you. You are quite safe from me, I assure you. Your beauty would taunt a saint, but I know too well the poison a fair face can hide. Beauty, my dear lady, is a lie to rob a man of his senses, make him weak. You'll not have that power over me."

They glared at each other, and to Alayna's credit, she held her counsel, lifting her chin in a mute arrogance—a gesture meant to annoy him, he was sure.

She was tempting. But he had not come back from the dead to tangle with a slip of a girl. Satisfied with her silence, he gave her a glowering nod of approval. He turned and left the room, shutting the door behind him with a deafening thud.

Alayna was left alone, breathless with overwhelming rage. This man—this Lucien de Montregnier—was incredibly obnoxious! So smug, so sure of himself. So certain he had won.

Well, he had, that much was true. And there was nothing she could do about it. Which was all the more infuriating. As she ruminated, Alayna paced within the confines of the chamber.

She kept looking at the bed linens. Of course, she

wouldn't tell anyone about de Montregnier's deception—
who would believe her? De Montregnier had been the only
one to see the unstained cloth. Now there was nothing to
prove her story. Angrily she ripped the coverings from the
bed. She would have liked to burn them, but that would
not have served her purpose any better.

At least he had promised he would not molest her, unless she was willing, he had said. Imagine the gall! Did he
think her some lusty chit who fell at a man's feet simply
because he was attractive? Did he think she would swoon
at the bawdy suggestions he had made, fainthearted and
hopeful for his favor? If he did, he was a fool! He was a
swaggering, conceited bully as far as she was concerned,
and she would find a way to thwart him!

Not looking where she was going, she almost slammed
into a large trunk. The place was teeming with them, oversize leather-bound chests of thick oak. And all of these
riches now belonged to de Montregnier. *His* castle, *his*
chambers, *his* food, *his* lands, *his* furnishings. He had won
himself a great prize. Everything, including her, it seemed,
belonged to him.

This fueled her anger. How she despised him, with his
high-handed arrogance!

She almost tripped again, this time over a thickly em-
broidered tunic. Edgar's. She flashed on the memory of
the other night in this very room when he had struggled
out of it, casting it aside carelessly in his eagerness for her.
The recollection brought a shudder. He had gotten down
to his leggings before he had succumbed to the effects of
his overindulgence.

It occurred to her that this, too, belonged to de Montregnier. Edgar's penchant for expensive clothing was
worth no small sum in itself. All part of de Montregnier's

booty. Alayna smiled at the thought of the dark warrior in Edgar's fancy garb. She hardly thought de Montregnier would favor the colorful and elaborately embellished garments. Good, it pleased her that this, at least, would be wasted.

Still he could sell them and fetch a goodly amount. No doubt de Montregnier would prove to be as greedy as his predecessor. The poor folk of the shire would certainly fare no better with the new lord than they had with the old.

It was then the idea struck her. A terrible, awful, wonderful, enticing idea that she told herself at once she could not possibly dare.

Could she? Immediately, and against all good sense, she knew she could. She knew she *would*.

Alayna flung open a trunk. She hastily lifted a few pieces and looked them over. Oh, yes, this was a delightful idea!

So he does not wish to be cheated of one thing of Gastonbury's? *Well, my Lord Conqueror,* she thought, a pleased smile stretching her lips, *I will cheat you at least out of these splendid clothes, and anything else that I can think of.*

Chapter Four

It was much later when Alayna entered the infirmary, her mind filled with plans for the trunks stuffed with Edgar's clothing, which now resided in her chamber. Her good mood did not last long.

Many of the men who had suffered serious injury in battle were now succumbing to the inevitability of their wounds. The place held the specter of death like a thick, pervasive stench. She moved about from one bedside to the next, feeling a numb horror at the sight of the dying, her high spirits now gone.

Eurice came to her side. "You look ill, Alayna."

Alayna sighed. "Not ill. I have been manipulated by Edgar and am now harassed by de Montregnier. Yet I stand here and see this carnage and realize that my problems are trivial compared to all of this death."

Eurice looked to the fallen men lying on their pallets. "Men make war, Alayna. 'Tis their way. They took their oaths to serve the Baron of Gastonbury, as their fathers did before them to all of the barons through the years, some good, some bad."

"Edgar was a wicked, evil man." Alayna shivered. "And I fear his successor is not much better."

Eurice raised her brow. "He seems fitting. Everyone is speaking of him, and not much bad. There is hope he might prove worthy. He gave a free and fair choice to enter into service, one he did not have to give."

"He gave nothing," Alayna snapped. "That speech was simply a pretty package for his ultimate insinuation into the barony. De Montregnier knows if he has the support of the vassals, Henry is unlikely to depose him. For the sake of peace and to preserve his own seat of power, the king will approve of the man who has the loyalty of the people. Tell me, did anyone decline his gracious invitation?"

Eurice shook her head. "Nary a one."

"Of course, who would? Why these poor folk would follow the devil incarnate after Edgar."

Eurice made a sign of the cross against the mention of the Dark One. Alayna smiled at her nurse's superstition.

"Eurice, I have found several trunks in Edgar's room. They contain an array of finery such as you have never seen. The extravagance is sinful, and it put me in mind of the need we saw in the village."

"Those poor wretches—" Eurice nodded "—what have they to do with Edgar's clothes?"

"He laid waste the countryside to fill his stores with food and wine, this castle with riches, those trunks with expensive garments and God knows what other extravagances. We must right that. Taking this treasure and redistributing it to the common folk might give some meaning to all that has befallen to me."

"Nay! It is thievery to take those things," Eurice

wailed. "They belong to the new lord now. He can have you swing from the gibbet for stealing."

Alayna smiled wickedly, savoring de Montregnier's anger should he ever learn of her scheme. "He will not kill me, though it would vex him sorely if he knew of my ambitions."

"Please have sense," Eurice continued, shaking her head in disapproval. "You were always headstrong, but now you must learn patience, discernment...."

"He is not going to release me, Eurice, he has made that quite clear. He thinks me a possession of Edgar's and therefore forfeit to him. He said he will not let me go until he is sure I can no longer be of use to him. Who knows how long that will be? I will not let him get away with it, not without making him regret it."

Eurice looked at Alayna aghast. Understanding dawned on her face. "You plot to steal Edgar's trunks to thwart this de Montregnier! 'Give some meaning to all that has befallen me.' Listen to you! You think to take revenge against him with this childishness."

"I am going to do it," Alayna said, her voice steady with determination.

A low groan diverted the women's attention. Seeing it was one of the wounded men, Alayna quickly abandoned their quarrel and rushed to his bedside.

She remembered him from yesterday when he was brought in. An older man, perhaps too old to fight, who had been conscripted by an unmerciful master. There had been some hope he would survive if his blood loss was not too great, but his health waned and now he was close to death. Pale and faltering, he was making a great effort to speak. "A priest," the man begged in a thin voice.

Alayna realized that he was requesting last rites to ease

his passage into heaven. "My God, Eurice, he seeks absolution!" she gasped. "He wants a priest. Fetch one, quickly!"

"There is no one here," Eurice whispered. Alayna stared at her disbelievingly.

"What do you mean we have no priests? We have men dying here, honorable men who deserve extreme unction to be absolved of their sins."

"The bishop commanded his priests to the abbey and Lord Lucien had no choice but to let them go. There are no longer any priests here."

"A friar, then."

"Alayna, there is no one!"

"He is dying," Alayna fretted. "He should be comforted." She looked down at the man. The poor soldier was in and out of awareness, barely coherent, muttering for forgiveness. She could not stand to see his agony. With a quick prayer for her soul for the blasphemy she was about to commit, she lowered her voice and murmured some Latin blessings she had memorized from daily mass.

Eurice stood in mute horror of the sacrilege she was witnessing but made no protest.

The mumbled words apparently convinced the man his request had been fulfilled. He reached out for Alayna's hand, crushing her fingers in his gnarled grasp. She did not let go even when the pain stabbed up her arm. His grip weakened and his face relaxed until he was at peace.

She sat in silent tableau with the man she had not known in life yet companioned in death, when a shadow fell across the bed. She looked up to see de Montregnier standing over her, flanked by two of his knights, Will and a youth whose name, she had learned, was Pelly.

Lucien stood with his feet braced apart and arms folded

over his chest, wearing the same smug look he had favored earlier. That, and her own unexplainable visceral response to his presence, made her suddenly angry.

"Come to view your handiwork, have you, good knights?" she snapped.

"Alayna!" Eurice gasped in reproach. Lucien did not seem to take offense.

"Was this one known to you?" he asked quietly.

" 'This one' has a name, though it is not known to me. My introduction to him was made after he had been mortally wounded by one of your men. Perhaps it was even yourself that felled him, my lord, for you surely did your share of the killing. In your enthusiasm for revenge against Edgar, you neglected to consider the faithful villeins who were bound to serve their lord and defend the castle. Good people, whose fault lay only in that they were required to serve your enemy."

Lucien gave her a hard stare. "I sought to minimize such tragedy. It is why I offered the challenge to Edgar to meet me face-to-face." His men gaped at him, apparently astounded that he had offered this. He usually explained himself to no one.

"Aye, after you slaughtered his fighting men!" Alayna accused.

"You have a quick tongue and a shrewish way," Lucien snarled.

Alayna narrowed her eyes. "Did you come here to gloat over your victory or disparage me? It poorly speaks of your character either way."

"I need make no explanation to you for being here. This is my castle, and this is my chapel. And these are my villeins."

"Chapel?" Alayna mocked. "I think not, for chapels

are made of prayers and alters, are they not? This place has none of that, for it is full of broken men and thin pallets made quickly with the haste of need. The stench of death fairly chokes you when you enter, instead of the sweet smell of incense and candles. A chapel, you say? Nay, 'tis a place of despair.''

"Well, it makes no difference either way, does it?'' Lucien's eyes glared. "'Tis mine! Need I remind you at every turn that I am now the lord and master here?''

"'Tis a grand testament to your prowess as a warrior that you see spread before you, but it does you little credit as our new lord and protector. 'Twas a deplorable performance in lordly protection you showed us yestermorn.''

Lifting a dark brow, Lucien eyed her sardonically. "This day has seen many noteworthy events, not the least of which seems to be this—a woman is making complaint about my 'performance.'''

Alayna colored at his innuendo and Will snorted momentarily before bringing himself under control. He was sobered by Alayna's indignant look. He smiled apologetically, but she only notched her chin higher.

She was angry enough to be reckless, yet she realized the hopelessness of arguing. She could never outmatch de Montregnier, for he would say the most outrageous things to shock and offend. With a sigh, she said, "Your rude comments are not necessary, my lord. I did not wish to antagonize you, though I find that, indeed, I seem to do so without much effort.'' She looked at the men lying in their humble beds, shaking her head distractedly. "Perhaps I have been a bit too vehement, but tending the fallen is not an easy duty. It grates on one as much as the loss of precious freedom.''

Lucien eyed her carefully, clearly suspicious this sudden

penitence might not be entirely sincere. When nothing else followed that last comment, he turned away, dismissing her apology without comment.

He spoke loudly in the vaulted chamber. "Those of you who were not in the bailey this morning, hear me." He repeated his offer of pardon in exchange for their pledge to honor him as their new lord. The terms were the same as before.

No one said a word. Alayna was silently glad, thinking that these men, embittered by their injuries and the death of their comrades, would refuse. At last, to see de Montregnier thwarted!

Then, unexpectedly, a murmur rose up as Hubert, a castellan of Gastonbury who was a good and noble man, rose slowly from his pallet. His wife, the Lady Mellyssand, caught Alayna's eye. Mellyssand had been the only person at Gastonbury who had befriended her, offering Alayna comfort when she was forced to marry Edgar. In the absence of Alayna's mother, Mellyssand had counseled her on what to expect in the marriage bed. Further, Alayna suspected Hubert had been largely to blame for Edgar's inability to consummate their marriage, for it had been the kind man's voice she had heard raising toast after toast to his newly wedded overlord.

Hubert limped to stand before de Montregnier. The room hushed. Hubert spoke. "Aye, I will accept you as my liege lord. And if the king's justice finds your claim false, I will commit my armies to serve any challenge you wish to make to that decision."

De Montregnier remained outwardly impassive, but after a moment's hesitation, or what could have been shock, he reached out a hand to firmly grasp Hubert's forearm in the gesture that men-at-arms shared as a sign of truce.

"I knew your father, Raoul," Hubert said. "He was friend to my own sire. He was a man of honor, a man who was admired. I had recognized your name, but I have been racking my poor brain these last hours to place your face, for you appeared familiar to me. At last I seem to have come up with some recollection. You were a lad, I remember, who was already showing remarkable skill with the sword. I recall your father's pride in you, and a bit of jealousy myself, for though I was older, I was not sure I was your better."

Lucien accepted this stoically, nodding. Hubert moved aside, calling the others to come forward.

When he had finished his business, Lucien came again to stand before Alayna. He raised his brows at her expectantly, as if to say what do you think of that?

"I see it pleases you to have your plan working so well," Alayna said.

"I am pleased. I have everything that I want."

"My mother taught me a bit of ancient wisdom," Alayna said lightly, "It teaches us the lesson that we must be careful what we wish for. We might just get it."

He nodded to her as if he understood, but Alayna did not know if he truly fathomed her meaning.

Chapter Five

Alayna would have never suspected that the new Lord of Gastonbury was feeling less than triumphant on this, the eve of his great victory.

As he made his way to the master's chamber, Lucien wondered at his strange mood. He was tired, which was understandable. He had barely slept in the two weeks previous to the siege—the anticipation had been too intense. Yesterday and today he had fought hard, fought with everything in him. Fatigue was natural, of course. But this day had brought him the realization of his great dream. After all was said and done, there should be something more than weariness for him tonight.

He raked his hand through his hair with a vengeance and exhaled. He should feel exhilarated! Sweet revenge was his at last. Yet the darkness inside him still burned as strongly as it ever had.

Certainly there was all that nonsense with the young widow. She was a minx, that one. She put him to mind of his mother. Well, actually she was not very much like his dame except for her sharp tongue, though it was not cruel and used to wound as his mother's had been, but rather self-righteous and angry. He did not really blame her, he could even empathize to a degree. He understood bitterness and the instinctive need for freedom; he had lived eleven years as a slave. But he was not about to let the soft lull of sympathy jeopardize his victory. The lovely Alayna was a powerful pawn in this gambit he played and, her feelings not withstanding, she was his.

He was suddenly struck with a clear image, one of eyes narrowed in contempt and a full, a pouty mouth set in a stern line, chestnut-colored hair swirling wildly around a sculpted face. He might as well admit, Edgar's virgin bride was much on his mind. She was a spitfire, defiant and irreverent, and he had an aversion to women of a head-strong nature. She did, however, have a vitality he found stirring. That was it! That was what troubled him so deeply tonight. It was that unanticipated response that disturbed him. It was so unfamiliar that it eclipsed his mood and dominated his thoughts.

Annoyed with himself, Lucien scowled. As he passed a timorous servant, she bobbed a quick curtsy and smiled, but the dark expression he shot her caused the poor woman to shrink away.

He was not a man who played the fool for women. He had never needed to. His status as Norse slave had done nothing to discourage female interest during the cold Viking winters. Summers, too, for that matter.

While he had lived under the savage rule of one of the Northland's most prodigious warmongers, his strength and skill in battle had distinguished him quickly as one of his master's fiercest warriors. First pressed into service as a foot soldier, he had eventually become so valued that old Hendron would not dare slither from his lair without his English slave, who soon became his finest warrior.

Whether due to this status or his withdrawn, aloof manner, he had been much sought after by the women of the lodge. This never fazed him, nor did he think much about the beauties who had graced his bed. They were only important for the short time they had amused him, and then they were gone.

Nothing and no one had mattered except the secret dream of revenge. Agravar, of course, had been his one friend, but no one else had penetrated his brittle constraint, least of all a woman.

He had moved amongst his comrades in arms, much envied for his skill both in battle and in attracting the amorous interests of women, yet set apart, encased in the isolated chrysalis of carefully nurtured hate. But it was not only that which had kept him apart. He was never their equal. Old Hendron had made sure that though his warrior-slave enjoyed sufficient freedoms to keep him content to fight for him, Lucien had never known a moment's peace from the brutal and humiliating treatment his master doled out to remind him of his lowly position.

That was the past, only the past. He knew it, but somehow it seemed impossible those years were behind him. He would feel differently inside if it were truly over, wouldn't he? Some spark of life, something to replace the vivid pain that had driven him thus far.

Maybe he would feel it in the morning, when he was rested and had a chance to put the rebellious Alayna out of his mind.

Lucien entered Edgar's chamber, closing the door quietly behind him as if afraid to disturb the reverent silence of the place. No ghosts now, he was relieved to note, none of the disturbing press of memories that had earlier afflicted him when he was here before with Alayna. He saw the bloodied linens in a heap on the floor and smiled at the mental image of her tearing them off the bed. The evidence of her temper amused him.

There was another feeling there, as well. He was surprised to find himself a tiny bit ashamed of his deception.

The entrance of a young servant girl interrupted his thoughts. She carried a tray heaped with meats and bread, which she placed on the table by the towering hearth. He had ordered the food sent up to his chamber, wanting to escape the hall. Having forbidden his band of mercenaries the typical amusements of the victorious—none of his new villeins were to be harassed or assaulted—he was content to have set Agravar and Will to watch over the proceedings. He himself needed no such diversions. Tonight, he sought solitude.

Lucien realized he was ravenous. "Girl," he called, making her jump. "Fetch some water and see it is well heated for me to wash."

Lucien ate quickly while she was gone. When the servant returned with the water, he stripped to his chausses in preparation for a quick bath.

Indicating the heap of garments he had worn in battle, he said, "Beat the dust from my clothes, and hang them on pegs to air. There is no time to wash them, but I'll not bear the stink of battle another day."

She gave him a quick look, taking in his state of undress. Lucien was not too fatigued to notice the womanly curve of her hips under the crude garments. He had thought her young at first, for her face was round and flushed. But at closer glance, she was indeed a woman full grown.

Finishing his bath, he toweled himself off. She was not as graceful as he was used to, but pretty enough. Perhaps the company of a woman would ease the unrest that plagued him, and banish the haunting thoughts of flashing green eyes and an arrogant chin tilted at him in defiance. Lord, just the thought of Alayna made his jaw work in irritation.

"What is your name?" he asked.

"Glenna," she answered in a small voice. There was something about her, something that made him a bit suspicious of her play of innocence.

"How is it you were chosen to see to me tonight?" he inquired. "Were you not afraid like the others?"

"How did you know the others were afraid?" she blurted.

He smiled tightly. Women were so transparent. The girl had probably volunteered, moving quickly to put her pretty little self before him in hopes of winning his favor. The status of the lord's leman was not a bad lot. The chosen woman shared her master's bed, and in return won prestige and privilege. This one was crafty, pretending shyness as a ploy to catch his eye.

As if sensing the end to her ruse, she met his gaze a little too boldly, allowing herself a better look at him. Lucien watched her eyes slide over him, gradually darkening with desire. Her face and form were lush, and by rights should have been inviting, but he could barely seem to summon any interest. He mentally compared her to a slimmer form more to his liking. Stubbornly he pushed the intruding vision of Alayna aside. "Did you serve the old lord?"

She understood well enough what he was asking. "Aye," she answered.

"You know what I seek?"

Glenna nodded, her eyes alight with anticipation. She

stepped forward to close the gap between them and placed her arms about his neck.

"I know, my lord. I will not disappoint."

Lucien felt his back stiffen in response. Even as she touched her lips to his, he knew he had made a mistake. He did not want her. He felt not the slightest stirring of desire at the voluptuous form pressed against him. He had wanted to quell the distressing preoccupation with another, but he was immediately aware that he would find no solace with this one.

He quickly reached his hands up to peel the fleshy arms from him.

Thinking he was breaking away to move to the bed, Glenna started for it, her hands already working to remove her woolen shift.

"Nay," Lucien barked, "I am far too tired to dally tonight. Leave me."

She looked startled, then smiled slowly as if in understanding. "If you are worried that your fatigue will afflict you, I will help you. Let me take—"

Lucien caught her outstretched arms by the wrists. "That is not my concern. I simply wish to be left alone."

"But you—"

"A passing thought, one I acted upon too quickly."

A flash of anger in her dark eyes surprised him. "Perhaps some other night, when you are better rested, you can call upon me. You will find me most willing...and accomplished."

"No doubt," Lucien murmured, presenting his back to her in dismissal.

"If there is anything else you require, at any time, call upon me."

She was annoying him now. "Go," he said curtly, not bothering to turn around.

He heard her leave and breathed a sigh of relief. He chided himself for his impulsiveness. Something about the girl disturbed him, something *wrong* about her. Or perhaps it was just his imagination. He was not normally given to flights of fancy, but then it was a strange mood he was in tonight. He grunted self-deprecatingly, wondering if perhaps he had gotten a knocked head in the fighting, scrambling his brains a bit.

But it was no injury that had driven him to consider the inadequate arms of the servant. As he flung himself atop the furs and let sleep descend, he knew that damnable witch Alayna had cast some sort of spell upon him. Never mind, he decided, no woman would divert him for long. He was much too disciplined for that.

He came awake with a start, instantly alert, knowing himself to be in a strange place. As memory washed over him, he relaxed back down amidst the furs.

His sleep had been dreamless. It had not improved his mood.

He rose from the bed, grimacing as his feet hit the cold stone floor. The chill of the lingering winter was bracing and he could see his breath like a puff of smoke in the air. He crossed to the hearth to stoke the fire, getting the blaze going before pulling on the thick woolen tunic he had worn yesterday. Abstractly he fingered the holes in the well-worn material. He could afford much better now. He should see to it when he found the time.

A sound at the door made him swing around, his hand darting to take hold of his sword lying across the table.

He had it unsheathed and at the ready before the intruder crossed the threshold.

It was Glenna. "I thought you might need some assistance this morn," she purred, not at all daunted by the gleaming steel he held. "Would you like some food sent up? Or perhaps some help in dressing?"

Lucien put down his blade. "Whatever I want, I will see that it is done myself. Go to the kitchens and ask if they can make use of you there."

Glenna smiled, ignoring his order. "Do you not have use for me here?" Her hand came up to lightly touch his chest.

He grabbed her hand and pushed it away. "Do not let me see you in my chamber again."

She paused, as if considering whether to obey. His anger rose, blinding him for a moment. Alayna had challenged him, but with her he had understood it. She had fought him as one who is backed into a corner. This servant's defiance caused his temper to flare almost out of control.

If she had not had the presence of mind to leave him, he might have done something rash. He had never lifted a hand to a woman, no matter what his opinion of that sex, and it would do his purposes no good if he began his reign here by beating one of the servants.

Lucien laid his weapons out neatly on the table, ready to be cleaned, and finished dressing. A footfall behind him alerted him to a new presence. He lifted his head to see Agravar standing just inside the doorway.

"So you decided to quit your lazing about and rise at long last," Agravar said with a smirk. "Your late morning has nothing to do with that pretty piece I just saw leaving here, I trust."

"'Tis just sunrise now," Lucien grumbled, "and nay,

that inane servant did not stay with me last night. You
know me better.''

"I thought I did," the Viking answered mysteriously.
He looked about the room, appreciatively eyeing the ornate
furnishings and elegant appointments. "I see you have
wasted no time in doffing the crude ways of the soldier in
favor of this lordly elegance.''

Lucien followed his gaze. The furnishings were numerous, large and thickly carved, hardly suited to his Spartan
tastes. A thought crossed his mind as he considered the
room. Something was different. Now that he saw it again
in the light, as he had the first time yestermorn, it seemed
somehow changed. As if something were missing. With a
shrug, he abandoned the thought. He turned to Agravar,
giving him a grim look.

"It will need to be stripped of these odious reminders,''
he stated, indicating the incompatible finery.

Agravar grew serious. "I hope it did not disturb your
sleep to be in this place. I know well how those memories
torment you. I thought perhaps you would wait before taking on this particular one.''

Lucien shrugged. "It was not difficult, actually.''

Agravar chuckled. "There is nothing like the diversion
of a woman to ease a troubled night. A willing maid can
make all the difference when a man has a restlessness in
him.''

Lucien shook his head at his friend. "I did not have the
damnable girl!''

Agravar laughed. "I believe you. I know your habits. I
would think that another would be more to your taste.''
He crossed to the window, easing open the shutter to peer
into the courtyard below. The castle was already bustling
with activity as the serfs hurried to complete their morning

chores. "One cannot help but wonder how the widow has fared this night."

"More likely she laments the loss of the riches Edgar brought her." Lucien shot him a scowl. "Do you bring news?"

"Aye. I have dispatched the scouts to the areas you assigned. The landholders return to their fiefs soon."

"Did you instruct the seneschal to prepare the written accounts of the household?"

Agravar nodded.

"Good. I want the entire contents of the castle inventoried, and the village, as well. Also, set up a forum where disputes can be brought before me. I want to establish justice quickly so that none can take advantage of the confusion to better his own lot."

"You cannot prevent that," Agravar said abstractly. Lucien was aware the Norseman was observing him.

"What is it?" Lucien snapped.

"What?"

"There is something troubling you. Out with it. There have never been any secrets between us."

Agravar paused, shrugged, then settled into one of the hearth chairs. His hand played with the hilt of a knife on the table. Lucien saw it was the dirk he had used to slit his hand yesterday.

"You seem no different, Lucien. There is no less bitterness in you this day than all of the others since I have known you."

Lucien's head shot up as he leveled a wary glare at Agravar. His companion continued unperturbed. "It went as you planned. Our army met with little resistance and you yourself dispatched Edgar. You acted with honor and have won all you sought. Yet I cannot help but wonder if it is all truly settled.''

Lucien sat on a footstool by the raised stone of the fireplace, taking up his sharpening stone and one of the weapons. He drew the steel across the stone, making a cold, ringing sound. It was an activity familiar and calming.

Agravar said, ''Nay, I see that it has done little to quell the demons that plague you. Nor mine, old friend.''

Lucien shrugged, a casual gesture belied by the tension in his voice. ''There is still much to be done. This is not over. My dame remains untroubled, safe in her convent. Is that not the greatest jest, Agravar—my mother has made her home these last eleven years with a gaggle of nuns?'' His expression looked grim, not in the least amused. ''I must reckon with that woman when the time is right. Perhaps therein lies my peace.''

''Peace,'' Agravar mused. ''Is such a thing possible for us? Or are we too used to the killing to rest now that all we have sought is within our grasp at last? Why do we not take it, then, and be satisfied?''

Lucien shook his head in honest bewilderment. ''Domesticity, Agravar. Perhaps it does not suit us. What a stagnant prospect—to be a country baron without battle to stir my blood.'' Nodding, Lucien's confidence in this explanation grew. ''Aye, that is it. I fear this soft life I have won for myself. This is what ails me.''

''I have been thinking,'' Agravar said. ''Perhaps the time for hate is over.''

''The time for hate is over,'' Lucien repeated in a soft, almost wistful voice. He eyed the blade he had sharpened, savoring the clean lines and purity of form in the simple weapon. The incongruity of honing the razor-sharp steel while having this conversation struck him, and he smiled to himself. He sheathed the dagger and took up another. "How does one learn to live without the very sustenance of survival?"

Agravar paused. "Perhaps we cannot. But I tire of the constant battle. It would suit me, I think, to put aside the ways of war and settle into a moderate life. To mount these broadswords upon the wall and look on them as ornaments, telling the tales of the battles we had once waged to our children, and their children after that."

Lucien grimaced at the picture, then eyed the array of weapons that awaited his attention. No ornaments, these, they were the tools of his trade, the only life he knew.

Agravar spoke again. "I am the bastard son of a Viking raider, a symbol of my noble mother's disgrace, despised before I was even born." There was no emotion in his voice, it was a tale he had talked of often to his friend. "When I traveled to my father's lands to meet my sire, I thought that finding him would bring me peace. You know as well as I how that turned out. Hendron was nothing but a vicious warmonger, no father for a son to admire. I found instead a brother, for we share the common bond, you and I. I, like you, used rage to fashion myself a warrior. I never thought of a life other than war. But my bitterness has run out. I am tired of this cursed life as an outcast. I weary of the fight."

"You wish to go to the soft ways of country squire, do you, friend?" Lucien scoffed. "Well, I am not done with my vengeance. Peace will come when I have finished what I have set out to do. When Gastonbury is mine by Henry's decree, and my mother is groveling at my feet, then I shall rest easy."

Lucien wiped the last of the dried blood from his sword

and carefully placed it in the scabbard. When he was done, he faced Agravar.

"If not for you, I would not have come this far. You gave your own father up to me, and that is a favor I shall not forget. But my grudge will end for me when it will, Agravar. Seek your lot elsewhere if you must, but the time for gentle living is not yet here for me."

Agravar shook his head. "I will remain."

Lucien nodded stiffly and preceded the Viking out the door. As they walked into the hall, they spoke tactfully of other matters.

"I have ordered the kitchens to prepare a celebration this eve, not of victory but of new loyalties and fealty ties. A calmer feast than was seen last night."

"Tonight is soon," Agravar considered.

"I want it so, before the castellans who were here for Edgar's wedding leave for home. A feast may do much to heal the breach."

Agravar gave him a long look, then smiled. "Perhaps, old friend, you are more suited to this life than you believe."

Chapter Six

Lucien wore his usual dour expression as he took his seat at the head table to break his fast. He ordered the ornate canopied chairs Edgar had used taken away and seated himself on a plain stool.

The faces of the others in the hall, a mixture of his soldiers, who were looking bleary-eyed from last night's revelries, and the guarded expressions of the Gastonbury folk, stared back at him. His brows lowered and they looked away. Hushed conversation buzzed like a faraway hive, for the mood was full of expectation.

Alayna entered. Their eyes locked for a moment before she turned away to sit at a trestle table with a few of the knights' ladies.

She looked beautiful this morning, more so without the disheveled hair and grime-streaked face of yesterday. Dressed plainly, she wore a simple gown of soft fawn with trailing sleeves to reveal a cream undertunic delicately embellished with a touch of gold thread. It was much less a show of finery than most in her position would favor. Her hair was caught demurely in a net snood, with some renegade tendrils twirling seductively around her face and

neck. She wore none of the makeup that was making its
way into fashion lately and the chain of gold links that
encircled the gentle flare of her hips was her only ornamentation.

Could it be she was unaware that this simplicity only
added to her allure? Lucien wondered, then decided no. It
had been his experience that everything a woman did was
calculated for effect. Certainly this woman wanted to appear—what was it about her?—harmless. And that could
hardly be so. She had made her intentions toward him
clear, announcing herself plainly as his enemy. Thus, he
could only assume she was trying to appear modest for a
reason. His instincts were alert, warning against her innocent facade. But what was it she was contriving?

Alayna was aware of Lucien's covert scrutiny. She
could almost feel the touch of his eyes, making her nervous
though she was determined not to let it show. Keeping her
own gaze carefully averted from his direction, she made a
point to relax, pretending to enjoy the company of her
companions, a group of gossipy knights' ladies whom she
found boring at best, and at worst irritating.

"He does not wish us to rebel," one woman whispered.

"Well, if he wishes Henry to favor him, he needs to
demonstrate he can keep the peace, keep control," a young
blonde added, blushing at the surprised looks her insight
won from the others. "That is what Geoffery says anyway."

"He is not afraid of rebellion, Anne. Your Geoffery is
correct, he does it for his ambition, not of fear. What has
he to fear? He has already defeated us."

Anne leaned forward, casting a sly look over at the dais.

"Well, if he is looking for a welcome, he should come see me."

"Him? Did you not notice Sir Will? He could make me swoon with just a word!" said another with a roll of her eyes.

An older woman scoffed, "You would swoon at a word from old Gerald!"

Alayna forced herself to laugh along with them, though she was having trouble attending to their conversation. She was tired, having spent the better part of the night going through Edgar's trunks, now safely deposited in her chamber. It was difficult deciding how to best make use of them. She had the sumptuary laws to consider. A peasant was not allowed to wear certain materials or colors reserved for the nobility and clergy. But Alayna had no choice but to interpret the dress code guidelines broadly. She was determined the stolen garments would serve her intended purpose, and the peasants of the shire would sport a king's ransom worth of finery.

Lucien continued to glower at her from his seat on the dais. Her laughter sparkled louder.

"Lady Alayna," a voice said, and she looked up to see Sir Will smiling at her. The ladies around her twittered, offering their anxious greetings to the knight. He gave them a cursory nod. "You seem to be passing a pleasant morn."

"Pleasant enough," Alayna answered. She liked him. He was an outrageous flirt, but she sensed in him a kindness, as well.

"May I sit with you?" Will asked. Alayna nodded. He sank beside her on the bench. "It is good to see you doing so well this day. You seem none the worse for the trials of late."

"Really?" she answered.

His eyes stared warmly into hers, and Alayna realized he was singling her out for his attention. The other women stared at her with envy.

"Well, I suppose no one expects everything to return to normal immediately," Will said, "but laughter is a good medicine."

A new voice cut in, drawing their attention. "Indeed, your merriment is intriguing, my lady. Newly conquered peoples rarely can be heard laughing so soon after their defeat. Please, share it with us so we may all enjoy along with you."

Alayna's head snapped up. It was, of course, de Montregnier, and he did not look in the least interested in sharing her amusement. His voice was even enough, but his expression was daunting. It was as if he sensed she had put on the show of gaiety to gall him. By the look of him, she had fairly succeeded.

The women sat in tense silence.

"'Twas only a diverting story that made me laugh, for 'twas most ridiculous," Alayna said, and shrugged.

"Please, demoiselle," he urged, "let us in on the hilarity."

She narrowed her eyes. "'Twas nothing, I said."

"But I insist," he countered. "If you keep eluding the question, I will be left to think that you have been caught discussing *me*." His gaze matched hers, brilliant black and hard.

She realized he was bullying her apurpose, but she could not keep herself from snapping, "Not you, but of a completely different man. The jest was of a lowborn cur who captures a castle and its people, then struts about as its lord. 'Tis a most funny anecdote."

She heard a sharp intake of breath from someone, and immediately, she knew she had gone too far. A quick glance about confirmed her fears. Pelly, who stood behind his lord, looked positively apoplectic, and even Will's steady smile had faded. The only one who did not look stricken was de Montregnier himself.

"How delightful," he purred, his eyes telling a different story. "When I have time in the future to waste on the obtuse meanderings of a woman, I would like to hear more about it. The circumstances of your comedic tale are not dissimilar to my own. Oh, had you not realized? I wonder if this poor fellow is also plagued with witless women who laze about grazing endlessly at the morning meal." He let his insult settle over her before offering a small, diabolical smile. "Have a pleasant morn, my lady. Will! Pelly!"

In the wake of his departure, Alayna became aware of the awkward stares of the women around her.

"My," said Anne, "you certainly made an impression."

The women erupted in laughter. Alayna pulled herself up straight. Rising, she excused herself, hearing the poorly repressed snickers hissing behind her as she went.

A short time later, she was back in her chamber with her nurse, still smarting from de Montregnier's stinging words.

"Ah, look at this tiny piece," Eurice exclaimed, holding up a small tunic she had fashioned for a tot.

"Methinks it needs some ermine," Alayna teased, placing a strip of the stuff around the neckline.

"Lord have mercy on us—serfs in ermine! The new master is sure to string us up if he sees that!"

"'Tis well he does not know what we are about, for

surely this fur would wilt under his dour sulk." Alayna shrugged.

Eurice looked at her curiously. "Do you not think he is handsome?"

"Are you daft?" Alayna bristled. "Handsome? With all of that scowling and glowering, one can barely distinguish his features. Besides, I was too angered to notice—I swear I could hardly see for all of the red before my eyes."

"'Tis difficult not to notice. Even if his features were not fine, he would be appealing for his proud bearing. Did you not even notice how tall and broad he was? How strong he looked?"

Alayna wondered what game her nurse was about. Her voice dripped with sarcasm. "Aye, Eurice, it did occur to me when he was dragging me into the chamber to wipe his own blood on the bed linens that he was indeed very strong. Then, later, as he was insulting and threatening me, I was quite impressed with his good looks."

Eurice's smile was cryptic as she concentrated on her stitching. "Yet you did not notice his face?"

"He is too often frowning," Alayna snorted.

"The man is haunted," Eurice said.

Alayna considered this for a moment before she stabbed her needle into the cloth once again. "Perhaps. Now he has earned himself one more ghost to plague him."

They fell silent, working until it was time for the midday meal. Alayna was relieved to see that Lucien was not in the hall with the others. She was, however, annoyed to learn that preparations were being made for a feast that evening. Everyone was talking excitedly about it, half in shock at the gracious way their new lord was conducting his first days in power. The people of any castle were used to war, it was a staple of life and they accepted their lot with bland resignation. Now there was tremendous relief after the ironfisted reign of Edgar. It irked Alayna to see how easily de Montregnier was winning approval.

After she had eaten, she visited the infirmary and was heartened by the improvements she found, especially Hubert, who was recovering nicely. When she had seen to her self-appointed chores and was satisfied that she was no longer needed, she returned to her chamber and took up her needle again.

Alayna decided not to attend the evening's festivities. Against her nurse's protestations, she reasoned, "I shall simply send down word to him of illness or fatigue, some excuse. I'll not subject myself to his onerous company again."

"Alayna," Eurice warned, "do not tempt him!"

"Nonsense, he will not mind. He hates me as much as I do him. Even if it does vex him, de Montregnier would not be so coarse as to make an issue of it."

Eurice left her with a disapproving look. Alayna changed into a soft linen tunic, curling up by the blazing fire to sew before retiring. It felt good to put the aggravating de Montregnier out of her mind. Without warning, her peace was interrupted by the abrupt thud of her chamber door being flung open. Terrified, she sprang to her feet.

It gave her no relief to see that it was de Montregnier who stood in her doorway, his face like a thundercloud. He pinned her with his dark glare for a moment before he spoke. "I just received word that you would not be joining us. Your message said you were ill. Odd, you seemed quite fit earlier today."

His voice was a low growl, snarled from between clenched teeth. It took Alayna a moment to find her voice.

"Aye. I do not feel well. It is probably only fatigue, but I beg your pardon from the evening."

"But I do not grant pardon, lady, for you seem to have recovered nicely from whatever mysterious ailment has afflicted you. In fact, you look the very essence of health."

He let his eyes travel slowly as if assessing her fitness. His languid perusal made Alayna instantly aware of her flimsy shift, no doubt rendered almost transparent in the light of the fire. Blushing hotly, she turned away, grabbing her dressing gown. When she had put it on, she turned to face him once again.

"Your manners are abominable, de Montregnier, as usual, though I do not know why I would expect a lowbred cur such as yourself to ever demonstrate anything but the rudeness you so often favor."

Lucien raised a brow. "That is the second time you have said that. What makes you think that I am lowborn?"

Alayna scoffed at him with a harsh laugh. "It is obvious that you are unused to gentle company. I think you enjoy playing the rogue to shock and offend. I know nothing of your breeding, and indeed, have learned that right of birth is rarely an indication of character."

"Take your late husband, for example," Lucien said smoothly.

Ignoring his comment, Alayna continued tersely. "Your behavior speaks of your ignorance, all matters of ancestry behind."

"Aye, 'twould no doubt amuse you to learn of the history of my ancestors," Lucien said darkly.

"You act the blackheart, and then bray like an ass when called one. You are a puzzlement, de Montregnier. Were I at all interested, I would find your behavior quite curious.

You are terribly inconsistent—almost as fickle as a woman!''

Her barb hit home. His face grew dangerous. "As for behavior,'' he snarled, "yours leaves much to be desired. Your lies and deceptions to avoid me are hardly admirable, though I expect no less from a woman. However, you are the widow of the late lord, and as such I require your presence at the feast. You look well enough to me. Your previous incapacitation seems to have been resolved. Now, dress promptly and join us in the hall. I will wait the meal for you.''

"Nay!'' Alayna exclaimed, incensed at this arrogant command. "I will not play the lady of the castle when you sit as its lord.''

Lucien moved forward with the unexpected swiftness of a cat until he stood just before her. She had to tilt her head back to meet his glaring look. Up close, she could see his eyes were a clear brown with dark lashes, unusually long for a man. Trying to look undaunted, Alayna forced her chin up.

"Do not play this game again with me, lady, for you know well you cannot win. I will have your presence in the hall this night at my side. Think on the privileges you now enjoy, for I have been more than generous in allowing you your freedoms. These are arrangements I can easily alter.''

Her eyes widened at this threat. Before she could muster a suitably caustic reply, he spoke again, his eyes softened as a teasing light appeared. "Your rebelliousness surprises me. It is most foolish. Though you have many faults, stupidity does not seem to be one of them. You would do well to try and please me. Is that not what your sex excels at? Cultivating power by weaving charm about a man, much like a spider wraps its prey in her web before devouring it. And who knows, demoiselle, perhaps you will not find my favor all that onerous.''

"What makes you think I would ever want the least favor from you?'' Alayna gasped. "You men think so highly of yourselves, assuming any woman would be flattered to be graced by your attentions. Well, some of 'my sex' care not a whit about pleasing a man. Make no mistake, your good graces are the furthest thing from my desire. What I seek is to be as far away from your arrogant, odious presence as I can get.''

She lowered her voice as she continued in a tone of solemn avowal. "I will wait on King Henry's decision, but I have no doubt that day will win my freedom, and when I am free, I will spare you no thought other than an occasional shudder when I think of you. Now get yourself from this room, for you have no authority over me that I recognize.''

Lucien regarded her dispassionately for a long moment before he stepped away. He went to the door and, just as Alayna was feeling triumphant, called over his shoulder in a flat tone.

"Keep to your solitude, then, cold lady. I see now that your waspish tongue and shrewish disposition would sour our celebration. My guests and I will do better to make merry without you.''

Alayna stood openmouthed at this statement, stunned with the impact of his words. She was unable to make any reply as he stalked out of the chamber, closing the door behind him with infinite gentleness.

Chapter Seven

The room was enveloped in silence, the only sound the soft echo of his fading footsteps beyond her chamber door. She stood alone, unable to move, with his last words echoing in her head.

Dear Lord, he was unbearable! How dare he forbid her from the celebration!

Restless, she began to pace in front of the hearth.

How could he stand there and have the gall to suggest she curry his favor? Was he mad? He must be, or too intoxicated with his newfound power to have any sense.

She turned on her heel and stomped back toward the door.

He was a cold, selfish, unfeeling brute. He was so full of himself, so impossibly arrogant that it was amazing he had not exploded with self-importance already.

Picking up a carved ivory brush, she flung it at a wall as she circled back to the window.

God's mercy but she hated him. He was almost pitiful, so obvious in his attempt to goad her into bending to his will. She was not deluded by his ploy. Of course, he was counting on her anger to prod her into going down to his

damnable feast. Well, he was mistaken if he thought she
would be so easily duped.

She flounced down onto the window seat, looking with
unseeing eyes out onto the bailey. It was a familiar perch,
for she had favored this spot during the long, dark days at
Gastonbury before de Montregnier's arrival.

Seated here again, she was struck with the vivid recollection of the despair of those times. Could it truly have
been only days ago? It seemed a lifetime. Dear Lord, at
least she was no longer with Edgar.

It was an incongruent thought, but it was nonetheless
true.

She loathed de Montregnier with his high-handed arrogance and his quick-witted barbs. Yet she was without a
doubt much better off for his having defeated Edgar and
taken over Gastonbury. Brutal and insensitive he was, but
she could not honestly hate his prowess on the battlefield,
for it had saved her from the unthinkable fate of living as
du Berg's wife.

De Montregnier wished to use her for his ends, but he
had never really caused her any damage. All he had done
was detain her. True, he was a dishonorable liar and a
ruthless schemer, but at least he was not a lecher, or worse.
He had not harmed her. And she had to admit she was not
completely blameless. She had done much to antagonize
him.

It almost certainly would have gone worse for her with
another.

Perhaps she *was* acting a bit peevish. Not without cause,
to be sure, yet still more thin-skinned than her normal
habit. There was something about de Montregnier that riled
her to her worst displays of temper. She suddenly realized
she was not very proud of that. Most assuredly, she was

ashamed to be hiding in her room to avoid a confrontation. What would her mother say of such cowardice?

Alayna came to her feet. She did not stop to examine her motives. With a sense of determination, she flung open the lid of the chest that held her finest gowns. She would have no help dressing, so she chose a simple, long tunic of deep rose brocade. Pulling it on quickly, she rummaged through another trunk to find an unadorned girdle of gold and a delicate filigreed circlet for her hair. She fetched the ill-used brush and roughly applied it until the mass of curls gleamed in a shimmering cascade down her back. She placed the circlet on her unbound tresses and slipped her feet into the soft slippers that matched her gown. Thus garbed, she smoothed her hands down the front of her dress, took a deep breath and hurried to the hall.

When she entered the room, she was aware of the hushing of conversations as she moved to the high table. The last time she had sat there, Edgar had been the host. Now, clad in his customary black, Lucien de Montregnier had the master's chair. He watched her with smug assurance as she came to take her place beside him.

"I beg your pardon, my lord, for the delay. I have come to attend you at your celebration, as you requested."

The words cost her only a little, but it was worth it to see the smirk melt from his face. It was obvious he had been expecting her to be blustering or sullen. This gracious apology had stunned him. Ha!

She was disappointed in how soon he recovered. Lucien merely waved his hand at the chair next to him. "Be seated and let the feasting commence."

With effortless grace, she sank into the chair at his left. A small scuffle drew her attention, and she turned to see Will and Pelly struggling over who would be the one to sit on her other side. Eventually Will gave his young friend a hearty shove and took the advantage. When he was safely ensconced in the coveted position, he turned to give Alayna a winning grin, choosing to ignore the dark scowl Lucien bestowed on him. Pelly sank into the next seat, looking quite perturbed.

Alayna could not help but to be amused by their antics. She rewarded both men with a genuine smile that immediately alleviated Pelly's sulk. Alayna's mood was lightened, as well, and she was delighted they had obviously annoyed de Montregnier. She decided that she may enjoy the evening after all. In this spirit, she applied herself to pointedly shunning any conversation with him, focusing her attention on the charming Sir Will.

The handsome knight was very attentive. He amused all with his lighthearted manner and frivolous tales of his own courage and bravery. However, he told these stories with such obvious exaggeration that they were transformed into delightful parodies.

Lucien was keenly aware of her presence at his side. After recovering from the shock of her humble apology, he saw it for what it was—a carefully calculated ploy to take him off guard. This woman was not as predictable as most, he would give her that much.

He was immeasurably annoyed when the serving wench set down the trencher and chalice between himself and Alayna. It was customary for these things to be shared between two people, and as the new lord, it was logical that he be matched with Edgar's widow. However, it was decidedly awkward. He scowled, flickering a glance to Alayna, who appeared horrified at the prospect of sharing the meal with him. She looked at him accusingly, and he realized she thought he had planned it. He felt a surge of perverse pleasure at her vexation.

"Does anything please you, my lady?" he inquired as a servant held a tray for them to make their selections. The sarcastic solicitousness in his voice made her bristle.

"Nay, my lord. Nothing here pleases me," she countered, her meaning clear. Lucien rewarded her with a grim smile.

"Take this tray away, it does not please your lady," he commanded.

Her eyes widened, locking with his amused ones. She had not expected that. The next servant presented her with a generous assortment of meats. Lucien could see that she was hungry from the look she gave the heavily laden platter, but he knew she would never admit it.

"And what of these? Is there naught here that pleases you?"

She did not answer, hesitating with the wariness of an animal who senses the trap but is unsure in which direction it lies. At her momentary lack of response, he waved the food away. Another tray passed untouched. When the next was proffered, she reached up quickly.

"I will have the pies," she said.

"Ah," Lucien said to the servant. "My lady wishes a pie. But wait, these pies look paltry! Why, they are too thin, with hardly any substance to them." She looked puzzled. He knew quite well there was nothing wrong with them, and so did she. "Take these away. My lady wishes fat pies, stuffed with meat and spices, not these skinny things."

The servant was shocked, and his moment's uncertainty gave Alayna the time to snatch several pies and deposit them in front of her. "These will do fine," she said, and smiled to the servant, turning an angry look on de Montregnier.

He chuckled softly, inclining his head slowly to concede her the victory.

Her manners were dainty enough, but her appetite was substantial. She ate every last morsel. When he offered her the chalice, she made a point of turning the cup so that her lips would not touch where his had been. Lucien smiled ruefully at that bit of drama. In their short acquaintance she had distinguished herself as the most difficult, exasperating woman he had ever met. She was not a bit intimidated by him. No one had ever been unmoved by his temper, his damning scowls, yet this slip of a girl had the audacity to check him at every turn. It should infuriate him, and most times it did. But why, by God's teeth, did it amuse him so?

Noticing his dark look upon her, Alayna met his stare bravely. "Now 'tis my turn to ask you, my lord, for you look unhappy. Though you usually appear as if you have swallowed a lemon, you seem particularly dour right now. Are you, then, displeased?"

Lucien stiffened at the gibe. "I have important matters on my mind, demoiselle. Do not forget there is much I must accomplish before the justiciar arrives."

"Ah," she said, "and your worry over your spurious claim weighs on your mind."

Spurious claim? She was at it again.

"I am a man of action, experienced in the ways of war, not government. But I suppose I shall acclimate myself soon enough. I have no such anxiety that all will not be exactly as I intend." He leaned forward. "And that everyone here will do exactly as I intend."

She sniffed delicately. "Well, 'tis a daunting job. If a

man were not up to the challenge, it surely would appear to be an intimidating task.''

He looked at her lazily, allowing a small smile to tug at the corner of his mouth. He picked up the chalice and took a long drink.

"Actually, I find myself looking forward to it. I thrive on challenge, be it of arms or wits. I have no lack of confidence in my ability to prevail in any situation.''

"Aye, your confidence, as evidenced by your frequent boasts, seems indeed endless.''

He shrugged. "'Tis only fact. I have never been bested.''

"Yet.''

"Are you telling me you think you will gain some advantage over me? Do you believe for a single moment that I will not get, from you and everyone else in this castle, exactly what I require? If you do, I must warn you how wrong you are.''

"Thank you for your immense generosity, my lord baron,'' Alayna replied, "but I need no assurances from you.''

"The future will tell, will it not?''

"Aye.'' Alayna nodded primly. "Let us wait for our debate to be determined by the test of time.''

He lifted the chalice in mock salute. The heat of his look made Alayna uncomfortable. Annoyed, she turned away.

As the meal progressed, the crowd grew rowdy, drinking their fill on the fine ale that flowed freely. Alayna did not like the shifting mood. She had no wish to be present if the occasion was going to degenerate into a raucous melee.

From beside her, Will said, "Do not let them concern you, lady.''

"Am I that obvious?"

"I am afraid you are not very good at hiding your thoughts."

"A fault of mine," she said.

His eye flickered gently over her face. "I do not think so."

She glanced back to the vociferous group of hired soldiers. "They seem rather reckless."

Will leaned back in his chair, a self-assured smile on his face. "It will become apparent that recklessness in de Montregnier's household is a very dangerous choice."

She frowned. "Your master seems not the least bit interested."

He looked past Alayna to Lucien, who was occupied with Agravar. His smile did not waver, indeed it seemed to deepen at his lord's lack of attention. "Aye, my lady, it does appear that way, does it not?" He squinted into the crowd. "There is someone waving at you. Over there."

Alayna saw Mellyssand seated at a trestle table trying to get her attention. She rose, saying, "Will you excuse me?"

Will came to his feet beside her, bowing low over her hand and saying with emphatic earnestness, "Pray do not tarry, or I shall grow too lonely."

She laughed lightly, then glanced apprehensively at de Montregnier. He was not paying any attention, she noted with relief. As she stepped off the platform, she was acutely aware of the many eyes that followed her. It seemed she was becoming something of a curiosity. They must all be wondering about her after her numerous clashes with the new baron. No doubt they thought her a lunatic to irritate the formidable man. Perhaps they were right.

"Alayna!" Mellyssand exclaimed, giving her a quick hug. "We have not seen you today."

"I have been occupied with much to do," Alayna said evasively. She could not very well divulge her recent activity of cutting and sewing stolen garments.

"How goes it with you, child?" Lord Hubert asked. He looked good, with a healthy amount of color. The hands that held hers briefly were warm and strong. "I am surprised to see you here. I had heard you were not well."

Alayna blushed, "I am fine. And you, you look much improved."

He nodded. "Thanks go to the ministrations of my devoted wife."

"That is not what you say when I insist on rest!" Mellyssand exclaimed with a laugh.

They exchanged a fond look before Hubert turned back to Alayna. "How do you find our new lord?" he asked. Before Alayna could respond, he added, "He is a good man, as many are finding."

Alayna shrugged. "I cannot say I particularly care for him."

Hubert seemed surprised. Apparently he had not heard the gossip. "What he has accomplished here is astonishing. The people are hungry for a fair leader, and they have forgiven him much in a short time."

Alayna held her tongue. She would get nowhere trying to dissuade Hubert of his admiration for de Montregnier. "I suppose he will be good for Gastonbury, but I am anxious to return to London. I await word from my mother, for I have had no message from her since I arrived. She must be dreadfully worried about me."

"Why do you not send her word?" Mellyssand asked.

"I have not troubled Lord Lucien with the request."

"Fear you he is too busy to hear of your need? Indeed, more pressing matters do prey upon him," Hubert considered. "Perhaps it is best not to bother him now. I will see to it for you if you wish."

Alayna paused, thinking of the opportunity. Of course, if Hubert knew of de Montregnier's attitude of wanting to "keep" her, he would not be so willing to lend aid. But she could not pass up this chance.

Pushing away niggling remorse, Alayna accepted his offer. Mellyssand began to talk of other matters, but Alayna's mind soared with excitement, calculating how soon she could expect her mother to arrive. Three days for the messenger's journey to London, then a few more before her mother could make ready, then three days travel—no, more for she must take into account that the number of people in her mother's retinue would slow them down. A sennight. Or a fortnight at the most!

She cautioned herself not to show too much excitement, lest she cue Lucien. Presently she excused herself and made to return to her seat on the dais, still much preoccupied with her plans. Oh, how she relished the thought of de Montregnier's rage when her mother rode through the gates and demanded her release. What he would do, she couldn't even guess. But it was one confrontation she would meet head-on.

She didn't notice that a man had stepped into her path until she almost collided with him. Her head snapped up to find herself before a hefty fellow with blackened teeth and grizzled beard. "Oh!" she gasped. "Excuse me, please."

She made to step around him, but he slid aside to check her. Alayna recognized him. He was one of Lucien's mercenaries. "Laidy Alayna o' Gassonbry," the man slurred.

"Please move aside," she said coolly. Her chin went up in her trademark gesture of defiance. That made the man chuckle, and he lifted his hand to touch her face. Alayna slapped it away. She turned her back on him, thinking to retreat, but he grasped her arm and yanked hard, bringing her around to face him again.

"Are you insane? Let go of me this instant!"

He and his fellows roared at her imperious manner. Another man, tall and rangy with a drooping mustache, casually moved behind her, pressing himself against her back.

"If you do not let me pass, I shall call for aid," Alayna demanded. Darting a look to the head table, she found Will gone and Lucien standing with his back to her, deep in conversation. The din of the hall was so loud she doubted if he would hear her even if she called to him. Damn, he watched her like a hawk any other time. Now when she needed him, he was ignoring her.

"Aye, I'll wager Lor' Eggar gave ye a good tumble, for sure," the disgusting man said. The stench from his breath made her gag. A round of laughs from his comrades emboldened him. "Made ye hot to 'ave it, did it? Care to gi' a poor knight a try? It ain't fair, ye see. We all fought hard, an' now we jes' want some reward. How about it, me laidy?"

Alayna recoiled from the heavy hand that reached out once again to grab her. She was about to shriek when suddenly, and without any apparent explanation, the smile of her tormentor drooped. His eyes rolled downward. Alayna's gaze dropped to the dagger that had suddenly appeared in his side. A dark stain was greedily consuming his tunic. She recognized the weapon from the worn hilt. It was the same one Lucien had used to slice his hand!

Whirling around, she saw him standing on the dais, glaring with the most thunderous look she had ever seen. "Get out," Lucien said. It was a low growl that carried across the crowd, drawing attention and creating an unnatural hush.

"I am injured!" came the mercenary's cry. He spread his hands before him with his blood smeared on them in dark exhibition.

Lucien did not react. "Get out," he repeated.

The man's comrades rushed forward to help him, urging him to obey, but he pushed them away. "We was only 'avin' a bit of sport. Are we supposed to act like saints?"

"You knew the terms when I hired you. These are my people now, and I am sworn to protect them. This is the last time I will say it—get out."

"You owe me money. You hired me to fight for you, an' I did."

Lucien regarded the man impassively. "Pay him. Pelly, call the seneschal and have a purse given to him. Then escort him to the castle gates and see that he leaves posthaste." His dark gaze never left the man. "I do not want to see you again at this castle, or on any of the lands which tithe to me."

With that, Lucien seated himself, implicitly dismissing the matter as settled.

Alayna stood awkwardly for a moment before hurrying to distance herself from the miscreants. She was again aware of the stares she drew as she made her way back to the safety of Lucien's side. It would have eased her embarrassment much if de Montregnier had offered some word of comfort to her, but of course he did not. When she reached her seat, she said tightly, "Thank you, Lord Lucien."

Interrupted in midsentence, Lucien turned slowly to face her. His features held a mocking look. "You are quite welcome, madam" was all he said. Dismissing her, he turned back to his conversation.

Why did he always have to treat her with such obvious contempt? She wondered why he had bothered coming to her rescue.

She might have said as much if her attention had not been drawn by the sound of a voice calling out. She looked up to see a man standing boldly before the dais. She recognized him as Lord Garrick, one of Edgar's cronies and a castellan of some power. "Lord Lucien!"

De Montregnier turned to meet his summons with a wary look. "Aye," he answered carefully.

"I beg your indulgence on a matter that has been troubling me." Garrick's glare of animosity was barely concealed. "You have among you a criminal and a deserter. I demand justice, for the young Pelly was in training with me before serving in your army. He ran off and took up arms against me, his sworn lord and liege, not to mention Edgar du Berg, who was his overlord. That is treason, sirrah, and I would see that you address it as the law commands."

"Would you?" Lucien answered. He stared fiercely at the castellan.

"Now that you are Lord of Gastonbury, you know well the importance of keeping fealty bonds, despite all else."

"Aye, I value loyalty above all else," Lucien said.

"Furthermore, he was but a squire when he turned tail and ran like the fainthearted cad he is, yet he sits among you as a knight fully vested. He is a liar, as well!"

"I vested him," Lucien answered. "I found him worthy."

Alayna shot a sideways glance at him and saw he seemed outwardly calm, the only sign of his ire was an insistent tic in his cheek where he was clenching his jaw.

"I wish to know if you will honor my complaint against his crime."

Lucien regarded Garrick coldly, rubbing his fingers over his mustache in thoughtful contemplation. "And what would you have me do?"

"He broke his oath. He deserves to be put to death!"

"You have no right to speak of oaths and honor," Pelly exclaimed, leaping to his feet. Heads turned to view this unusual display from the young man who until now had barely spoken a word. "You treated the men in your training like animals—nay, worse! Young Cedric was not the first who died. We did not receive instruction in weaponry, but in fear!"

Garrick reddened. "Quit yourself, lad, and mind your place. Your betters are speaking."

Pelly's boyish face screwed into a mask of outrage. "Aye, you would wish me to keep my peace. There are too many tales you would prefer not known."

"Enough!" Garrick roared. "I'll not let you spread lies about my household to this company to justify your dishonor."

Lucien spoke quietly, yet all listened with rapt attention. "That you would challenge my judgment so publicly shows either unbelievable audacity or unbridled confidence. Either way, it makes for a formidable opponent. Are you my enemy or my faithful vassal, Garrick of Thalsbury?"

"I gave my promise," Garrick admitted grudgingly.

"I should think you would be treading carefully here, when I can strip you of the lands you hold."

"You would not dare!" the man sputtered. "I have given you no cause. I met your bargain."

"They are, after all, mine. Am I not the rightful Lord of Thalsbury?"

Lucien smiled slowly at Garrick, an evil smile that chilled Alayna to watch. She was stunned at this news. She had known only bits and pieces of his identity. But to learn that he was the heir to one of Gastonbury's most lucrative fiefs was a shocking revelation.

Lucien was still, but Alayna could sense the tension coiled tightly inside like a snake about to strike a deadly blow. "So that makes me Edgar's vassal, yet I took up arms against him. Am I a criminal, also? I tell you this, the bonds of fealty are binding on both ends. Edgar broke those bonds. So I am free by virtue of his crime to act on my own. So is Pelly free, from you and Edgar both. Do not press me about oaths, nor quote to me the law, for the contract of loyalty binds both lord and vassal to protect and serve." Lucien paused, giving Garrick a long, slow perusal. "If I hear of you making complaint on this again, I will treat it as insurrection. Am I clear?"

Garrick glared but did not protest.

De Montregnier continued, "Pelly is my man now. He has sworn himself to my service and I to his. Trouble him no further, for the order of the old baron is gone, and this is my burh."

Garrick opened his mouth to protest but apparently thought better of it. He snapped his jaw closed and, with a baleful glance at Pelly, nodded his assent quickly. The repudiation did not sit well with the spiteful man. He continued to glower with ill-concealed malignancy from his seat.

Lucien managed a brittle smile. Turning to Alayna, he

lifted a brow to enhance his smug expression. "What say you now of my lowborn status?"

Alayna bristled. "I always thought your behavior bespoke more of a barbarian than a gently bred lord."

To her dismay, Lucien answered her with a hearty laugh. "Your wits are as sharp as your tongue, lady. Indeed, I have much of the barbarian ways in me, since I grew to manhood in their company."

She rose with as much haughty control as she could muster. "May I be excused, my lord? I am fatigued."

Lucien paused imperiously, as if considering her request. "Aye," he said with a sigh, suddenly bored. "I think 'tis best. If you were to stay you might tempt me with your malicious tongue, and I believe my guests have had quite enough diversion for one evening. Good eve to you."

Alayna was speechless, which for once was good and well, for if she were to give voice to her reaction to that last barb, she surely would have screeched in a most unseemly manner. As it was, she kept her peace, demurely inclining her head before taking her leave.

That night brought little rest until she was able to calm her thoughts and focus on the hopes that rested with the letter she would send through Hubert. When her mother arrived and demanded her freedom, it would wipe the smirk off those dark, handsome features. Aye, Eurice was correct. He was quite handsome. His looks were haunting, but his boorishness chafed. She could barely wait to be free of him.

Her mood was instantly lifted as she grasped that thought tightly and pulled it with her into her dreams.

Chapter Eight

"That is the last."

Eurice and Alayna sat in Alayna's chamber, putting the finishing touches on a small tunic. It had taken over a fortnight to refashion the elegant clothes into usable pieces. During this time, Alayna had seen little of de Montregnier, for she was often in her chamber, and the new lord seemed content to leave her be.

"Now what, my dearling?" Eurice said. "These need to be delivered to the village and we cannot do that without Lord Lucien's permission."

"So I will get it." Alayna shrugged, as if it were a matter of ultimate simplicity.

Eurice gave her a reproachful look. "And how do you propose to achieve such a feat?"

Alayna considered this for a moment. "He does seem to be set against me and unlikely to do me any favors. But he has no reason to suspect us of any wrongdoing. Perhaps if I just ask him outright, as if no ruse were afoot, my naturalness will give him no cause to speculate."

"You would not dare to be so brazen!"

"Do you have a better solution?" Alayna asked.

Considering this, Eurice shook her head but warned, "Remember your temper, Alayna. Do not vex him."

Alayna playfully made a face in response. "You think I do not know how to be nice?"

This only made Eurice roll her eyes heavenward.

Alayna set out to find de Montregnier. She knew she must be on her best behavior. She reminded herself to think of the treasure she was about to give away right out from under his nose. That should make her pleasant enough to get through the interview.

After a quick search, she found him in the armory with Agravar and a scribe, taking inventory of the stock of fine weaponry Edgar had amassed.

"Pardon, my lord," she said politely. Lucien's head snapped around at the sound of her voice, his brows drawn down in an immediate frown. Alayna felt her ire rise with just that look, a feeling she immediately repressed.

"Lady," Lucien rumbled expectantly. Behind him, Agravar nodded but gave no voice to his welcome. She was a bit intimidated by this Viking, though he had done nothing to alienate her. It was simply his size and foreign looks that made her wary.

"May I speak with you, my lord?" she inquired.

"Is this a matter that can wait? We are busy here."

She swallowed, determined not to rise to the bait. "Nay, I must speak with you on a matter of some import. It will only take a moment."

He nodded his head as if he were granting a cumbersome favor. A glance at the scribe sent the man scurrying away. "Very well, what is it?" Lucien said.

"It concerns the village that lies just before the forest. The folk there are sorely troubled by poverty, living in conditions which I have found difficult to ignore since my arrival."

"I am aware of it," he snapped.

"I wish to see to their needs and distribute certain garments I have made for their use."

Lucien regarded her impassively. "Well?"

"I require transportation and escort," she choked, trying valiantly to refrain from snarling. "And of course I need your *permission* to leave the castle."

"Well, you have it," he said.

Agravar interceded smoothly. "I will see to it. Let me know what it is you require, and I shall make the arrangements for you."

These were the first words she had heard from the giant. She would not have expected such a gentle response from such a rough-looking man. And a friend to de Montregnier as well.

Lucien only glared at the Viking. "Thank you, *friend,* for your help," he said sarcastically.

Agravar grinned back. To Alayna he said, "I'll instruct the groom to provide you with the necessary supplies." With that he quit the room, leaving Alayna and Lucien standing awkwardly across from each other.

"Your charity is touching," he drawled caustically.

Her eyes flashed briefly. "Nay, sirrah. 'Tis your charity that is impressive."

He let the cryptic remark pass. "Your mission serves me as well, for I have in mind to take stock of all of the people in this burh and their needs so as to fully service my properties. I will send my man with you to assess their conditions, and the two purposes can be served thusly."

She was somewhat surprised at his concern for the impoverished peasants, though it was in his own best interest to do so. Peasants were considered expendable assets, yet a baron's fortunes relied on the tithes and taxes they supplied. It had always struck her as singularly foolish, not to mention intolerably inhumane, to ignore the plight of the poor upon whom the noble rested his feet. De Montregnier's insight displayed wisdom in tending well to their needs.

Still, it was gratifying to see his concern, and she found herself saying, "Is there any other way I can be of service?"

He considered her for a moment before turning back to the array of weapons he had been inspecting, perusing them in a distracted way as he paced thoughtfully. "Aye, lady, perhaps you may. I would be interested in your evaluation of what you find, for there are times when a woman notices things a man may overlook. Will shall go with you, and you may give your report to him...."

Lucien's voice trailed off as he stared at the rack of swords in front of him. His body stiffened and his face froze in a strange expression. If Alayna did not know it was impossible, she would have thought it was fear that she saw on his dark features.

"What is it?" she asked tentatively. Glancing in the direction of his unwavering gaze, she did not see anything of note, only the neat row of broadswords aligned in the iron rack.

He made no reply. He did not even move.

"Are you ill?" she inquired again. She was becoming alarmed. Had he some malady? Should she call for help?

She moved closer to lay her hand on his arm, trying to shake him from his trance.

"Please answer, you are frightening me."

He looked at her. His eyes were strange, glazed and

unfocused. It was chilling, that haunted look, more so than any scowl he could conjure. He murmured something inaudible.

"What? I cannot hear you," she urged.

"My father's sword," he rasped in a dry voice.

Alayna was stunned. She turned once again to survey the weapons displayed on the rack. His father's sword? A man's sword was his most prized possession. The only way it could be stripped of him was in defeat. Had Edgar battled the late Lord of Thalsbury? "Here, in Edgar's armory?"

Lucien nodded slowly. "Aye."

Breaking away from her grasp, Lucien moved forward slowly. He sank to his knees in front of the line of naked blades, drawing one out with deliberate care. He held it reverently in his open palms.

She would have asked if he were certain, but it was clear to see the weapon was unique. It was finely wrought with delicate etchings in the blade. The handle had a scrolled hand guard and was encrusted with a singular sapphire of enormous size. It was a magnificent piece of workmanship. There could be no mistaking it for another.

His voice came again, deeply laden with emotion. "We were set upon. My father and I and a few of his men had ridden out in a small hunting party." She strained to hear the choked words that tore from his throat. "It happened too quickly, for they were lying in wait for us. My father never drew his sword." He looked down at the object he held in his hands.

"What happened to you?" she asked, not able to resist.

"I was taken."

"Did you escape?" she prodded.

"I saw my father slain, then I was hit myself."

Alayna was at a loss for words. Though her curiosity was wildly aroused, she was reluctant to press him for more. For lack of knowing what else to do, she stayed with him like that, kneeling beside him as he cradled the lost sword of his father, long dead, apparently somehow a victim of Edgar du Berg.

When Agravar returned, his features immediately drew into a dangerous look as he took in the scene before him. Alayna hastened to reassure him. "He was glancing at the weapons when his eyes fell upon this one, and it were as if he was struck ill."

Agravar said nothing. In three long strides, he was at Lucien's side. Without any gentleness, he grabbed his friend by the arm and yanked him up to a standing position.

"What is it, Lucien?" Agravar demanded.

"He said that this is his father's sword," Alayna offered.

Agravar's eyes widened in shock. "Is it true?"

Lucien answered, "Aye."

He seemed to be finally recovering, the familiar scowl settling over his features. Averting his eyes, he unsheathed his own sword, carefully replacing it with the larger weapon. His movements were slow with a deliberateness that spoke eloquently of his feelings. When the blade was in place, he turned back to his companions, his tone firm and steady once again. "Did you make the arrangements for the journey?"

"Aye," Agravar answered.

"Have Sir Will ride escort. Before they leave, send him to me, for I have a task for him while he is there."

Agravar nodded. Lucien turned to Alayna, his expression guarded. "All is set, demoiselle. Was there anything else?"

Alayna stood before him, feeling conspicuously awkward after witnessing his unwilling display of emotion. "Nay," she answered, and quietly excused herself.

The outing was set for two days hence, but her excitement was overshadowed by what she had observed in the armory. It disturbed her to have seen the fearless warrior, and a man whom she was happy to despise, in such a vulnerable state. She had glimpsed the conqueror of Gastonbury in an unguarded moment, witnessed an intimate look at his inner demons. Seeing him like that made it more difficult to hate him.

Thus, it was with an unaccustomed sense of guilt that she prepared the trunks of stolen clothes to be transported to the village.

When the day arrived, Alayna was happily surprised to see a beautiful mare saddled and waiting for her. The freedom of riding out of those gates, albeit temporarily, was exhilarating and she was immediately caught up in the adventure.

Will was his usual charming self and soon had her laughing at his witty jokes and amusing stories. He gave her an entertaining account of the men in de Montregnier's army, from Pelly to Agravar to the youngest knight-in-training. For each, he had some exaggerated and humorous tale of misadventure. Yet, he did not similarly jest about Lucien, speaking only in reverent and respectful terms when referring to his liege.

They rode past the cluster of huts crouched along the road, straight into the square where the villagers were as-

sembled for the day's business. Noises and smells assailed
the traveling party as they drew closer—the din of bartering, the nervous bleating of sheep, the mournful wail of a
cow sold for slaughter, all intermingling with the high-
pitched laughter of ragamuffin children weaving among
the stalls in a game of chase.

The sounds fell off until the clamor ceased into abrupt
silence as the traveling party drew to a stop.

Alayna paused, suddenly uncertain. She looked to Will
for a lead but saw he awaited her orders. With a start, she
realized that she was Lady of Gastonbury, and by rights
the duty of addressing the inhospitable crowd was hers.
She drew herself up straight and inhaled a deep breath.

"I am Lady Alayna of Aven—Gastonbury," she announced. How odd it seemed to own that title. "I am
widow of the late Lord Edgar du Berg, who was defeated
in battle by our new baron, Lucien de Montregnier. He has
sent me to greet you in his name and has bidden me bring
you gifts of clothing and to see to your needs."

She was rewarded with blank looks. Nervously she dismounted and instructed several of the grooms to unload
the trunks from the cart. "Lord Lucien wishes you to receive them as tokens of his goodwill." It was a lie, but no
one knew differently. She suddenly wished that the fierce
baron was here now to handle this difficult situation.

She held her breath. No one moved. She glanced at Will,
not at all heartened by his expression. She spied a soldier
behind him fingering the hilt of his sword.

Alayna had no idea of what to do to defuse the escalat-
ing tension until she spotted one of the tiny garments she
and Eurice had stitched for a babe. She had seen a woman
holding a sparsely dressed infant of the right age. Snatching the small bit of cloth, she approached her.

Behind her, Will dismounted and moved close.

"Your son looks to be in need of this," Alayna offered, holding out the tiny piece of clothing. The woman made no move to take it. Alayna froze, feeling the hot flush of failure. Then the child the woman held smiled at Alayna, and that simple gesture gave her her cue. She held out her arms for the boy. Surprisingly the tot leaned out of his mother's grasp, and before the woman could say nay, the smiling lad was in Alayna's arms. He giggled and promptly grabbed a fistful of her hair, yanking again and again, laughing uproariously at Alayna's exaggerated yelps.

When she went to return the child to his mother, she was met with a warm smile. Timidly the woman accepted her son back and held her hand out for the garment.

"What is your name?" Alayna asked.

"Leda," the woman answered.

"And your boy?" Alayna smiled at the child who flirted shamelessly from the comfort of his mother's arms. "He is a beautiful child."

"His name is Thom."

"Hello, Thom," Alayna said, making him laugh as she prodded him with a quick tickle. "Leda, could you use some new clothes? Do you know someone who is in need?"

"Aye, lady." Leda nodded. When they had found something suitable, the young Leda encouraged the others, some of whom came forward and riffled through the trunks.

When they were finished, Leda stepped forward again. "Pardon, my lady, but if you would like a rest before returning to the castle, I would be honored to offer some humble refreshment. We do not have much, but I have fresh bread and my mother makes excellent cheese."

Alayna was touched at the offer and quickly accepted. Will insisted on accompanying her and they were shown to a small, neatly tended shelter that was no more than a hut. Ducking through the low doorway, they entered a single room almost bare of furniture, but well kept and freshly swept.

"Please, sit there," Leda urged, indicating the plank table and several stools.

Will and Alayna obliged. Thom toddled to them on unsteady legs, lifting his arms to be picked up. Alayna obliged while Leda hurried to unwrap the cheese and place it before them with a small loaf of bread and a tankard of ale.

She took a nibble of cheese, surprised at the excellent quality. "You said this cheese is made by your mother?"

"Aye, lady, she makes the best in the village. Folk barter for her cheese, and she can hardly make enough of it."

They were interrupted by a loud din from outside the flimsy portal. Will jumped up and lunged for the door, flinging it open with his sword at the ready, only to reveal Lucien poised just outside the threshold.

Will leaped back in surprise when he saw who it was. With a grateful sigh, he lowered his weapon.

Lucien, however, did not share his relief. His face was thunderous as he swept unceremoniously into the dwelling, quickly surveying the domestic scene before him. He seemed to tower over the women, his bulk accentuated by the tiny proportions of the room. His eyes locked onto Alayna, raking over her with a searing appraisal.

She felt burned at that look. Standing quickly to face him, she handed the frightened babe to his mother. "My lord?" she queried tightly.

"What are you doing here still?" he snapped. "I

thought you would have conducted your business and returned to the castle posthaste."

"We were invited to eat and rest."

Will said, "Is something amiss?"

Ignoring him, Lucien looked to the woman cowering in the corner, a protective hand raised to shield her son. "Who are you?" he demanded.

Alayna intervened. "How dare you challenge her! She was only showing us kindness and hospitality. I realize these qualities are unfamiliar to you, but you must allow that we are not in any danger."

His reply was interrupted as Agravar came running in.

"Have you found her?" he puffed.

The situation was getting ridiculous, three oversize knights crowded in the small room, two astounded women and a babe about to erupt into a fit of temper at any moment. Lucien let out an exasperated breath, running his hand through his thick hair. He whirled around and stepped out the door.

Will, who was apparently miffed at Lucien's lack of confidence stalked after his master. Offering her apology to Leda, Alayna followed, slipping by the Viking at the door. Agravar, awkward and alone in the small room with Leda and Thom, smiled sheepishly at the startled woman staring at him wide-eyed.

The Norseman shrugged. "My lord was worried. When my lady did not return as she should have, we thought she had come to some harm."

Leda did not answer. Thom stared with trembling lip at the big man. The child drew in a deep breath and let loose a bellow that was amazing for such a tiny fellow. At his first wail, Agravar quickly stepped backward through the

doorway, closing it after him, for he was anxious not to
incite the tot any further.

Outside, Lucien was walking in long strides toward the
horses. Will ran up beside him, grabbing Lucien's arm and
whirling him around. They exchanged words briefly, and
Alayna, who was hurrying to confront Lucien herself,
could see that Will was quickly mollified by whatever it
was that Lucien said. She, however, was not as easily
calmed.

"Why do you act thus?" she demanded when she
caught up with him.

"I had the foolish notion some harm may have befallen
you, though I should have known better. Heaven help anyone who tangles with the she-wolf!" he snapped, not
breaking stride.

"You do not fool me, de Montregnier. You had no
thought for my safety. You thought I had made to leave,
did you not?"

"Nay, I know you will not."

She smirked back at him boldly. "What confidence you
have, sir. Do you think that your company is so charming
that I dread to leave it?"

Roughly he took hold of her upper arm, dragging her a
short distance away from the others so they would not be
overheard.

"Take care," he threatened. "You will not abuse me
so with your wicked tongue. Though our differences are
many, I am still your lord and protector, and I will not
tolerate your disrespect."

When she opened her mouth to make her retort, Lucien
held up a staying hand. "Nay, demoiselle, do not vex me.
Be satisfied your delay here in the village caused me some
concern, for it had not occurred to me there may be some

lingering resentments about. If my arrival startled you, I regret it. But I was hardly thinking of proper courtesy.''

She shot him a glaring eye. ''Nay, say 'tis not truth! You were unaware of the proper courtesy? 'Tis nigh unbelievable that such a chivalrous lord as yourself would display such a lapse.''

Lucien blinked at her for a moment, not comprehending her sarcasm. Before he could recover, Alayna lashed out again. ''You burst in there, terrify an innocent woman and her babe, stomp about—''

''Stomp about?'' he queried dangerously.

''And all because you feared I had tried to run for freedom.''

''That,'' he snarled, ''is not something I fear. At times I believe I would not interfere were you to attempt escape. By the way you try me, I swear I would welcome it.'' His features held a cool look of superiority. ''But I know you will not.''

''Then you are a fool, for I will leave at my first opportunity!'' she challenged. She stood across from him, hands on hips, eyes flaring in defiance.

He paused for a heartbeat before replying. ''No, lady, you will not. Because you have not heard word back from your mother. You cannot leave before you get your reply.''

She felt no less stung than if she had been slapped. Speechless, she watched him as he drew out a scrolled parchment from inside a leather pouch tied to his belt. Alayna recognized the document immediately as the letter she had written to her mother and entrusted to Lord Hubert.

''Did you think Hubert would not clear any outgoing missive with me, especially one going to King Henry's court?''

With a swift motion, she snatched the letter out of his hand. "How dare you interfere, you despicable lout!" she cried. To her distress, she felt hot tears stinging her eyes and splashing out onto her cheeks. "You have lied and deceived to hold me against my will, kept me apart from my mother and the home I miss, trapped me in this hateful place, which has witnessed my worst and most profound humiliation. Yet why you wish me to stay is a mystery, for you only spurn and mock me at every turn. Whatever your selfish motivations are, they sicken me. You think only how you can keep me in your possession—all a part of your pathetic vengeance that has nothing to do with me. I find you cruel and small-hearted and loathsome!"

With a sob, she threw the parchment, striking him harmlessly on the chest, before running for her horse.

Lucien stood for a moment in the wake of her outburst before he stooped to pick up the discarded note. He fingered the letter with careful consideration. After a brief moment, he returned it to his pouch before joining the others.

There was a somber mood to the party that rode into Gastonbury's upper bailey later that evening. Alayna dismounted and took to her room without a word to anyone. Lucien similarly ascended to his chamber, silent and pensive, too preoccupied to register annoyance that the servant girl, Glenna, was there against his earlier proscription.

"Glenna, fetch Pelly to me," he said, moving to the hearth to stare into the flames.

Incredibly, the girl took a step toward him. "You are vexed, my lord. She tries you, I know. Let me—"

"Get Pelly." He almost roared it.

Glenna's eyes flashed fire, but she did obey.

As soon as he was alone, Lucien began to strip off his

travel-stained garments. He had no wish to revert to the lordly custom of having assistance dressing or bathing, preferring his old ways, even if they were the habits of a slave. It was only a few moments later when Pelly knocked.

"My lord?" Pelly said with a curt bow. Lucien stifled a smile. The lad's exuberance never failed to lighten his mood.

"Aye, Pelly. I have a mission for you. I want you to deliver this message to the Lady Veronica of Avenford at King Henry's court."

Recognizing the name, Pelly's eyes widened in shock. He took the proffered document. Lucien continued. "Tell no one what you are about and return posthaste."

"Aye, my lord," Pelly said, bowing and taking his leave.

In the silence of the chamber, Lucien finished undressing and ate the cold meal waiting for him. He eased himself into the great bed and doused the candle. Although tired, he found he could not sleep. It was a new experience, being kept awake by the pangs of conscience.

Chapter Nine

Alayna stood in the chilly morning air, huddled under a thick woolen shawl. The clouds overhead were heavy with the threat of rain, reflecting her own desolate mood as she said farewell to Mellyssand and Hubert.

"I wish you did not have to return home so soon," Alayna said.

"I will make Hubert promise to allow a visit right away," Mellyssand said, giving her a reassuring squeeze.

"Very soon, please."

"Hubert assures me Lord Lucien is a good man. He admires him a great deal, you know, and my husband is not light with his loyalty. Now, do not look so serious. Come, give me a last embrace for I must be off before Hubert loses his temper."

Alayna held her close for a long moment before Mellyssand climbed into the wagon beside her husband. Hubert was in a foul mood since his injury would not allow him to ride astride with his men. He scowled at Mellyssand and she patted his hand comfortingly. He grudgingly allowed himself to be appeased, gripping her fingers in apology.

"Fare thee well, my dear," he called, "though I know you shall. You are in good hands."

He raised a salute to Lucien, who stood a short way off as the trap clattered forward.

Alayna could not help a glance at de Montregnier. He met her eye, raising a mocking brow. Lifting her chin, Alayna nodded before turning away.

Eurice was waiting for her at the steps to the keep. "Come inside. The heavens look ready to explode."

"A fitting portent, do you not think?" Alayna quipped, pausing to look upward. "The skies give testimony to my fate, Eurice. You are so fond of interpreting these things. Do you not see in them a sign of my despair? I will rot here—de Montregnier's scorned possession."

"Do not fret, child," Eurice clucked. "All will work out as it is meant to."

Alayna shook her head. "I do not know why he keeps me here. He seems to despise me as much as I do him."

Eurice smiled. "De Montregnier is a man who likes to be in control of his destiny. In you he has found the one he cannot master. You tempt him, child, do you not see it?"

"I know it. It seems I cannot even be within a stone's throw of him before that dour look descends."

"That is not what I meant."

At Alayna's puzzled face, Eurice explained, "Alayna, it is not conceit to know the truth. You are a beautiful woman."

"He hates me!" Alayna scoffed.

"He desires you."

This was not only inconceivable, it was unacceptable. "But he avoids me, and when he does address me, it is with nothing but contempt."

Eurice gave an impatient jerk of her head. "A man such as Lord Lucien knows well how to discipline himself with a hard heart. He seeks to use that tool here with you."

"How do you know so much about him?"

"There is much that can be learned if one is willing to listen."

"Why does everyone insist on trying to explain him to me?" Alayna flung with a dismissing wave of her hand. "Does no one understand that I do not care?"

"Is that so?"

Alayna put her hands to her temples. "I am tired."

Eurice frowned at her. "You are feeling sorry for yourself again, and making your own misery. I have potions to mix." She started away, paused, then called over her shoulder, "Did you not consider, Alayna, that skies such as these cast no shadow on those below? There are many ways to interpret a portent."

With that, Eurice took herself off to resume her chores.

Alayna was about to return to the main building when she heard the pounding of hooves as a rider approached. She turned to see Pelly ride into the bailey, pulling up to an abrupt halt before Lucien. It appeared Pelly was relaying information of some urgency, for he spoke with emphatic gestures to his lord.

Some news to darken de Montregnier's mood further, Alayna mused diffidently, deciding to hide in her room lest Lucien cast his angry eye toward her.

The storm started, pounding rains and high-pitched winds that set Alayna's nerves on edge. Grateful as she was for the comfort of her chamber, she had a strange feeling of foreboding. She thought it must be due to the loss of her good friends, Hubert and Mellyssand, and her quarrel with Eurice, until a nervous youth brought a summons informing her Lucien wished to see her in his chamber. Anticipating another unpleasant interview, Alayna clenched her teeth as she followed the lad to the master's door.

Pausing just outside the room, her hand poised to knock at the portal, she took a deep breath and notched her chin up a bit. She would not have him see her anxiety.

She gave a swift knock.

"Come."

The imperious tone set her teeth on edge.

Lucien was standing with his back to her, facing the hearth. The firelight was behind him so that she could only see him in silhouette. Even this was a posture of arrogance, with his feet braced apart and his broad shoulders squared.

The chamber was well lit, both by the glow of the fire and the sconces burning on the wall. Looking about her, she saw he had removed many of the large, ornate pieces of furniture, leaving only a few objects of plainer design. The huge bed still stood against the wall above the hearth in the hall, arranged to take advantage of the heat rising up from it, but it was the only original piece left in the chamber. Despite the absence of ornamentation, it seemed somehow cozier, less intimidating.

He made her wait what seemed an interminable period of time before turning to her. When he did, she could not read his expression with the backlighting from the fire, but his manner made her uneasy. He seemed to radiate tension, alerting her defenses.

"Alayna," he said in an even voice. The sound of her name spoken so familiarly seemed strange coming from his lips. He looked to be struggling with something, some inner turmoil. Something to do with her? Again the dark flash of dread sizzled in her veins.

He paused, then started again. "I have learned of a challenge for the barony of Gastonbury." He moved away from the firelight, and Alayna glimpsed his face, stern and closed. Worry or vexation?

"The counterpetition comes from someone claiming that Edgar bequeathed his properties to him well before my challenge was made."

Her voice registered her surprise. "Then Gastonbury is not yours."

"Nay, not that. 'Tis true, the barony does not belong to me yet, not without Henry's blessing. But I have no doubt that will be forthcoming. This opposing suit is weak. The law should recognize my right to the title and lands, having honorably challenged Edgar and won. I am in residence, and I have the pledge of fealty of the vassals who tithe to the barony."

"Then what troubles you?" She was growing more uneasy. His manner, this unfamiliar patience as he explained his situation, lent the feeling of a trap closing in.

"Anything that even minimally jeopardizes the barony is of serious concern for me," he answered.

"But you said you have no fear you will be usurped," Alayna protested.

"I have survived long on the lesson of never underestimating the threat of my enemy and to always be prepared for the worst."

"What has this to do with me?" Alayna asked warily.

Lucien crossed to a table to pour himself a cup of wine. He downed it in one gulp before drawing a breath to explain. "As I said, I have everything that matters in my possession. I have the castle, the villeins and vassals. But most of all, my Lady Gastonbury—'' he paused meaningfully ''—I have you.''

A stab of fear made itself felt in her stomach. "What do you mean?"

"You are Edgar's bereaved wife. My suit would be greatly strengthened by an alliance between us."

His words fell like weights upon her, his voice seeming to come to her from very far away. *Alliance?* Her mind raced. He could not mean...

Unaware, or uncaring, of her reaction, he continued. "Therefore I have decided on a swift and simple solution to the problem. We will be joined in marriage on the morrow, and thus any claim to Edgar's properties will revert to me. With such a coalition, no other will stand a chance to wrest the barony from me."

"Are you quite out of your mind?" Alayna blurted, finding her voice at last. "*That* is a most ridiculous proposition. If I thought for a moment you were serious—"

"I assure you, madam, I am serious."

"Pray tell me what advantage such a match brings you?"

"Aside from the obvious joy of being wed to a gracious lady such as yourself?" he chided, the dark humor dancing dangerously in his eyes. "It should be clear that you are very valuable, indeed. Since Edgar had no issue, you as his widow would have inherited his properties."

Realizing what he was saying, she spoke softly, absently, as if to herself. "So I am the true heiress of Edgar's properties? How is it that it never occurred to me before?"

Lucien's brows drew down. "Because it would be absurd. You would have to defeat me in battle to enforce it, and I very much doubt you could." A cold smile crept over his face. "Unless you wish to challenge me hand-to-hand to decide the matter."

Missing his meaning, she snapped, "Not likely." At his broadened smile, she colored as she realized he was alluding to an intimate sort of encounter. "You are mad to suggest it!"

"So you have told me."

"Nay," she said, shaking her head in denial. "I'll not agree." Her lip curled in contempt. "Perhaps you have not been paying attention, de Montregnier. I despise you, I loathe the very thought of you, and live for the day when I can finally be free of your odious presence. To be joined with you as your wife would be the most horrible fate I could imagine."

"I have no illusions about your feelings," he said, and shrugged. "They simply are not important. The future of one of the largest shires in England is at stake. Marriage is for profit, despite any silly woman's ideas you no doubt entertain. Or perhaps not, for your first marriage promised great reward, did it not?"

"I told you, 'twas not my choice to marry Edgar. I was as opposed to him as I am to you," Alayna answered.

"'Tis of no matter. This is a game of serious consequence, and I intend to win. As your protectorate, I make the choice of your marriage, and so I choose myself. You can do nothing but obey."

"I will not," Alayna exclaimed, "I will never speak my vows! I will rebuke you at the altar! I will—"

Lucien was surprised at how much her resistance angered him. He had spoken truthfully. He had had no illusions that she would be well-disposed to the idea, yet he felt a welling of unwanted irritation in the face of her vehement refusal.

He spoke softly, enunciating each word. "You will obey."

"Nothing—nothing!—could make me agree. I would sooner be wed to a jackal!" she yelled.

The bite of her words brought an unexpected rush of something unpleasant, something suspiciously close to pain, that made him vicious. "You will obey. There is too much at stake here. You will agree or I will beat you myself and hold you in the dungeon," he roared. His rage was ruling him, something he had promised himself he would not allow to happen.

"Beat me then, you vicious lout!" she cried bravely, but his threat had put a fear in her, he could see it in her wary expression. Damn her, with that hurt look. He felt a pang of conscience, which only served to annoy him further.

To her credit, she was not daunted by his bullying tactics. With that annoying tilt of her chin, she uttered, "I'll never marry you."

She was maddening! Lucien stepped forward and took hold of her arm, pulling her to him with a hard yank.

"Aye, demoiselle, the morn will see you my wife," he gritted through clenched teeth. "And with our union, there will be none who can protest me as rightful Lord of Gastonbury." With a small shove, he released her. "See that you are ready when the time comes."

Alayna whirled and ran out of the room, leaving the portal open behind her. Lucien watched her flee, raking his hand through his hair in exasperation. What the hell had he done?

His head snapped up as Agravar stepped into the room. "Well, is she agreed?"

Lord, Lucien groaned inwardly, how had Agravar

missed overhearing that debacle? Surely their voices had reached clear down to the great hall.

"Did you speak to her gently? Did you explain the situation?"

"I acted like an ass!" Lucien shouted. Again the hand swept through his hair. "Why does that woman drive me to such distraction? I vow when I get within eyesight, my very mind deserts me. All she has to do is tilt that chin up and look at me with that contemptuous defiance she wears so well and all my good intentions are lost."

Agravar frowned, concern creasing his brow. "She did consent?"

"'Tis no matter, the deed will be done as planned. This union is too vital to be stayed by a girl's hurt pride. The important thing is that I keep what I have won."

Lucien's casual reply was belied by his restless pacing. Finally, in frustration, he slammed his fist into a washstand, splintering the wood.

"Did that help?" Agravar commented wryly. Lucien cast him a forbidding look. "Perhaps you should rethink this, Lucien. Whoever this other man is who claims Gastonbury may not pose any serious threat at all. You might not need the widow."

Lucien shook his head with determination. "Nay. We do not know for certain who has appealed to Henry, but it is in all likelihood Garrick. His suit may be judged to have merit, for he did indeed hold Edgar's trust and friendship. If he can find some way to discredit me, I am done. I did not come this far to lose now. I will do what I must."

"Consider what you are committing yourself to," Agravar warned gently.

"She will reconcile herself to the situation," Lucien growled. "I will marry the little hellcat and pay the price for it, too! God help me if I win Gastonbury at such a cost.''

To Lucien's utter amazement, Agravar seemed to be suppressing a smile, and doing a bad job of it at that. "It is ironic that Pelly's mission to deliver Alayna's missive to her mother brings us news of another claiming your spoils. Otherwise, we would have had no warning. The lady already brings you luck, friend.''

Lucien scowled, knowing that he was being needled. "She has been a thorn in my side since we arrived.''

"Then why did you insist on keeping her here?''

"Because I knew that she might prove useful, you dolt! Now stop badgering me, I have had enough of it from my previous guest!''

To Lucien's great annoyance, Agravar roared with laughter. "All right, old friend, I'll be off.''

The Viking made for the door, then paused. "What did she say at getting the message returned? Strange, I thought the news would have eased her.'' At Lucien's look, Agravar shook his head in disbelief. "Do not say that you neglected to tell her!''

"I was distracted,'' Lucien said irritably.

"Distracted?'' Agravar said. "I should say. Had you but mentioned the letter from Veronica, your lady may well have been much softened toward you.''

"It does not matter.''

"Strange you would forget.''

"This chit tries me as no other,'' Lucien complained.

Again the oversize warrior laughed, tossing back his blond head with a hearty bellow. "She bests you in this brief time in a way my father could not in eleven years. For all of his brutal treatment, he could never break you.

Yet, this girl has you tangled up. You had better take care—once wed, there is no telling what she can do."

Lucien's miserable mood must have shown on his face. Agravar sobered, offering, "Let me take the missive to your bride, and put her mind to rest on that matter. It may go easier for her on the morrow knowing its contents. Unless you do not wish for her to see it. Do you fear her mother?"

Glaring at his friend for a moment, Lucien was about to make some scathing comment, then thought better of it. "Nay, I will give it to her myself. There is little her dame can do, for by the time she arrives, her precious daughter will be wedded and bedded."

He brushed past his friend, too annoyed to notice his self-satisfied grin. Stalking through the corridors like a demon, he came to Alayna's door and pounded boldly. It galled him to have to wait, hard put to restrain himself from flinging the damnable thing open.

When Alayna answered, eyes red and swollen from her angry tears, and saw Lucien standing there, she almost slammed the portal shut again. Quickly he held out a slip of parchment to her.

"Pelly brought this for you," he said simply, and turned on his heel.

Confused, Alayna held the scroll and stared at the broad back of her enemy as he stomped away. Her mind flew over several suitable retorts, but she did not have the energy to vent them. With a resigned sigh, she opened the letter.

She glanced over the words, then stopped and reread the message more slowly. Their astonishing meaning flooded through her in a wave of exhilaration.

Her mother. It was from her mother!

She looked up, thinking momentarily to follow Lucien, but stopped. He was gone.

It was incredible. He had sent her letter, after all. And now she knew that her mother was set to accompany the king's justiciar when he traveled to Gastonbury, for Henry had forbidden her to come until the matter was settled legally. Veronica assured Alayna, in her inimical style, she would deal with the matter of her daughter's "detainment" as soon as she arrived.

But the missive read that Henry's man was set to arrive in June—two months' time! Far too long to wait. The morning would see her wed to de Montregnier!

Yet, somehow, that thought did not raise her hackles as it had only moments ago. *He had sent Pelly to London with her message.* Why did that simple fact make so much difference?

Just when she was prepared to condemn him for the most hateful, unfeeling man in Christendom, he did something like this. Showing…what? Did it mean he did have some consideration for her feelings? That flew in the face of virtually all other facts. Still, there was that time in the armory. He had been so different then. Vulnerable. Perhaps he did have a feeling side after all. And maybe he was not so immune to her as he would have her think.

Then again, it was much more likely that it served some purpose of his to have her believe so. He was cunning enough to know that the hope of her mother's intervention would give him the leverage he needed to gain her cooperation.

Fingering the crisp texture of the parchment, Alayna smiled to herself. De Montregnier thought himself invincible. But he had no idea of the position of influence her family held. Veronica was a wealthy and powerful widow, fierce as a lioness when it came to her daughter.

De Montregnier wished for a political alliance and so he should have it. But only for a time. It could all be undone quickly enough when her mother arrived. Two months. Not so long a time, really.

It would be an in-name-only arrangement, easy to annul—de Montregnier hated her almost as much as she did him. Let him think he had won. It would make her ultimate victory that much more sweet.

Chapter Ten

The morn of Alayna's second wedding day dawned clear and bright. She woke early and lingered in her room until a page came to tell her the ceremony was set for late afternoon.

Eurice was strangely tight-lipped about the whole matter as she helped Alayna dress in a simply cut gown of rich cream and wound her thick tresses in a knot so the veil could be affixed. Throughout this ritual, Alayna sat calmly, hoarding her secret hope of freedom and vindication like a shroud of comfort.

The chapel had been restored to its former purpose and Lucien waited for her beside the priest, some nameless friar who had broken ranks with the angry bishop. One glance at her groom, scowling his deepest frown and looking as if it were he who was being forced into this, and Alayna felt a surge of fear threaten to break her peace. But she dutifully spoke her vows in a voice that was clear and strong with a confidence she did not feel.

When they were pronounced man and wife, her new husband bestowed only the briefest of kisses upon her cheek, but the warmth of his lips touching her for even that fleeting moment sent a tremor through her body. Then, without preamble, he stalked off, leaving her standing awkwardly until Will came to her and offered his arm.

"Congratulations," he said tightly. Alayna tried to smile back, but the effort failed. Seeing she had been abandoned by her groom, Will led her into the hall where people stood about and stared at her, all seeming to be as dismayed by this sudden turn of events as she was herself. He stiffly excused himself, leaving her alone.

Damn de Montregnier, she fumed silently, directing a glare at him where he stood, busy with his knights and pointedly ignoring her. His rudeness should not amaze her, but it inevitably did. Did he not notice her standing alone with curious eyes crawling over her in hungry speculation?

It was going to be a long two months.

Off in a corner, a young servant girl stood, her gaze trained unwaveringly on Alayna. She did not flinch when Alayna noticed her, nor did she change the malevolent look in her dark eyes.

Crossing to where Eurice stood waiting for her, Alayna asked, "Who is that girl?"

"Which one?"

"Over..." Alayna paused, looking about the hall. The girl was gone.

"She was just there a moment ago. She glared at me with a terrible hatred. I never saw her before. I wonder who she was."

Eurice looked uncomfortable. "If you see her again, tell Lord Lucien. There would be some here who would be jealous of your good fortune and wish you harm."

Alayna almost choked. "Good fortune?"

"You are feeling sorry for yourself again."

"And have I no right to?" Alayna exclaimed.

"Alayna, I know you dislike him, but he has not been unkind to you."

"Even though he insults me and orders me about like a servant."

Eurice chuckled, patting Alayna's arm in a light reprimand. "It seems you have done your share of insulting." She sighed, shaking her head. "I only say that his worst crime has been to be disagreeable."

"And forcing me to marry him, what of that?"

Eurice nodded. "Aye, but how different is it than if the marriage were arranged by your father? Looking to gain from the union is no crime. If it were, all husbands would be dangling from the gibbet."

"Not a bad idea, that," Alayna muttered.

With a wave of her hand, Eurice surrendered, retreating into the kitchens.

Alayna puzzled over Eurice's defense of Lucien. Without the familiar comfort of her nurse, she felt more alienated than ever.

"May I offer my congratulations?" a voice said, making her start. She looked up to find Agravar standing before her, offering a slight bow.

"Oh, you surprised me."

"You look lost in thought," he commented.

Alayna no longer dreaded the imposing man. She sighed, "Congratulations are reserved for happy events, sir. Your good wishes make me feel the hypocrite."

He gave her a long look. "I know this marriage was not to your liking, but you will find Lucien an honorable husband."

"I can hardly imagine why he would be honorable to me as a husband when he had not been so thus far."

"You must understand that Lucien has waited a long

time for his vengeance,'' Agravar explained, leading her
to the head table and taking the seat next to hers, ''and I
suppose his methods seem rather extreme. But believe me,
if you knew what he had to endure, you would not think
so badly of him.''

''I just wish that it all had nothing to do with me,''
Alayna lamented. She gave him a thoughtful look. ''How
is it you and Lucien came to be friends? You are not alike
at all.''

''The circumstances of our friendship were rather
unique. But suffice to say we found that we had some
things in common and in many ways, my lady, we *are*
alike. I know he seems harsh, prideful and even stubborn
at times, but Lucien has strength of character I very much
admire. He survived conditions that would have reduced
other men, perhaps even myself, to mindless shells.''

''What was it that so tried him?'' she asked. She
watched Agravar hesitate, then smile.

''Lucien's tale is his to tell.''

Though his words put her off, his tone was gentle
enough not to dissuade her. ''In the armory, he confessed
he was taken by Edgar's men and sent away. How is it he
is able to return, and with wealth enough to fund such a
well-trained army?''

Rising, Agravar gave her a winning grin. She thought
at first he was not going to answer her, but then he leaned
down toward her and said softly, ''He killed my father and
stole his treasure.''

Swallowing convulsively, she did not doubt for a moment he was telling her the truth. Agravar bowed, just as
congenial as before, and left her once again alone.

Lucien knew he was in a strange mood today.

Perhaps part of it was shock. That had certainly been

his reaction when Alayna had come to the chapel, suitably attired and amazingly not shouting vile epithets. He had not realized until that moment that he had never expected her to capitulate, not without more threats and thundering from him. Aye, she had shocked him for certain with her calm demeanor and blank expression.

He was relieved, as well. And decidedly, inexplicably...*guilty*.

And why he should be feeling guilty he could not imagine. Yet, there it was, gnawing at him from the inside, coupled with a fair dollop of shame that stifled the satisfaction he should, by rights, have known.

God's teeth, was he developing a conscience?

He hoped not; it was something he could ill afford. Yet he couldn't say he was pleased with himself at this moment. In point of fact, he was incalculably enraged.

Not at Alayna, for once. She had done nothing. Perhaps at himself. But he could hardly help the circumstances that had prompted this rash marriage.

The truth was he was not happy to be wed to a woman who despised him so. What perverse fate had entwined his destiny with her, of all women? She had crossed him when no one dared. She had flouted his orders, chastised him in public, demeaned him with her haughty looks and impertinent barbs. She was by far the most exasperating, infuriating, fascinating...

He sighed, shaking off that last thought. Agravar was looking at him curiously. Lucien realized that he had heard nothing of what the Viking had been saying.

"What is troubling you now?" Agravar asked impatiently.

"I am too much distracted," Lucien said. "These constant battles are wearing on me."

"Are we speaking of Garrick or Alayna?"

"It does not improve my mood that I have taken a wife who would sooner see me gutted than look at me. Did you notice her? She might have been a vestal virgin going to her death pyre."

"What did you expect?" Agravar exclaimed.

Lucien exhaled. "Must I live out my days with a she-cat, forever spitting and hissing at me?"

"Strange, she said much the same to me not a moment ago."

Lucien shot a glance at his new wife. He couldn't help but feel a pang of regret upon seeing her seated alone. She looked as friendless as he felt.

"Maybe some words of reconciliation are in order," Agravar suggested.

Scowling, Lucien snapped, "I have made no apologies thus far, and I am not about to start now! This pretense is tiresome. I am leaving."

"But it is your wedding day!" Agravar protested.

"Aye, that it is. Be content that I do not declare it a day of mourning."

When Alayna climbed wearily to her chamber that evening, she did not expect to find it emptied of her belongings.

Momentarily confused, she stood in the middle of the stripped room. Slowly comprehension dawned. De Montregnier!

A small sound behind her made her whirl around to see the same young servant girl whom she had caught glaring at her before. Gone was the malevolent look. Instead her face was wan with an eerie blankness.

"A curse on you," she said dreamily.

Alayna stepped back, horrified. "What did you say?"

"He wants nothing of me, he sees only you. 'Twas that way from the beginning, but I thought my willing ways and your shrewish tongue would bring him to favor me. I wanted naught but to be his leman. But he has cast me out. Because of you."

Alayna was completely confused and more than a little frightened. Trying to sort out her message, she asked, "Of whom do you speak?"

Focusing on Alayna, the vacant look was gone for a moment. "I watch him, but he does not see me. But I see all. I see more than he knows." She paused, a look of stark anguish contorting her plump prettiness. "He spoke your name in his sleep," she whispered. Then, in a flash, the girl fled from the room.

Dear God, the girl was insane! As if Alayna's plight were not dire enough, she was now plagued with the ravings of a madwoman.

She could spare the deranged servant no more thoughts. The absence of her belongings could mean only one thing. Lucien expected her in his chamber tonight.

As to why he had done this, there could be no mistake.

He could barely stand the sight of her, and now he wanted to lie with her? It defied reason. But then, she had never been able to make any sense of that man.

What would happen to her if she refused to go? No doubt the cur would send a troop of soldiers after her, dragging her kicking and screaming if they had to.

If she refused, would he take her by force? She did not think he would. De Montregnier was many things, but a ravager of woman was not one of them. At least so far as she knew...no, he was not. She would simply go to him and tell him she would not submit to him.

As she made her way to the master's chamber, her mind was filled with one question: what would he do? It was a sin for a wife to deny her husband, and this same day she had promised before God to obey him.

Good Lord, what had she gotten herself into?

He was waiting. The door was ajar and he was seated in one of the hearth chairs. Rising, his voice was calm, almost soft, as he said, "Close the door."

She obeyed, bracing herself. "What have you done with my belongings?"

He walked toward her. "They are here."

His expression was unreadable. In the absence of his customary scowl, his features were even and pleasant, but there was a strange kind of look in his eyes. They seemed to burn like smoldering coals as he studied her. Unable to meet that scalding gaze, she turned away.

He came to stand before her. "I have been told I behaved poorly. Agravar, who is forever berating me for my lack of manners—especially with you—has made it a point to inform me of this fact. I suppose it is true." After pausing, he added, "I apologize for that." He was so composed, with a quiet sadness that was disturbing. It set her nerves on edge more than any thundering rage he could have mustered for the occasion.

He continued, "Understand I had no choice but to insist on the marriage. You know my reasons, so I will not belabor the point. But it leaves us in a rather awkward situation." He seemed to be searching for the right words. "We are off to a bad beginning."

"It is easy for you to be so gracious when you have won, de Montregnier," she breathed, not sure if she wanted to challenge his mood. How could she trust this unexpected gentleness?

"Aye, I have thus far. But tell me, demoiselle, what is it I have won?"

She frowned, confused. She had never seen de Montregnier like this, pensive and thoughtful, almost penitent. Only that one time in the armory. Something of that pain was in him now and it made her nervous and strangely excited.

What had he won? Everything! And now, he would ask even more from her, which reminded her of the matter at hand. "Why did you have my things brought here?" Was that her voice? It sounded so meek and unsure in her ears.

"Because they belong here, as do you."

A surge of emotion caught in her throat. "I did not think you would wish...I never thought...you have always seemed to dislike me so much—"

His brows shot up. "Have I?" He seemed to consider this for a moment, as if it were a singularly new idea. "'Tis a curious thought. Have I then been so unkind to you?"

"How can you ask that?" she asked, incredulous. He must be playing some kind of game with her, some cruel jest for his amusement. "You have done nothing but harass me since you arrived. You have acted the knave, through and through. I would have thought you hated me!"

He smiled halfheartedly. "I could say the same of you. Indeed, lady, you do seem to be able to try me as no other."

"'Twas you who started it," Alayna defended sullenly. "I only asked to be allowed to leave."

"But, as you know, I could not have that."

"Your precious revenge."

"Aye, my revenge," his disconnected voice repeated. "But we are beyond that now."

"We are the same as we were when we started. A few words spoken before a priest cannot change anything."

He did not seem to have heard her. "You thought I hated you?" he asked, as if the thought just now struck him as incredibly ridiculous.

"Of course I did!" she exploded irritably before she could check her words. She froze and waited for his response in wary expectation. Incredibly he gave her an indulgent smile.

"That temper of yours is something to reckon with. Do you know it makes your eyes positively spark green fire? And your mouth sets in the most irritating little pout."

"You are not making any sense," she snapped.

"You must know I find you beautiful. I admitted it the first time we met." He paused. "I did not intend to hurt you."

"Then why did you? Why must you always treat me like some nitwit child whose wishes are unimportant? Oh, assuredly, my feelings are nothing next to your grand scheming ambitions—you told me so yourself. So do not tell me that you never meant to hurt me. You did so, and you did not care a whit about it!"

"I did what I always do, what I must do to survive. Is it so unbelievable that I might regret that, even while I have no choice?"

"What amusement is this? You want me to believe you are actually *sorry* for everything you have done?"

He sighed heavily. "You really do think me a beast." He crossed his arms over his chest. "Sorry has nothing to do with it. It really is not so complex. I have had to fight for everything I have, and I have been doing so for a very long time. I simply do not wish to spend the rest of my life fighting with you."

"You should have thought of that before you insisted on this unsuitable marriage."

"Perhaps I should have."

Alayna studied his face to see if he was sincere, or simply mocking her. "Then you regret it?"

"What if I do?" He shrugged. "Married we are. And so what of it? Would you carry on your anger indefinitely?"

She shook her head in disbelief. "I thought this marriage was all for the sake of the barony. You have what you want. Why do you wish to…lie with me when you abhor the very sight of me?"

His eyes flickered over her in a way that affected her even more than his touch. "Nothing could be further from the truth. Abhorrence is not what I feel when I look at you, I must admit that, Alayna. Far, far from it."

Pressing her hands to her head, Alayna tried to stave off the crush of this discordant revelation. "I cannot be your true wife. I will never accept it."

He became very, very still. His features slowly gathered together like storm clouds to form the cold scowl she was so used to seeing. She watched, spellbound by his anger swelling to life, a rage she had caused with her heartless words.

"Did you not swear to do that very thing just today?" he said, his voice heavy with bitterness.

"I do not know why you want me!" she tried to explain desperately. "I did not expect this!"

"I do not give a damn what you expected. Now that you know what it is *I* expect, what will you do?"

"My God, I do not understand you at all!" she cried.

"Aye," he said darkly, his eyes suddenly flaring with black fire. "You understand me not at all!"

"Nor do I care to, I just wish to be left alone!"

"That is impossible, *wife!*"

Suddenly outraged, he stalked a few steps away then whirled back around.

"Do you have any idea *why* I have done all this, this 'precious revenge,' as you call it? Why I would exhaust my coffers to mount an army? Why I would take on a shire that has been run into the ground so far that twenty years will not return to me what I have already spent to put things to rights? And why, most of all, would I shackle myself with a wife whose only delight, as you have informed me again and again, is dreaming of the day she will never set eyes on me? Why, I ask you, why do you think I have done any of it!"

He was working into one of his terrible rages, but this time it was coupled with an anguish she could not fathom. It had the power to silence her in awe.

"Did you think it was greed?" he barked. "Greed! Well, seeing as I favor expensive luxury and flout my riches so freely, I can understand that misunderstanding. The trouble is I do none of this. Nay, lady, 'tis not greed that drives me, for I have no taste for ermine or jewels or any of the things that gold can buy.

"Power, perhaps? Is that what you think? Again, I ask you to witness how I have sat complacently in the comforts of Edgar's abundance and played the lazy baron. Rather, you have seen me drenched with sweat and grime, riding out at daybreak to work alongside the meanest of my serfs, coming back long after dark to the reward of a cold supper. I have not even asked the kitchens to wait the evening meal upon my return, for God's sake! So tell me, how have I abused my power?''

He was breathless, spent after his tirade. "So what, then—what is my reason?''

She whispered, "Tell me. I do want to know. *Why?*''

A harsh laugh escaped him and he glanced about the room as if searching for some assistance. "Peace. That is all. I have done all of this just to find some peace for myself.''

Silence descended like a finely spun web, binding them together. Alayna could not move, even when he closed the distance between them in a few long strides.

"Where is my peace? I have not found it. And now, with you as my wife, I never shall." If she did not know his arrogance, she would have thought his voice held a plea. "Put your bitterness aside. You are my wife, you shall be mother to my children. That decision has been made. Let it be, then. No more fighting, no more of this incessant struggle.''

"I never thought you meant this marriage to be real,'' she said softly.

"Well, I do. I mean it to be a real marriage in every sense. And I will give you no cause to deny it as anything else. I will not, like your ill-fated first husband, fail in my duty.''

His eyes were again dark and fierce. They burned into her flesh where they touched her and panic returned. His large hands grasped her shoulders, not hurting her but for the sheer affront that gesture of possessiveness sparked within. He was so close she could smell the clean masculine scent of him. It made her dizzy.

A small sound escaped her, a kind of strangled protest. Her rapier wit seemed to have deserted her as she realized she was his wife. She would have to give him everything he asked of her.

Her stubborness rebelled. In a voice devoid of connection, she said, "No."

Chapter Eleven

Lucien was aware he had failed miserably. Frustrated, helpless, he wanted to lash back, dole out some of the hurt she had just inflicted.

Roughly he yanked her to him. She fell limply against his chest like a doll. His hands came up on either side of her head, tangling in her hair as he fought to control the urge to crush his mouth against hers.

Nay. Nay! He had said that he wanted no more of these battles, and he had meant it. He did not want to start their marriage like this. He would not force her any further.

She was watching him, her eyes wide and frightened like a doe's. Her lips were parted and he found that he could not, after all, resist.

Lowering his head until his mouth barely touched hers, he kissed her. Slowly, slowly, he gathered her in his arms, almost sighing with the soft feel of her pressed against him.

God, he wanted her.

It had been hard to accept, but he had known it for some time, just as he had known that he was helpless to control it. It frightened him. He had never thought to need a woman, even in a physical way, which was surely all this was.

Yet this soft creature, so remarkably yielding, was filling his senses with intoxicating desire. Could it be he was imagining her response? She seemed to cling to him with a helpless kind of urgency.

He broke away, searching her eyes to see what secrets he could glean in those depths, but she would not allow it. She struggled to free herself.

"My kisses do not please you, madam?" he said, annoyed with his own show of weakness.

"You know they do not."

"I think you are lying. Do not disappoint me, Alayna. You have always been brutally honest." He forced himself to relax his grip, sending her stumbling back. "So tell me what may I do to please you."

"You will not do it."

"Let me guess—divorce you. Is that it?"

Her lip curled as she tilted her head to its familiar angle. "Why do you keep taunting me in this cruel game? I cannot wait to be rid of you and your imperious, pompous, boorish— You will regret it all when my mother arrives."

"And what do you imagine will happen then, my lady love?" Derision dripped from every word.

Alayna did not flinch. She leveled her emerald gaze at him and said, "Then I will see your head served to me upon a silver platter for what you have done."

Lucien was stunned by the vehemence with which she spoke and the sneer that marred her lovely features.

How could he have ever thought to have put the battle to rest?

"Why then, Salome, it seems that my days may be quite numbered until that fateful hour. I am all atremble." Her eyes darkened at his caustic mockery. "So, as the troubadours preach, let us make merry now, for tomorrow may bring sorrow and death."

His hands shot out, catching her by the shoulders, and wrenched her to him once again. "Come, wife," he rasped. "Let us make merry tonight."

His mouth closed over hers cruelly this time, crushing and bruising as he had wanted to do before. Gone were his good intentions, the careful tenderness, and much of his restraint, as well.

"Nay!" Alayna sighed, not even struggling. He paid her no mind, bending to devour the luscious curves that tempted him at her shoulder and the gentle sculpture of her throat. The scent of her, feminine and sensuous and so foreign to him, assailed his senses, weaving a spell that threatened to overtake his will. He was losing himself in her, her texture, her taste. She had gone limp against him, her pulse fluttering wildly against his lips when he kissed the tender flesh behind her ears.

She made a sound, like a soft moan in the back of her throat and shook her head to deny him, but it was another lie, so feeble he ignored it. His hands roamed daringly over her curves, lulling her into sensual abandon when, without warning, she cried out, "Nay!" and, catching him off guard, jerked out of his grasp.

"You do not know when enough is quite enough, Alayna!"

"Do not touch me again!" she cried shrilly. "I cannot bear it."

"What is it you cannot bear? This?" He made to reach for her, then stopped in shock as she recoiled. That small action had the power to wound him that no sword ever did.

"Am I so disgusting to you?" he said before he could check it. She stared at him, her mouth red from his kiss, her eyes like brilliant bits of ice. She looked so incredibly desirable he had to turn away before he lost what little control remained. "I am truly sorry if the idea is so repugnant to you. Go now, if that is what you wish. We will have it your way. Perhaps there is no turning back the trouble between us. But remember it was your choice."

She did not answer for such a long time that he thought perhaps she had indeed crept silently away.

"Why do you not simply take what you want?" she whispered. "You always do."

He turned back to her. "I will not take this."

"You do not fight fair, de Montregnier. Just when I am ready to despise you as the most loathsome of men, you finally give me the freedom I have been begging for all along. You would really let me go? Risk losing everything?"

He did not answer. Watching the play of emotions that flashed across her face, Lucien could trace her disbelief, her suspicion, her guilt and, finally, her resignation.

She said, "You know it is a sin, as well as against the law, for a wife to ban her husband from her bed. Do you set a trap for me? Well, you will have no cause to torment me with any punishment. I will allow you your rights." She shot him a resentful look. "Does that make you happy, *husband?*"

He almost laughed. Trust her to give him what he wanted, but dress it so that he could never take it, not this meek submission to wifely duty.

"Nay, Alayna, it does not make me happy."

"You are never happy."

"Perhaps that is my curse."

She gave him a derisive sigh. "What else do you want from me?"

He closed the distance between them in a sudden surge of determination. He saw the look on her face, a flash of fear, and something else. Damn her, why could she not just admit that despite all of the enmity between them, there also existed an unexplainable tide of passion? "Only this," he murmured harshly.

She did nothing to resist him this time. A low growl escaped him as he brought his mouth down to hers once again. Let her deny it now, he thought. Let her play the unwilling bride here in his arms, if she could, and he would leave her without another word.

She fought it. To the credit of her damnable pride, she tried desperately to hold out against the combustible feeling that exploded within them, but her body betrayed her as it had before. She melted against him, her arms reaching up to hold on as one who is drowning reaches for their rescuer.

He had only meant to summon her desire with a kiss, but he could not stop now even if he wanted to. A fire had spread through him and he abandoned himself to its urgent prodding. He had never held a woman and had it be like this, felt these feelings that coursed like life's blood in his limbs, leaving him in a mindless state of need.

He parted her lips and tasted the sweetness of her mouth. Suddenly he could not touch her enough, taste her enough, get her close enough to him.

She was his, completely at his mercy. Impatient, he worked to unfasten her clothing. Her gown slipped easily off her shoulders, but the thin chemise underneath was tied, necessitating a degree of patience to undo it that he did not have. Gripping two fistfuls of the fabric, he ripped it in two.

A soft cry escaped her when his hand touched her fevered skin. He savored the feel of her flesh, bared to his exploration, as his hands smoothed down her back, then up again to take the rounded weight of her breast in his hand. The hard press of its aroused peak against his palm sent a renewed jolt through his body that threatened to tear his very mind from him.

Pulling him close, she arched against that intimate caress. A thrill at such a victory nearly brought him to the brink of madness. This was what he wanted! She could not deny sensation. She could refute him on everything else, but the body had a will of its own.

He drew away. She was the most lovely thing he had ever set eyes upon in his life, made more so now with the flush of desire staining her cheeks. Her eyelids were heavy and she looked a bit dazed.

"You asked what I want from you. 'Tis simple. I want for you to freely give what is only yours to offer," he said. "Say me nay now, wife. Tell me to stop, and I will do it. But if you wish me to take you, then you must speak it out loud. I will not have you claim you were unwilling. Say you will have me or tell me no, for this is the last time I will ask, but I will not be satisfied with your pretense of mere submission, for it is more than that between us."

She stared back at him, a horror in her eyes as she realized what he was asking. "I said I would not deny you. I swore before God to honor and obey, and the law forbids—"

"Blast the law, Alayna!" he thundered. "This is between you and I."

"If I forbid you, you will beat me for disobeying—"

He gave her a vicious shake. "No beatings, I promise you. How can you think—? When have I ever lifted a hand to you? No threats now. Nothing but desire—yours and mine. Tell me what you want. *Tell* me."

Alayna stared at him, frozen, mute. The absolutely unthinkable part of it all was she *did* want him. She did not wish him to stop the exciting, terrifying whirlwind he had created. Every nerve in her body was aching for his scalding kiss and the smooth, warm touch of his hands. She would have begged him for the fulfillment of the fires he had ignited within her but for the shred of sanity that pulled her back from the terrifying edge of abandon.

He was watching her with black, fathomless eyes, waiting for her to succumb. Waiting for another victory for the unconquered warrior.

Yet, there in his eyes, too, was a desperate hope as he awaited her reply. But how could she trust it?

"Nay," she said, barely above a whisper.

"What did you say to me, lady?" Lucien demanded.

As soon as the words were out, she regretted them. What had she unleashed with that unlawful denial? She watched in horrified fascination as the mask settled back over his features and his grip relaxed.

Suddenly he grasped her neck in his open palms and pressed a cruel kiss to her lips. She thought he was going to go back on his word and take her anyway, but then he released her and stepped away.

She fumbled for the scraps of material that lay draped about her hips, covering her naked breasts.

"So, then, I'll leave you, just as I promised. But remember you were the one who chose it to be this way."

He looked dangerous, his eyes blazing. She thought it

must be her guilty conscience that imagined an awful pain in the charcoal depths.

"It appears I was gravely mistaken. I thought for a moment that there was more than ice running in your veins."

Before she could react, he was gone.

Lucien woke his master of the butlery to tap a fresh keg of ale and took a full skin with him up to the battlements.

He often walked along this stretch alone, enjoying the solitude and the unhindered view of his domain. His castle, his lands, his people, which he had wrested away from his enemy in a brilliant strategic attack that had won him everything he had ever dreamed of. His, all of it.

Who the hell cared? he thought miserably, running his hand through his hair. How had he ever allowed himself to come to this end?

Slamming the skin down, he prowled restlessly, his body tight with tension. He had almost lost control of himself back there. How he had stopped himself from tossing her onto the bed and taking her against her will, he did not know. Pride, he supposed. He had more than his share of that quality, he had been told not infrequently. Others considered it a fault, but it had gotten him through those dark years of torture and humiliation. As much as Hendron had tried, he had never been able to break that streak of stubborn determination.

Where had his damnable pride been tonight? Dear Lord, he had stopped just short of begging for her. So she hated him, found him so disgusting that his touch sent her near mad with revulsion, did she? But she did not—that was the thing. The little liar could not admit that in spite of her bitter heart, she was as vulnerable to the attraction between them as he was himself.

Damn her! Damn her for her beauty and those eyes that could flash with rage or go soft to limpid pools of green when wounded. And damn himself for the weakness that had made him susceptible to those manipulative wiles. He had even offered to let her go, for God's sake!

Well, she was not going anywhere. He had been insane to even think it. She could pout and sulk to her heart's desire, but he would not allow her sweet face to deprive him of what he wanted. She was the key to keeping Gastonbury. Let her despise him, curse him, do her worst. He had lived without the love of a mother, so too could he survive without the gentle regard of his wife.

He had the power to see to her undoing. For all of her cold rejection, she could not deny the unwilling response of her body. Aye, he had an ally there.

It was a game of power. He would never forget that again.

Anger and pride and bitterness came together, forging a new resolve that congealed into a hard knot inside him. It was a familiar brew.

Chapter Twelve

Alayna came awake with the unpleasant sensation of a smack landing smartly on her posterior. With a yelp, she sat up and whirled around to find herself nose-to-nose with Lucien. It took an instant for the clinging wisps of sleep to clear from her head.

"Rise, wife, and fetch my bath. I need to be off early today."

"I beg your pardon?" she said archly.

"It will do you no good to beg, woman, for you will not be permitted to loll about lazily in your room. Fetch the water and see to my bath."

"But those are the duties of a squire!"

"I have no squire. I do not need one, for I do have a wife."

She audibly choked on that. Implicitly dismissing her, he began to undress. When Alayna saw he meant to strip naked, she sprang from the bed. Stepping quickly into a gown, she sped to the kitchens to fetch the water.

A servant set it on the fire to warm, but Alayna assured him that he need not, grinning at the thought of the frigid bath she would deliver. She sloshed the heavy burden up the stairs, spilling it all over herself and leaving a trail of soaked rushes behind her.

Staggering into the chamber, she found Lucien seated by the hearth with nothing but a piece of linen draped over his lap. He was inspecting the leather ties of his belt, oblivious to her openmouthed shock at seeing him in this state of undress. She stood frozen in the doorway, gaping at the sight of his broad chest unveiled for her eyes. The muscles in his arms flexed in a most fascinating way as he worked the tie, testing its strength.

"Pour the buckets into the basin, and be about it quickly. I cannot waste the entire morning waiting for you," he commanded gruffly.

Terrified he would stand and let that inadequate scrap of cloth fall away, she hastened to quit the room.

"You will not leave my presence until you are given leave to do so!" he thundered, just as she was at the door. "Remember that in the future and it will save you a painful lesson in wifely obedience."

Her teeth sank into her bottom lip as she turned away from the portal. Pretending to busy herself tidying the room, she took special care to keep her back to him at all times. She could hear the splash of water as he washed, then the soft sound of the drying linen being rubbed briskly on his skin. She was assaulted by uninvited images of him rubbing the washing cloth over his body—the wide shoulders she had glimpsed, the thickly corded arms and long, strong legs.

His voice close to her ear made her start. "Very invigorating, wife. How did you know that I prefer a chill temperature for my morning ritual? It is excellent that you please me so well."

She gritted her teeth at his snide remark. "Are you through?"

"You may turn around, my love," he drawled sarcastically. "I do not think my appearance should offend."

He had dressed. She gave him a look as if she found the man before her wanting. "Oh, my lord, but you do offend."

He casually toyed with a tendril of her hair. It took every bit of her restraint not to yank the strand out of his hand.

"Take care, Alayna, for on the morrow, I may wish you to attend me at my bath," he said. He chuckled at her appalled expression, turning on his heel to exit the room. At the doorway, he called back, "Coming, my love?"

Sighing in disgust, she followed. They walked in silence into the hall and took their seats.

During his meal, Lucien commanded Alayna to choose meats and tidbits for him from the large trays proffered by the servers. She resented having to serve him publicly. It was the position of a servant or the squire to fill the lord's trencher, or for the man to serve the woman as a show of honor. Having to perform this lowly duty was his way of demeaning her.

She was sorely aware of the curious looks it earned from those gathered in the hall. Glowering at him, she dumped food roughly onto his trencher, making a great effort to splash him. Globs of gravy and morsels of food were thrown up onto his tunic. He cast a brief scowl at her game, but he only wiped away the stains without comment.

When the meal was done, he simply rose and quit the place without the courtesy of a farewell. It made her chafe, this public display of his scorn. Pretending not to care, she hurried out, thinking to find Eurice. After a short search, she located her nurse in a small room off the kitchens, mixing poultices from herbs and grease. When Alayna entered, the older woman only looked up at her briefly, wordlessly returning to her chores.

"Good morn," Alayna said.

Eurice gave her a baleful look. "My lady."

"What is it you are doing?" she queried, trying to smooth over the tension between them. "Which poultice do you mix?"

"Something to heal one of the villager's maladies, nothing more. 'Tis nothing important."

"It must be important, for it seems to occupy you day and night." Alayna's comment had a sting, one that Eurice did not miss.

Eurice looked up. "Do you think I have neglected you, child?"

Feeling abused by de Montregnier and piqued by her nurse's lack of consolation, Alayna snapped, "Abandoned would be the truth of it."

"And what is it that you require that I have begrudged you?"

"Your company, for one!" she said.

"And what do you think I can do for you? Do you think the pining of an old woman will help you now? You are wed, and your path is set. You need nothing from the likes of me."

Alayna's eyes narrowed suspiciously. "Has de Montregnier done something to forbid you from me?"

"Nay," Eurice denied. "The baron has not troubled me. He would not do such a thing. He is nothing like Edgar was, and a woman could do much worse than him for a husband." At Alayna's look of disgust, she added, "You must try harder, Alayna. It is a wife's duty to acquiesce to her husband."

"Bah!"

Eurice's eyes narrowed, and she asked quickly, "Did you turn him away last night?"

"Nay, I did not. He…" How could she explain? "I told him I would submit."

"Ah," Eurice said, satisfied, then grew suspicious. "And how do you fare this morn? Do you need something for the pain? And the bleeding, has it stopped?"

"A-aye, the pain, it does trouble me. But do not worry over it—"

"You never lied well, Alayna!" Eurice snapped. "He did not bed you!"

"He did not want me!"

Eurice snorted harshly, "That is another lie. The man has been prowling about for weeks trying not to look at you. Are you so blind you cannot see how you plague him?"

"He wanted…more than I could give."

"Whatever your husband wants, it is your duty to submit." Eurice stopped, considering something for a moment. "What was it he asked?"

"For me to admit that I wanted him." There, Alayna thought. Surely Eurice would understand why she could not yield that.

"Oh, child." Eurice chuckled. "You are so young and proud. Would it truly be so hard to tell the truth?" At Alayna's surprised look, the woman shook her head. "You have a handsome, virile husband who desires you. Forget the old resentments, Alayna, and concede to him."

"I cannot!"

"Your mother and I were wrong to indulge you so. We meant to love you and teach you well, for you were a beautiful, bright, enchanting child. But I see you have become spoiled.'' Tears stung Alayna's eyes. The woman's words were like an assault. ''You need not coddling now, for that is the way of a child, and too long were you kept as one. Rather you must now make your way as a woman. Now you are a wife, and someday may become a mother. It is time you grew up, Alayna.''

There was truth here, but she could not bear it. Speechless with hurt and indignation, Alayna whirled and ran from the room.

That night at the evening meal, Alayna made sure to keep her own counsel. She did not bicker with de Montregnier, she did not dump his food sloppily onto his plate, nor did she splash his wine when she poured it into his chalice.

''Your lady wife is unusually quiet tonight, Lucien. Have you frightened the poor girl into this unnatural silence?'' Agravar questioned.

Lucien had noticed the difference, as well. ''Aye, she does indeed seem to be behaving more appropriately this evening,'' he said. ''No hostile challenges, no rapier insults. I nary know how to conduct myself without the constant barrage of old.''

Feeling a particular satisfaction at Alayna's show of obedience, he did not take note of Agravar's frown of displeasure. ''She does seem to be somewhat…less spirited,'' Agravar commented.

'''Tis good and well,'' Lucien said, and smiled, gloating freely, ''for she was much too headstrong. It just shows a woman who is high-strung must have a firm hand to guide her. This done, she will know how to act as a proper wife should.''

''And what would you know of proper wifely behavior?'' Agravar snorted. "Your dame did nothing to honor your sire. And save that damning scowl for someone upon whom it will work.''

Lucien did not lighten his expression. "You are correct, my mother did not show me how a goodly wife should act. Rather her instruction was in the way of how one should *not* behave. And I intend to cherish the harsh lessons I have observed from her. I will not tolerate prideful displays, petulant tempers and vanity.''

"With all due respect, Lucien, I have observed none of these qualities in your lady wife," Agravar chided gently.

"Nor will you,'' Lucien answered darkly.

Still smarting from the confrontation with Eurice, Alayna could not shake her somber mood.

It did not help that every movement of Lucien's made her want to jump out of her skin. His presence burned her with a preternatural heat. She could not keep her eyes off his hands, large and sun browned with long fingers that were calloused and hard. Her traitorous mind kept imagining them on her skin, as they had been last night, hot and possessive. She shivered, forcing her eyes away only to be drawn back by the unwilling tug of disturbing memory.

If he touched her again with those hands, could she deny him?

She would go mad if she had nothing to think about for two months but Lucien's hands, she decided. Maybe she would work on getting some things together for the villagers. De Montregnier seemed interested in the contentment of his people; perhaps he would be amenable.

"Whatever suits you,'' Lucien replied when she asked. Rising, he mumbled something to Agravar and left. Alayna stared after him, then shrugged. Who could understand him?

Moments later, a nervous young servant approached. "Your master commands you to attend him in his chamber," the lad recited stiffly.

Alayna felt the simultaneous flush of anger and shame. To her acute embarrassment, several smirks were directed knowingly her way. "Tell my lord I will be there presently," she murmured.

The youth shifted uncomfortably, "My lady, he instructed me to bring you back posthaste."

"But I am otherwise occupied, and I wish not to retire just now."

"Our new baron has need for you, lady," one young woman teased. "His appetite for food has been met. Now he seeks to satisfy his other."

The woman laughed at the ribald comment. Alayna had no choice. Lucien himself would bluster into the room and drag her back with him if she refused.

She gathered the remnants of her dignity and rose in a smooth movement. Tilting her chin a notch, she followed the boy to the master's chamber.

Chapter Thirteen

Alayna found him in one of his sulks, brooding in his chair by the hearth. She would have liked to vent her spleen after such a humiliation as he had dealt her, but she saw that he was in no mood. He glared at her as soon as she entered, snarling, "In the future, madam, I will expect you to accompany me to our chamber after every evening meal."

She made no reply. "Is that understood?" he demanded. Alayna nodded mutely, preparing to make herself ready for bed.

Confused, she stood for a moment, unsure. She was too modest to undress with him present. And she could not sleep in her clothing, like a servant. As if reading her thoughts, she heard a chuckle rumble from the direction of the fireplace.

"Go ahead and disrobe. 'Tis nothing I have not already viewed." She saw his eyes darken as he watched her. "Aye, and I would gladly see that vision again, wife." She watched him apprehensively. He seemed strange, thoughtful and agitated, as if he had been ruminating on unpleasant thoughts.

With a fluid movement, he rose from his seat to come to stand before her. "Surely it is my right to see my bride in that state of natural beauty, unhampered by the constraint of clothing, that a man longs for? Would you deny me, Alayna?"

She shook her head, meaning she would obey him, but then made no move to do it.

"You are quiet tonight. What blessed event has caused the stillness of your acid tongue?" He slid his hands up her arms, over her shoulders, to splay his fingers around her neck. "Why do you hesitate? Is it that you need help? I am glad to assist you, but I recall that yestereve I did not do a very capable job in your undressing."

He was mocking her, of course, for last night he had destroyed her garments. She knew if she resisted, the end would be the same, for he would surely make good on his threat and tear her clothing from her back.

Praying he meant only to taunt her, she stepped out of her gown. When he looked at her expectantly, she reluctantly drew the undertunic over her head to stand shivering before him in her shift.

She kept her eyes lowered, not wanting to see the disapproval in her denial of his request to see her naked. The shift was flimsy enough, being of fine linen but it did offer some degree of shielding.

"Are you not fond of that piece of clothing?" he needled. She crossed her arms protectively over her breasts.

"Please, my lord," she whispered.

Lucien lifted her chin so that he could see her face. "'Tis rare that I see you like this, soft and meek. I wonder if 'tis real or just another ploy to melt a man's heart."

"You cannot expect me to strip and stand before you. Even you would not be so cruel to require it from me."

His eyes flickered over her, softening.

"Aye, I will allow you your modesty, for now." Still he did not move away. She wished he would leave her, for her body was trembling violently with his nearness.

He had not forced her last night. Did he regret his not having taken her? Did he mean to right it tonight?

"You are beautiful, you do know that, my lady wife?" He drew her into his arms and kissed her gently. She held her breath against the soft touch, her heart thumping wildly in her chest. She feared he would feel the pounding of it against his own breast. She could feel the muscular hardness of the whole length of his body. His mouth felt warm, his tongue touching hers in a heart-stopping invasion that left her limp.

Her mind calmly reminded her of her anger, of all that he had done to hurt and offend, yet she felt herself slipping away, caught up again in the sensations that had assailed her yestereve. Waves of flittering pleasure teased her belly and sparked the fires of arousal to life. She moaned as if in protest, but it came out throaty and passion filled. She tried to turn away from his mouth, but he only swept down to devour her shoulders and neck.

His mouth was like a branding iron searing her flesh with kisses of fire. The calloused hands she had studied so diligently at supper slid down over her curves, kneading her womanly shape. She was falling down, down, swallowed once again by the mindless demands he so expertly aroused.

He broke away again, leveling a searching look deep into her soul. "It is as before, Alayna. You will have to say me yea before I will take you. I have made a vow not to take an unwilling bride to the marriage bed, and so I ask you now—do you consent?''

Would he truly always leave her alone as he had promised? she wondered. Is that not what she wanted? If so, why did she not speak the word and gain tonight another reprieve?

"Why do you hesitate?" he prodded. "Can it be that you are considering the benefits of my bed?"

"Nay, you braying ass!" she exclaimed sharply, unnerved. Lucien only smiled ruefully.

"Before you decide, my cold, cold wife," he said bitterly, "let me give you a sample of the delights you decline." With that, he pulled her back into his arms. His kiss was now passionate and demanding, swiftly taking her over. Then suddenly, he released her. As she stumbled back from the unexpected absence of support, he swept her shift neatly over her head, leaving her naked before she realized what was happening.

"I am improving," he commented, noting the intact shift as he tossed it aside. He pulled her back to be kissed. His hands roamed freely, shockingly, over her silken flesh. He cupped one breast, drawing his thumb over its taut peak in agonizing excitement. She whimpered and tried to wrest herself away though she was not at all sure she wanted to be free.

His mouth left hers to follow where his hands had been, capturing the hardened nipple in his mouth. She stopped struggling, suddenly going limp. Tangling her hands in his long hair, she held him close as he swirled his tongue in a wicked caress. Her knees buckled, and if not for his strong arms, she would have fallen.

He pressed his advantage and slid lower, bending over her as he pressed her down on the bed. She felt as if she were floating in a maelstrom of sheer sensation, all thought suspended. He was sweeping away her will with each passing moment.

His breath was ragged, his voice a hoarse whisper in her ear. "What say you?"

Alayna felt ravaged, neglected, angry and impatient all at once. Her body screamed for something she did not understand. Yet she despised him all the more for having this power over her. "You know my answer."

Lucien shoved her from him roughly as if in disgust. When he turned away, she made to retrieve her shift, but Lucien's voice shot out with a sharp denial.

"Your pride was indulged quite enough this evening, you'll not be permitted another allowance. Your perversity surprises me, Alayna. In your efforts to deny me my rights as your husband, you treat yourself badly, for you deny your own pleasure, as well. Do you not wonder what lies beyond the touching? Have you not thought that there is fulfillment in what is aroused between us? I will tell you that there is, sensations you have probably never dreamed existed." He considered her callously for a moment. "But not for you, my ice maiden, for the cold grip of pride cannot be melted by mere kisses. But I will not be denied all of my rights, so leave off the shift and climb into bed beside me." He looked away, fighting visibly with his anger. "We will continue to test this cursed pride that afflicts us both."

She buried herself under the furs quickly, squeezing her eyes shut as he disrobed. As he lay beside her, she held her breath. Moments passed. He made no move for her.

The morn dawned clear and the yellow rays of sunlight invaded the room through the slivers between the window's shutter boards. Alayna nuzzled sleepily into the warmth against her side, sighing in her sleep in oblivious contentment.

Awake beside her, Lucien smiled to himself as she pressed her cheek to his shoulder, arching her back to mold her body to his side. His body was responding to her unwitting sensuality, but he kept still, savoring the feel of her against him and anticipating the moment she would wake to find herself clinging to him like a lazy kitten. He was not going to rob himself of that bit of pleasure by his growing impatience.

She roused, stretching languorously before opening her eyes to stare full into his face, not more than a breath away. Her eyes focused, widened, and just at the moment when she made to push away, Lucien tightened his grip to keep her at his side.

"Good morn, my love," he drawled.

"What are you doing?" she sputtered.

"Why nothing, my little love pet, just sleeping when suddenly I was wakened by the impertinent press of you against me. I confess, it did shock me, but I must admit I was not displeased."

She was incredulous. "You are lying, sir, for I would never voluntarily touch you, even while asleep."

"And yet you have the evidence before you," he said, smiling.

"'Tis some trick."

He studied her eyes, sparkling like green crystals and fringed heavily with black lashes, seeming as if they could look clear through to a man's soul.

"Why do you fight me, Alayna, when you know your body craves what I can give you?"

"You are despicable!" she gasped, trying anew to free herself, though still to no avail.

"Do you wish me to test you?" he rumbled dangerously.

Before she could cry out her refusal, his hand reached out to bare a breast. She tried desperately to cover herself, but he easily caught her hands in his and held them out of the way. Her eyes flickered to his face, blanching when his hand covered her exposed flesh. He watched her eyes grow dark as he crooked his forefinger and gently grazed a knuckle over the sensitive peak. She bit her lip, but otherwise made no move or sound.

Alayna forced herself to lie still. She must not allow him to affect her this time.

She could have succeeded if his hands had not begun their rousing travels, sliding smoothly over her flesh to create shivery flutters to wash over her. Her body was alive suddenly and her will to resist drained away with unbelievable swiftness.

He bent over her, bringing his mouth to pause just before hers so that it was she who closed the breach, reaching up hungrily for the offered kiss.

"Say it," he murmured.

It was nearly impossible to stifle the words as they welled up in her throat, but she could never, never give him that.

"Nay, Lucien," she whispered. "Do not ask it of me. Take what you want and leave me my dignity."

He paused, the sound of his breathing labored as he fought for control. "You are a fool."

With that, he rose abruptly, leaving her to gather her wits. He was dressed and out of the chamber quickly.

* * *

Lucien was nowhere about when she descended into the hall.

Alayna flung headlong into the arrangements for her second trip to the village, spending the better part of the day with the seneschal, Alwin, inventorying the castle stores. Though she had seen evidence before of Edgar du Berg's great fondness for greedily amassing wealth, she was still stunned as she sorted through the excess and made her selections.

"I must ask my lord husband if he approves of my giving away so much," Alayna said to her companion, thinking aloud as she planned.

"Lord Lucien left instructions that you were to be given freedom to choose whatever you require," the kindly man announced with a broad smile. He had been Edgar's man and, though he never said a word against his old master, it was clear that he held the new lord in high esteem. "Said he trusted you, he did."

When she had recovered from her incredulity, she began to order the stock for her wagons with a renewed enthusiasm and the project was well on its way by the end of the day.

It was not until supper that she was told Lucien would not be returning for several nights. Pelly shyly informed her that his master and Agravar had ridden out with some of de Montregnier's men to clear the forest of a band of thieves who had been nesting there. She was assured he would return in time to escort her to the village as planned.

She was surprised at the sharp stab of disappointment. Ignoring it, she vowed to put this time to good use, determined to spend a good deal of it on her knees in the chapel praying for prudence. And chastity.

It was several days later when she was in the stables,

speaking with the master of the horses about the proper number of mounts and wagons for her needs. Like the seneschal, the head groom had been instructed to cooperate fully with her. Unlike Alwin, however, the burly man had no patience with his new mistress.

"Seems like we should be worried about ourselves and not them folks down there," he muttered under his breath after hearing her instructions.

"If not for those people down there tilling their fields, you would have nothing on your table!" Alayna snapped. "Nor would your lord. It serves him to see to their needs. Now do as I have told you and do not let me hear another complaint."

He shrugged indolently, slouching away. "And another thing," she called after him. "You may accompany us. Perhaps a closer look will teach you some Christian caring. If not, then some good hard labor will do you good."

He turned away silently, kicking a wooden pail out of his way in disgust.

Alayna let out a long breath when he was gone, a bit amazed at the sharp rage that had come upon her. Sitting on a plank that had been placed over two crates, she rested her head against the wall. Perhaps she was overtired, she reasoned. The mission to the village had taken on a momentum she had not anticipated and she was busy with the preparations almost day and night. Yet neither her frenetic level of activity nor her fervent prayers for self-control had done anything to banish her unchaste thoughts. Dark eyes and a wild mane of hair haunted her mind like a demon torturing its poor victim.

A movement out of the corner of her eye caught her attention. It was Will standing in the doorway.

"Will, did you wish to see me?" she asked.

The knight hesitated a moment. "Nay, lady, 'twas just that I was making sure you are well."

Touched by his chivalry, she said, "That is kind of you, but unnecessary. I am sure that I am quite safe within these castle walls."

He was visibly uncomfortable. "Just the same, I shall keep watch over you."

It was his awkward manner more than his words that made her suspicious. "Did de Montregnier send you to spy on me?"

"He has asked me to see to your safety, aye."

"Does your baron fear so much that I will attempt an escape that he must send you to mind me like a child?"

Will only shrugged, refusing to rise to her challenge.

She snorted. "I doubt 'tis my safety that worries him, but rather the notion that I may make good my intention to leave here as soon as I am able. God forbid it, that the great Lucien de Montregnier be robbed of one vestige of what Edgar once laid claim to. Never mind that I am a human being, a woman with feelings, and most notable among these sentiments is loathing for that arrogant man!"

She sprang to her feet and stomped a few paces away, jamming her fists down on her hips while she seethed at the audacity of de Montregnier. To put a guard on her!

Will ignored her distraction. "Alayna," he said softly. "I would speak to you."

She blinked. "Aye?"

He hesitated, as if he were wrestling with a great decision. "I know you are unhappy. Lucien...he treats you badly. I beg you to consider an alternative."

"Alternative?"

He paused for a heartbeat. "Me."

"What?" she exclaimed.

"Think what I am offering. I would protect you, take you away. Surely you have noticed my admiration. If things had been different, I would have wooed you myself. As it is, I cannot stand by and see you so miserable. What I am trying to tell you, Alayna, is I care for you."

"Please, speak no more," she said, stepping away. She was married before God, no matter what her feelings were about it. She would not play Lucien false with another.

He reached out and closed his hand over her arm. "Alayna, do not dismiss me so quickly. Think on it, on what I can offer." Their gazes locked for a swift moment before he pulled her to him and kissed her, all of his longing, all of his need pouring out in that stolen embrace.

She held herself stiff and unyielding in his arms until he released her. Breaking free from his relaxed grip, she wiped her hand across her mouth.

"Do you seek to dishonor me, Will?"

"Nay," he breathed. His blue eyes blazed with his desire, but his voice remained sober. "I have never been a man of honor—I have no illusions about myself. I am a soldier for hire, a mercenary. I was employed by de Montregnier to help him gain this land. But you see, I found I wanted to serve as a knight should, out of loyalty, not money. Then, he had to marry you, and he does not even cherish you as you deserve."

He looked away as if he could not bear the sight of her any longer. "I would honor you, and love you with all of my heart."

"No, Will. True, my lot with Lucien is not to my liking, but running away with you would not be right."

He looked crestfallen, smiling sadly as he turned back to her. "I should not have spoken."

As he made to leave, Alayna placed her hand on his

arm. "Do not brood on this, Will. I will speak of it to no one. But know this. You are dear to me, but I do not love you, and if I were not the wife of your lord, I would still decline your troth. I love no man."

"Do you not?" he asked mysteriously.

"I will leave de Montregnier when the time comes."

Will regarded her for a moment before speaking. "I compromised you in a way no gentleman should a lady. I was selfish when I sought you for myself, and you were right to turn me away." He gave her a long look. "I knew what it would do to Lucien should you come to me, yet I risked it."

"Oh, certainly, it would goad him into quite a fit to be cheated of the least of his prizes."

"Alayna, are you so blind? It would devastate him." His voice was choked with guilt. "You see what a knave I am?"

"Nothing would devastate de Montregnier," she snorted, "least of all a woman, and certainly not me."

Will only shook his head slowly. "Come, let us get inside before someone finds us and starts to gossip. We will do as you say and forget this unfortunate conversation."

He followed her back to the main building where they entered the castle in silence. Alayna headed straightaway to the chamber that was hers and Lucien's. She was distracted and troubled, but not by Will's imprudent actions.

She could think of only one thing as she wandered around the empty room, feeling an inexplicable press of loneliness. Will had kissed her, taken her fully into a passionate embrace.

And she had felt nothing.

What was wrong with her that a man of gentleness and

courtly manners, handsome and pleasant, who by rights would make any maid swoon, interested her not in the least? Instead, she was susceptible to a brooding cur who loved to bait and mock her, who brutishly forced her to submit to his amorous assaults in the hopes of wresting the ultimate victory from her. De Montregnier was right on one account—she was perverse!

Chapter Fourteen

On the morn of Alayna's second trip to the village, the wagons were already loaded and waiting when Lucien and his men rode into the bailey.

"I see you have not disappointed me, my lord husband," Alayna said when he pulled his mount alongside hers. "Though you wait until the last possible moment"

Lucien shrugged. "It could not be helped. Let us be on our way." He kicked his horse past hers and led the group out through the castle gate, choosing to ignore her haughty look. She was spoiling for a fight this morning, but for once he was not up to it.

He had not meant to be rude to her. It just seemed to come, as it always did, when she flashed those green eyes and tilted her head at that intolerable angle. And why did she look so unaffectedly appealing, even dressed as she was in a simple gown of gray and her hair pulled back?

When they arrived at the village, they rode directly away to the marketplace. Lucien watched warily for signs of the rancor Alayna had met before, but was gratified to see rather hopeful expectation in the faces of the folk who watched.

"Bring the carts up, and get some help unpacking them," he ordered. The crowd seemed to recoil at his harsh tone. Was he truly that intimidating? he wondered. He knew he was when he meant to be, but he intended no ill will here. Softening his tone, he continued, "There is much to be done. Each of you see to your assigned duties."

He saw Alayna rush over to greet a woman who was holding a babe. She swept the child into her arms and laughed enchantingly as the tiny boy waved his arms. The woman followed Alayna and the child into one of the huts, leaving Lucien to stare like a dumbstruck fool after her.

He had never seen her laugh, he realized. Not like that, completely carefree and without any bitterness. She was never that way with him.

"It gets no easier, does it, friend?" Agravar smiled. Lucien scowled and the Norseman chuckled. "Why do you insist on this game when you have but to take her, and you will be relieved of this distraction?"

"Thank you for the sage advice," Lucien snapped, "but considering your long acquaintance with women, you will understand if I do not become overly enthusiastic at your direction."

Agravar winced as if wounded by Lucien's retort, then immediately fell to laughing once again. Lucien only deepened his frown.

"My lord," Pelly interrupted, "I have with me a man of the village who has requested a word with you."

The man, a brawny fellow of perhaps two score and ten, waited nervously. Lucien made an effort to frown less. He wanted respect from these people, not the fear Edgar had inspired.

"My lord baron, several of the village men wish to

speak with you," the man said. His hands were busily wringing his cap. "Would you consent to join us in the gathering room above the tavern?"

Lucien indicated for him to lead the way. Dismounting, he followed him to a small, dusty room accessed by a dark rising of narrow timber stairs. Several men were seated on stools, silent as Lucien and Agravar ducked inside.

One of them, an ancient with a glorious mane of snow-white hair and a flowing beard, indicated an empty stool. Lucien declined.

"You are the new baron," the old man said. His voice was surprisingly strong. "We thank you for your generosity of the clothes."

"I gave no one clothing," he said.

The elder raised a brow. "Your lady, before you took her to wife, presented the poor of the village with gifts of clothing. She said they were from you."

"Ah." Lucien nodded. "Then she was the one who was being generous, for the gift was hers."

"She told us you were unlike Lord Edgar. She said you were fair. We have heard others report similarly to us. We want to know simply this—how do you intend to deal with us?"

Lucien admired this man—he was courageous and he was direct. He sat down on the stool which had been proffered earlier.

"Tell me of your village," he commanded simply.

The group exchanged glances. The ancient nodded to the brave one who had fetched Lucien to them, and he stepped forward, his hands still worrying his now mangled cap.

"If it pleases your lordship, my name is John. I have lived in this village all of my life, and I can tell you we never suffered as greatly as under the late lord." As if suddenly wary of speaking ill of the dead, John crossed himself and muttered, "God have mercy on his soul."

"Tell him about the tithings, John!" someone called.

John's head bobbed, "Aye, my lord, they nearly broke us."

Another man, a redhead with the burly look of a Scot came forward. "Aye, and terrorized us, he did."

Listening to story after story of the harrowing years under the reign of du Berg's barony, Lucien was much impressed by the group. He saw they were, for the most part, good and honest people, not adverse to hard work, but despondent after years of oppression by their nobility.

He listened patiently. When their appeals had drawn to a close, he stood and paced thoughtfully before them. "There are several matters which I will be able to remedy immediately, namely repairing your shelters and providing the necessary provisions for your families. These things have already, in fact, been initiated. Once completed, I will expect you to then use this advantage to further your own lots. Be assured I have no interest in harboring the same ill will of my predecessor, but neither will I be taken advantage of. I expect every man to work, and I will have my share as is my right as lord. But I will take only what I need. And that, I can assure you, is less than a tenth of what you were used to giving Lord Edgar."

A stunned murmur rippled through the gathering, followed by a hush as they awaited his next words. "As for the other matters," he continued, "I will take them under advisement."

The elder stood on wobbling legs, a glowing look of appreciation on his leathered face. He nodded, saying, "We thank you, my lord."

Lucien motioned to Agravar and the two took their leave. Once outside, Lucien said, "Have the men inspect the place and make a list of what will be needed. Do what you can today, and then report back to me."

"The castle is in need of a cheese maker?" the woman asked.

Alayna nodded at Leda's mother. "Indeed, good woman, the castle always has need for cheese such as I sampled. I will see that room is made for you and your family."

The woman seemed unimpressed by the compliment. "Have you something then for my daughter?"

"Aye," Alayna assured her. "Leda shall attend me. I am in need of a maid."

Satisfied, she pressed on. "One last thing. If we are to come to the castle and serve his lordship, I must know what manner of man he is." She leveled a meaningful gaze at Alayna. "Will my daughter be safe?"

Alayna was taken aback by the woman's frankness but understood her concern. Many a lord felt that any girl working in his keep was his to sample, and took full advantage of their superior position to assert this right. Though the question was a reasonable one, asking the lord's wife was a bit unusual.

She gave her response without prevarication. "He does not abuse his authority and he respects his servants and villeins. He has a growing esteem among his people. He would not harm your daughter, or any other maid. He even forbade his men from the usual...carousing when they first arrived."

She was surprised at the glowing terms with which she spoke of de Montregnier, even more so since they seemed to reflect her view of him fairly accurately. With somewhat of a start, she realized her husband was an admirable man in every area but where she was concerned. There, his scruples seemed to desert him, for she did appear to bring out the worst in him. That realization was not new, but the strange longing it brought on was.

"Very well, we will come," the woman said. Leda clasped her hands together and let out a small cry of joy.

Alayna was delighted, and thought how Lucien would also be pleased. Somehow, she liked the idea of pleasing him.

Leda and her mother packed their meager belongings to accompany them back to the castle that very evening. While they were about this business, Alayna busied herself playing outside with Thom, attracting the interest of the other village children and it was only a matter of time before they were all engaged in a rousing game of tag.

The sound of laughter drew Lucien's eye. He turned to spy his wife playfully chasing a groups of ragamuffin children. Pausing to watch, he could not suppress a small smile.

How he had missed her. He had thought the distance and time of this past week would clear his head, lessen the overwhelming need of her that threatened his mettle. Instead, his wretched longings had grown with each passing day, but he had forced himself to stay away, hoping they would extinguish themselves if not fanned by her stirring presence. Yet, the respite had done nothing but sharpen his desire.

She saw him, immediately sobering, the joy melting from her face and she composed herself quickly. He felt a tightening in his stomach at the change.

"My lord," she said breathlessly, coming over to him. He noted the wary look. "I would make a request. I have met a young woman whose mother is an excellent cheese maker. I thought she would do well to serve you with her talent."

"What is the point?" he said. He felt a pang of ire at her careful speech, liking it much less than the unguarded abandon he had witnessed just a moment ago.

"I asked them to come to the castle," she said cautiously. "I thought it would please you and I could use Leda as a maid, if you do not mind."

"I do not mind," he snapped, frustrated by the unintentional harshness in his voice.

She dropped a curtsy. "Many thanks, my lord," she murmured.

He supposed this show of compliance should please him, yet it did not. But for once, he kept his displeasure to himself.

They entered the castle walls just after dusk. Alayna went immediately to the chamber, undressed and slipped into bed before Lucien could come in, hoping that he might not trouble her if he thought her asleep.

He did not leave her much time to make a success of her intended ploy. She had not yet snuffed the candle when he entered, causing her to curse herself for not having been faster. A quick glance showed his absence had not improved his disposition. He looked tired and he was scowling.

"Fakery is unbecoming, Alayna," he said flatly.

She was chagrined that he guessed her intent. She flounced under the coverlet, drawing the fur higher in a show of petulance. "Neither are tantrums," he added dryly, ignoring her to see to his own disrobing.

"Is it only you, my lord, who is allowed to show any anger?"

Lucien shrugged, slipping easily into the role of antagonist. "I am the master of this shire."

Alayna glared at him.

"And remove that ridiculous garment," he commanded. "You look like a servant, sleeping in your clothes."

She grew angry at the rebuff, though she knew it to be true. The noble class slept upon furs, and they slept naked. Only serfs slept in clothing. She must make a laughable sight in her pathetic attempt to shield her body from him.

When she hesitated, he turned a baleful eye toward her. "Is that another garment you have no love for?" She shrugged her shift off quickly before diving under the furs.

Lucien turned back to the task of removing his boots. She could not help but watch him as he undressed without the aid of a page or squire. It made her wonder about him. If he were a born noble, the Lord of Thalsbury, how is it he held not one personal servant to dress him or care for his belongings, which were of fine quality and well made but few in number?

"Why do you not employ a squire to attend you?" she asked out loud before she realized she had given voice to her thoughts.

He looked up, surprised at her curiosity. "I am used to attending myself."

"But now that you are lord here, do you not think—"

"I prefer my privacy."

She fell silent after a small "Oh."

Lord, he was fearsome. His dark looks were handsome, but his thin beard and mustache gave him a sinister look.

His wild mane of hair was soft, she had learned. It added a sensuality to him that she found strangely appealing. As he undressed, his muscular body was revealed, sculpted and firm. The finely wrought muscles rippled with fluid movement as he bent to unlace his chausses.

He was a fine-looking man. Alayna felt the first stirrings of passion. Good Lord, she was lost if just looking upon him whet her desire. She glanced away.

He snuffed the candle and joined her in the bed. She cringed, breathless in anticipation of what would happen next. She didn't know what she feared the most—feeling his hands on her, pulling her to him once again, or hearing the even breathing indicating he was asleep and would not be troubling her tonight.

His hands touched first on her arms, traveling lightly along silken skin to caress the rounded shoulder. She tried to turn her mind away from the thrilling sensations his touch aroused. A sense of destiny settled over her, for this was the night. She knew her reaction was too strong and her defenses too weak to refuse him once more.

His voice, soft as velvet, floated to her in the darkness. "I tire of this game. I vowed to take you as a willing wife, but I will have you no matter what, for I can wait no longer for you to quit your silly woman's games."

"I have already said I will not resist you," she whispered into the air. From behind her, she felt him slip closer, pressing his full nakedness along the back of her. Her breath caught sharply in her throat, for she felt the hardness of his desire pressed against the back of her thigh.

"Nay, 'tis not what I seek," he said softly just below her ear. Shivers went through her. "I do not wish wifely obligations. You know what I want."

Aye, thought Alayna, *my complete, unconditional sur-*

render. She grew desperate. "A lady does not enjoy such pleasures, but submits herself to use by her husband only for the purpose of lawful begetting of children. As your wife, pledged before God, that is all I can offer." It was the catechism of young girls educated and influenced by prudish nuns and resentful priests and she didn't believe a word of it.

"You are a liar," he said softly, amusement making his voice light. It sounded like an endearment. She was weakening. She was almost gone.

"Did not your mother teach you the ways of lords and their ladies?" she tried desperately. "Women of virtue are not supposed to indulge in lustful beh—"

"Cease this gibberish prattling," he declared. His fingers dug into the tender flesh of her upper arms. "And never again speak of my mother to me!"

He gave her a quick shove as if suddenly repelled by her. "I am tired of your devious ways. You go out of your way to goad me. I give you chance after chance to redeem yourself, yet still you will not respond to a gentle hand. I could have you beaten. I swear, madam, I could do it myself without a qualm, for if ever a woman deserved it, it is you! But I fear I would be tempted to throttle you and thereby silence that nagging tongue forever."

He was out of bed, stepping angrily into his leggings. Alarmed, Alayna cowered in the furs.

What had she done? she wondered. She had not meant to anger him. There was some wound there she had prodded with her clumsy chatter.

"I'm sorry," she said softly. She knew he heard her words, for he stopped his movements for a moment.

Apparently they had no effect, for he left anyway.

Chapter Fifteen

He stayed away. Alayna had no idea where he slept, but he did not return to their chamber for nearly a sennight. She barely saw him during the day, and even when she did, they did not speak. Although it was what she wanted—to be left alone—she could not enjoy the respite. Her mind kept ruminating over the strange events of their last night together, trying to discern what it was she had said to make him so outraged.

She was still much preoccupied with her absent husband as she sat sewing in the chamber toward the end of the week. She liked to sew, found it very relaxing. It brought about pleasant memories of nights with her parents by the great hearth where her mother had taught her how to place small, even stitches in the fabric. Here they had spent time together as a family, laughing and telling stories and mostly teasing one another. Her father would look at her mother with adoring eyes, and Alayna would feel the love they shared surround them all like a protective cocoon.

She wondered if a man would ever look at her that way. Certainly de Montregnier never would.

She picked up a tunic of Lucien's and fingered a small

hole in the seam. She could fix it easily enough. Smoothing out the fine wool, she spread it over her lap. His clean masculine scent still clung to it. It was pleasant, making her sigh as she threaded her needle with black thread.

A loud commotion out in the bailey drew her attention. Adjusting the slats in the shutter, she peered down onto the courtyard below. A small crowd was gathered in a circle. In the center, a man struggled against two others whom she recognized as a pair of Lucien's mercenaries. Stripped naked to the waist, his back was crisscrossed with scarlet welts. Alayna flung open the shutter to get a better look.

A crisp snap cut the air as a thick strap of leather slithered to life, landing on the man's back to open another long wound.

Alayna was frantic. What was this? Where was Lucien, why did he not put a stop to this punishment?

Then she saw him, bare-chested and braced, standing a short distance from the man's mutilated back with the whip curling around his feet like a restless snake as he drew it back for another blow. The sweat glistened on his body, making him appear more powerful than she had ever seen him before. She watched in fascinated horror as he raised his arm to wield it once again. His muscles strained, bunching as he poised for a moment to gather his strength before bringing the weapon down to bear. The man cried out, jerking against his handlers.

Lucien's vengeance was not stayed. He swung again. Again. And yet one more time, until at last his arm was still.

He stood for a moment, sweating from the exertion, his chest heaving as he paused. He strode to the man, who was hanging limp from the terrible attack. Grabbing a fistful of his hair, Lucien jerked his head back to speak to him.

Lucien's message was brief. He let the man's head loll forward, casting the whip aside before stalking off toward the stables. He seemed terribly angry. That rage had been directed at her so often. Alayna could sense it as if it were a tangible thing reaching up to her even as she sat safe inside her room.

Turning back inside, she realized she was shaking violently, almost sick from the brutality she had just witnessed. Worse still was the visage of de Montregnier, his violence at last unleashed. She sank back onto the cushions, fumbling for her sewing, but her hands lay still for a long time and when night came, she slipped into the great bed alone.

She had just doused the candle when a thunderous sound shattered her sleepy silence. Alayna sat up to see the outline of a figure she knew well; Lucien stood framed in the arched doorway. He had flung open the door, though it was by no means barred against him, and now waited for the last echo of the crash to die down into silence.

"Good, you are not asleep."

He crossed the threshold and slammed the door behind him. She watched him with growing trepidation, trembling at the predatory way he was advancing into the room. The memory of his doling out the savage punishment she had witnessed this afternoon burned in her mind.

"My wife," he drawled. "My beautiful, cold, spiteful, vindictive little fury. Have you missed me, sweetling?"

Alayna's voice shook as she answered him, "I have been here waiting, I—"

"Have you?" he thundered. He was walking awkwardly, lurching, actually. Alayna could make no sense of his strange behavior. She shrank back amongst the furs, afraid.

"And do you await me every night, my love, longing for me, wondering if I have not found solace with another?" He laughed cruelly at her telling response, knowing he had hit the mark. "So you have missed me!" he exclaimed. "Well, fear not, my icy maid, for I have had no use for another."

Suddenly Alayna realized the wild talk, the stumbling gait and slightly slurred speech meant only one thing. "You are senseless with drink!" she cried.

"'You are senseless with drink,'" he mimicked with a falsetto voice. His voice deepened as his humor left him. "Aye, drunk I am, but not nearly enough. I can still see you, my delicious, untouchable little viper, and so I have not drunk enough. I still smell you, that sweet, musky scent that is all yours—and so my senses are not nearly blunted enough. Who can blame me, really? A wife such as you would make a man long for the blessed oblivion of his ale."

She stood, transfixed, hearing the horrible things he was saying, knowing that some of it was true. She was no wife for any man to envy.

"Aye, look at you, with your hair loose and around you, those large eyes looking at me like a doe's. That mouth ready to be taken, but it is all a lie, is it not? Beauty is the greatest lie a woman tells a man, for it promises delight but delivers naught but misery."

With a swift movement, Lucien snatched her to him. His breath smelled of the ale he had consumed, and his brown eyes were fierce.

"You tempt me, woman. I have withstood the most terrible punishments a Viking lord, renowned among savages for his singular talent in that area, could serve up. And all without ever wavering in my purpose.''

She dared not breathe, fascinated with the revelation. He had never spoken of his past.

''You tempt me to throw my honor to the wind and break my vow to have you as a willing wife. How can it be so easy for you to do in such a short time what old Hendron could not do in years? But for you it is ridiculously easy, is it not? None could ever claim what you have sunk your slivered claws into. My body betrays me, and my will deserts me. You tempt me beyond my endurance, little vixen. You are madness itself.''

His mouth swept down on hers with a growl. Mindlessly she clasped him back, welcoming the cruel kiss and returning it with an ardor that took him completely off guard.

He wanted her, and with the exhilarating realization of that fact, she had to admit that, despite all that lay between them—the anger and the fear—she wanted him, as well. Her desire for him was like a desperate, wild thing, with no thoughts or reason to tame it any longer. Let him ask his question tonight, and she would say him yea. She would beg him to take her if that was what he required.

When he pulled away suddenly, her eyes flew open and her head snapped level to meet his gaze. She opened her mouth to speak, but the look of him stopped her. His face wore a look of tortured emotions more disturbing than any scowl that had ever afflicted those handsome features.

''Do you know who it is who kisses you, lady? Do you know whom you embrace?'' His voice was strangled. He shook her with a mild jerk. ''Say it, say who I am.''

''Lucien de Montregnier,'' Alayna whispered. He was frightening her anew. He shook his head, demanding, ''My title.''

"Lord of Gastonbury," she whispered.

Her blood shriveled in her veins at the cold laughter that tore from his throat. "Nay, lady, not that in truth. I am but a slave. Did you not know that—a slave!"

He released her at last, leaving her numb.

Slave? Her mind absorbed what he was saying, flying quickly over the things she knew. In the armory, at the shock of seeing his father's sword, he had said that he had fallen with his sire, but not dead. Taken, he had said. Taken as a slave!

What had he said just a moment ago? A master who excelled at cruelty. A slave for all of those years! Could it possibly be true? She stared at him with a petrified look, for once not frightened of him, but of the truth that she was hearing. He smiled a lopsided smile at her, weaving a bit.

"Do you know what I did today?" he rasped. "I flogged a man for trying to assassinate me." He came close again, this time not touching her, only leaning in as if to impart some great secret. "Do you know how many times I was whipped when I was a slave? Nay, of course you do not. Neither do I, for there were far too many to count." She had to look away from the intensity in his eyes. His mouth was close to her ear. "And today I had to do that to another man. Can you imagine what it was like?"

Silence, and Alayna instinctively understood. "You had to do it, Lucien," she said softly. Her gentle words surprised her, and she was shocked to feel the wetness of a tear sliding down her cheek.

"Aye." He nodded, looking away. "I cannot appear weak." His eyes grew pained again as they focused on something far away. "Still," he breathed.

She laid her hands on his arm, feeling the strength that

lay there under her palm and she marveled at how she had always thought him invincible, beyond the reach of other men, and certainly beyond hers. Her empathy for him overwhelmed her, and to both their surprise, she stepped close to draw him into an embrace. Placing her hands on either side of his head, she drew him down to be kissed.

Lucien closed his eyes against it. She would be his tonight, he knew, but he was confused and he had drunk far too much. He could not take her, for his need would make him savage. He would hurt her; he knew he would. Hurting was something that would feel good just now.

Abruptly he set her away from him, saying, "I am fatigued." He stepped away from her and began to undress. Alayna stood stock-still, a scarlet flush staining her cheeks, before slipping into the bed. She turned on her side away from him. He extinguished the light and fell in beside her.

When Alayna awoke the following morn, she found Lucien still sleeping. She carefully eased herself out of the bed, dressed quickly and went down to the kitchens to fetch the water. Making sure it was well warmed, she directed several servants to bring the buckets back to the chamber, stressing they must be quiet.

She did not open the shutters to admit the day's light, but crept quietly around the room in deference to Lucien's rest, lighting the fire and tidying the litter of clothing strewn on the floor. Straightening, she found him awake and watching her with a baleful eye.

"What hour is it?" he said hoarsely. He looked cross, she noted, wondering if it was the lingering sickness of last night's indulgence or if she had done something to unintentionally provoke him.

"'Tis well into the morning, my lord," she answered.

Running his hand through his thick hair, he eased back

into the furs, looking down in surprise when he saw that he still wore his leggings. He cast Alayna a questioning look.

"I have fetched water for you. It sits by the fire to avoid chilling."

He rose silently, weaving momentarily before finding his equilibrium. Once more the hand swept through his hair and he shook his head as if to cast off the fogginess that clung to him.

He could remember little of yestereve. Vague, incomplete images were all he could recall. Alayna's horrified face, her in his arms. He cringed inwardly at the thought he may have treated her roughly, then cringed again as the effect of concentrating pierced his brain.

"Do you wish me to summon Agravar?" she asked.

"Why the devil would I need Agravar?" he said, but his voice held no bite. "I will see him soon enough in the hall."

"I did not think you would wish to go out today. I mean, since you are so sick—"

"I am not sick," he protested unconvincingly, moving carefully to dress. His limbs were sluggish and his irritation at himself grew with each clumsy movement. "Get yourself out of here before I say something to start another war between us. I warn you that I am cross this morn." Alayna skittered out the door.

With his familiar scowl firmly in place, Lucien entered the vaulted hall where many still sat lingering over morning meal. Ignoring the head-splitting chorus of greetings from his men, he stalked to the dais and collapsed into his chair between Alayna and Agravar. He shoved away his trencher and called for some ale.

Agravar exchanged a conspiratorial look with Will.

With a devilish smile, he gave Lucien a hearty slap on the back and spoke in a booming voice.

"How goes it, my lord baron? Did you sleep well?"

Lucien winced, leveling a murderous look at the Viking. "Well enough."

"That is gratifying," Agravar said. "Though you look rather peaked. Are you sure you are well? Perhaps it is nourishment you require—these sausages are quite tasty. Here, have you tried one?"

The aromatic food turned Lucien a paler shade. He pushed it away, choking. "Nay."

Alayna had to smother a giggle. She was amazed that Lucien, for all of his glowering, took their taunts in stride. She had not noticed he sometimes made a game of his dour disapproval. Perhaps he was not as perpetually cross as he seemed.

The Norseman pressed his advantage now as he called out loudly for the steward. "Come fetch my lord baron some other victuals, for he cannot abide the sausage you have prepared!" Looking to Lucien, he inquired, "Perhaps some eggs smothered with gravy? Or would you prefer some stuffed partridges with elderberry sauce left from last evening?"

"I am not hungry, Agravar," Lucien snapped, a thin sheen of sweat breaking out over his face.

"Perhaps some fresh air would suit you, my lord," Alayna offered timidly. Every one of them looked at her in amazement.

Agravar was the first to recover, booming loudly again, "Nay, my lady, our Lord Lucien must have nourishment to sustain him in his duties for the day. Why, without proper nourishment, we men would be weak and frail,

given to unaccountable vapors and sicknesses of the stomach, would we not, old friend?''

Their merry game was again commenced. Lucien
seemed determined not to succumb to the natural repug-
nance for the food that was passed before him, but his
tormentors were more dogged. When Agravar offered a
plate of steaming sweetbreads, Lucien rose abruptly and
darted for the garderobes. At least his tormentors had the
graciousness to wait until he was out of earshot before
erupting into laughter.

Alayna pretended disapproval, clucking primly before
dissolving into giggles herself. When her husband returned, he looked much improved, giving his men a wry
smile.

"Enough lingering over breakfast, you lazy louts. Let
us be off to our business."

The men arose from the trestle tables, the servants scurrying to clear the place so they could be about their other
chores. Lucien paused, surveying the scene, looking somehow satisfied at this ordinary activity. The downward lines
of his mouth shifted to a more pleasant vein, and he turned
to Alayna with a soft look in his eye.

"What will you be about this day, my lady?"

She stared at him until she could recover. "I—I plan to
work with the cook and seneschal, looking into the castle
stores and making arrangements for some bartering with
the peasant folk." Why was his gaze making her blush?
"I thought, since there is excess, that we could share the
overage. It seems they would be apt to appreciate it, working harder and be healthier." She faltered, "Is—is that
acceptable?"

Lucien smiled crookedly, apparently pleased. It was the
first smile that Alayna had ever seen on his face that was

not cruel or taunting. She was overcome with a strange weakness in her knees.

"That is quite acceptable. We seek the same for our villeins. It is quite an asset for me to have a lady such as yourself for my cause." His smile deepened, and Alayna watched in fascination as his features were transformed into a countenance of relaxed boyishness. The harsh lines eased, and his eyes lost their brooding skepticism.

She could make no response, for she had no functioning of her brain with which to think of anything to say, nor of her mouth with which to form the words.

Taking no notice of her incapacitation, he offered her a small bow of courtesy before following his men out.

It was difficult to keep the pleased smile from spreading across her lips. Dreamily she played with the gold cup before her, musing on his kind words, his uncharacteristic charm.

What was happening to her? she wondered. Just last night, she would have welcomed him to her bed and given him all he asked, and more. Now, this morn, he seemed so much less fierce. She was actually sorry when she heard the sound of horses riding away.

Sighing, she rose, still lost in thought when she almost collided with a servant who had come to clear the table. Mumbling a distracted apology, she glanced up. Recognizing the servant who had spoken to her so malevolently on her wedding day, Alayna gasped.

"My lord seeks to make amends." The girl was sneering at her, a bitter smile twisting her mouth into an ugly line.

"What?" Alayna demanded, trying, for once, to be imperious, but only succeeding in sounding frightened.

"Do not think he seeks nothing but to soothe you to get

what he wants. He needs you, for Gastonbury. He is a man who gets what he needs—always. But he does not want you. There lies no more warmth in his heart for you than for his old Viking master.''

Alayna's eyes snapped wide. ''How is it you know of my husband's past?''

''Oh, my fine lady, there is much that I know about your husband. Men have other choices when their uppity ladies do not suit.''

Her implication was clear. ''You lie!''

''Are you sure, my lady? Methinks he does not visit you until late. I guess that he does not find your bed to his liking, and he is a lusty man, I can tell you. Ask him sometime about young Glenna, and see what he tells you.''

''How dare you speak to me this way, you wretched girl!'' Alayna was shocked to hear her own voice nearly a shriek. ''Now, get away from me else I will have you punished for your impudence.''

Glenna's eyes looked a little wild. ''Nay. He will not allow it.''

With that, the girl scampered off, as silent and swift as a wild mouse.

Numb, Alayna's mind raced over a myriad of thoughts, all confusing and raw. Lucien had denied that he had taken another while apart from her, but it could be a lie, although he had little enough cause to do so. If he chose to be with another, there was nothing she could do about it. She had denied him the invitation he had sought to her bed. It was possible he had found another, one more willing, as Glenna had said. And the pretty servant seemed very willing to ease the discomfort of her lord.

What an idiot she had been! She had let herself be drawn to him, even when every instinct had rebelled against it.

How easily she had fallen into his arms every time, shamefully responding to his ardent seductions like some common serf in awe of the great warrior. He played the gentle lord, it was true, but it was only for gain.

All his tender kisses, those rare gentle words, the careful revelations, all of these things meant to catch her off guard and bring her to his bed. Then there would be no annulment and he would keep his barony. Gastonbury was the only thing he cared about. He wished to use her, nothing more.

Did he even now share the jest with his men—? *"Did you see how pliant she was this morn? A bit of a trick, no less. I but throw out a crumb and she snaps it up like a hungry dog."* Oh, he was getting to know her weakness well. And it was true that she had a growing weakness for him.

With a strangled cry, she stumbled up to her chamber. She hated him. Oh, God, how she hated him. His cunning seduction cut deeper than any insult.

She could not see him again. She could not bear it!

Quickly doffing her slippers, Alayna slid on her heavy boots and grabbed her cloak. She had no plan, no idea of what she was about to do. She only knew she needed to escape. Escape Gastonbury, and escape Lucien de Montregnier.

It was a miracle she managed to slip out of the castle undetected. Lucien was so sure of her, no one said a word as she walked purposefully out of the postern gate and took the north road.

Chapter Sixteen

The dungeons lay in the bowels of Gastonbury castle. They were merely a smattering of tiny cells carved out of the earth, each containing only a thin pile of straw and a shallow ditch that served inadequately as a garderobe. The stench was horrible, rising up to meet Lucien as he descended the steep stairs that plunged downward into the unrelenting dark.

There was a familiar tightening in his chest, a feeling that came upon him when he was forced to confront a particularly lucid memory of his past. He had almost been paralyzed after having to flog the prisoner yesterday. It had been necessary; indeed, it was the least of what the assassin deserved. Now, after a persuasive night alone with his pain, the prisoner might be more willing to talk.

He entered a small chamber where Agravar stood beside the bound captive. He composed his face into his fiercest expression.

"My lord baron," Agravar said, bowing respectfully. Lucien almost laughed at his friend's exaggerated reverence. The Viking was playing his part to the hilt. Lucien played his, nodding distractedly.

"Has the prisoner decided to tell us who hired him?"

"He is still being most foolish, sire."

"Then there is no cure for it. The purse paid must have been fat, indeed, for him to retain such loyalty to his employer. A pity."

The prisoner, bent and weary, his face too dirt smudged to be recognizable, made no reaction. Lucien watched the eyes.

"Aye, my lord. Though I know that you did expressly forbid it, I must confess that I tried to bribe the man, offering him a huge purse for the information. He declined."

Actually, they had discussed the attempted bribe, but had thought it wise if it seemed it was against Lucien's wishes. Lucien didn't want to appear eager to bargain.

"Really?" he commented dryly. "I will see to you, Agravar, when we are done here."

The Viking bowed his head in mock shame.

Lucien walked away, saying casually, "No purse would buy that kind of loyalty from a brigand, for they would sell their own mother for a sou." Nay, money could not buy that kind of loyalty, but fear could. "We could kill him, but then, we would know no more than we do now."

"True," Agravar agreed, "it would do us no good."

Lucien paused thoughtfully. "I do not wish this man's death."

Lucien watched the prisoner react. Curiosity, he saw with satisfaction. Just a brief flash. The cur had thought himself dead, now there was hope. Very good.

"Release him," he commanded. Agravar acted stunned at that announcement. The prisoner's head came up and for the first time he looked at his jailers.

He was experienced, Lucien thought, he holds himself

well. But there could be no more experience on this earth than his own.

"Release him?" Agravar challenged.

"Aye, we will let him return to his life. Yet we will enhance it for him, give him a new challenge, as it were. We will send out a rumor that he spoke of his illicit master to you and I. In return for this information, this man won his freedom, so we let him go." He grinned evilly. "Now, why else would we do such a thing unless he cooperated?"

"Nay!" the man shouted, jumping up.

Lucien let out his breath.

"'E—'e'll slay me, me lord. Please, don't make me go out there and face 'im. 'E does terrible punishments, 'e does—much worse'n ye. 'E'll kill me girl, and I 'ave a son."

Lucien turned a chilling look on him, unmoved by his pleas. "You know the terms."

The prisoner hung his head. "But my fam'ly."

"We can shield them, take them to another place where they will be safe."

The man thought about it for a moment, looking inconsolable as he weighed his options. "I'll give ye 'is name if ye promise to get my kin away from 'ere."

"Who sent you to kill me?"

The answer came as expected. "Garrick of Thalsbury."

Lucien had suspected as much. It would give him great pleasure to plan his retaliation against Garrick.

"Let it be done as we agreed," Lucien said to Agravar, then he turned to leave. He forced himself not to run up the treacherous stairs. Up to the sunlight. With this wretched business behind him, he was thinking of Alayna.

He headed straight to his chamber, thinking to find her there, sewing, as was her habit at this hour. He was disappointed to find the room empty.

Weary, he sat by the hearth. How empty the place seemed without her. The sickness of this morn had made him weak and he was still reeling from his dealings with the assassin. When would the past stop haunting him? He would rest for a bit, he decided, leaning back against the wall and closing his eyes against the world.

When had he ceased to thrive on the struggle? Where once it had been his life's blood, now it left him restless and dissatisfied and yearning for something....

Alayna. If only those arms would welcome him, if only that quick tongue would speak gently instead of flinging sharp-witted barbs to whet his temper.

As he slipped into slumber, he wondered where she was.

He was awakened by the feel of a soft, warm mouth on his, pressing shyly, lightly. Alayna! His arms came up to catch her to him, hands tangling in her hair as he pressed his mouth up against hers, opening it to taste fully of the sweetness there. He came instantly awake, aware all at once of his pulse slamming through him in violent courses, the arousal in his loins, and the ache of a sudden, unbearable urgency. He was still afraid it was a dream, some terrible, wonderful dream of his own making.

He opened his eyes, expecting to see sultry green. He found himself instead staring into the brown eyes of the servant girl, Glenna.

Springing to his feet, he almost knocked her on her backside. It was as if she had suddenly become fire, scalding him with her unwelcome closeness.

"I do not mind if you think of her," she pleaded in a wheedling voice. "Take me and pretend that I am she."

"I told you before never to come to this chamber," he

snapped. The hairs on the back of his neck stood on end. He sensed there was something very wrong with this girl.

Her arms snaked toward him. He knocked them away. "She hates you, you know. Why do you pant after her?"

"Listen to me, girl," he commanded firmly. "Take yourself away and do not return. And never speak to me unless I ask you a direct question, do you understand?"

She stared at him a moment, her eyes round. "I am to be your leman, honored throughout the castle. It is because of her. She is so vile to you, how do you not see it? I hate her!"

Despite his many threats to Alayna, Lucien had never struck a woman no matter what the provocation. But he did so now, quickly slapping his flattened palm across Glenna's cheek. It was a light blow, meant to snap her out of her hysteria.

Slowly her hand came up to her reddened face and her eyes narrowed. With a sob, she ran out of the room.

Lucien's rage receded, replaced by an unsettling feeling. Where the devil was Alayna? He knew she spent most of her time in this chamber, away from the gossiping tongues that dogged her in the hall. Suddenly his instincts flared to life and he was alarmed.

Storming out of the chamber, he stopped a young servant boy who was laboring under a load of firewood, "Have you seen your mistress today, boy?" he demanded.

The lad shook his head. Lucien broke into a run, skidding to a stop when he saw another servant, a woman. "Where is the Lady Alayna?" he asked.

"I know not, my lord," she answered.

"Drop what you are doing and find her. I want everyone in the castle to search. Do not stop until she is found."

"Aye, my lord." Lucien almost collided with her, then

paused impatiently to let her pass, grabbing another man who happened by.

"Have you seen the mistress?" he urged.

"Nay, lord, not since the morn."

"Where did you see her?"

"She was in the hall, just after the meal. I saw you speaking to her and then you left and she stayed while I was sweeping."

"Did you see her speak to anyone?"

"Only a servant girl."

Suspicious, Lucien inquired, "The girl, who was she?"

"I believe 'twas Glenna, my lord."

Wild with anxiety, Lucien bellowed for some pages to find Will and Agravar and Pelly. He bounded back up the steps to the chamber again where he tore through Alayna's trunks. In disgust, he threw the garments down in a heap. He was not familiar with her wardrobe; he would not know if anything was missing.

Footsteps made him whirl around. A young woman stood uncertainly at the door. It was Alayna's maid. "Are any of your lady's things missing?" he yelled.

The poor woman fairly tripped over her own feet as she hurried to examine the clothing jumbled together on the rushes. "Only her cloak and the dress I saw her wearing today, my lord. And her boots are gone."

Wordlessly Lucien swept out of the room, almost colliding with Will. Agravar was fast upon his heels.

"Alayna has run away," he stated grimly.

"Run away? To what purpose?" the Norseman snapped.

"The little fool has finally made good on her threat to escape me. Her boots and cloak are gone."

"We must find her," Will exclaimed. "She could be in danger."

Lucien's eyes darkened. It was something he had not considered. If any harm came to Alayna, he would not forgive himself, for it was his fault for not seeing that Glenna was deranged from the beginning.

They decided to split into small riding parties to cover the most area. Agravar and Pelly took a band of men down to the village to explore the huts there and the forest beyond. Lucien and Will went through the postern gate, combing the trails of the woods above and beyond the castle, traveling along the river.

"Let us split up," Lucien said. "You head south, follow the trails until you come to Deaston Manor. She may have sought shelter there. If she did not, come back and join me."

"You head north?" Will asked.

"Aye," answered Lucien, his jaw set. "Garrick may have a hand in this. I ride to Thalsbury."

The road Alayna traveled was nothing more than a thin strip at the base of a sheer cliff face, winding along the bank of the river. The water level, high from the recent rains and the spring thaw, was ready to spill onto the bank and into the already narrow ribbon of road. When the rain began again, Alayna cursed her luck. She thought briefly of returning to the castle, then rejected the idea. She had no desire to face de Montregnier just yet. She would find an opening in the cliff and take shelter in the woods beyond until she could think of what to do next.

The downpour was heavy and in no time she was soaked through. The sturdy gray wool of her cloak weighed her down. She slipped and stumbled in the mud. Fearful of the rising level of the river, she began searching for some means of escape in the sheer wall of rock. Water started to wash up onto the road, swirling about her ankles.

Exhausted from struggling for each step, she wondered how far she had come. It was dark, though if from dusk or the heavy storm clouds, she could not tell. She had no sense of how long she had been out here. Her strength was giving out, and she could barely maneuver in the sucking mud and rising tide. She was aware of the giddy rise of panic inside her, making her lurch desperately, frantic to return to the castle, but her efforts won her little progress. With a sick feeling of despair, she knew she could not make it.

She thought of Lucien, all of her previous anger now dissolved by the potent wash of fear. She would gladly humble herself if only he would come.

As if summoned by her prayer, a shape appeared amidst the gray sheets of rain. It was a lone rider coming from the direction of Gastonbury on a dark steed. There was no doubt in Alayna's mind as to who he was—Lucien!

He was here, and she knew no matter what his wrath would bring, she at least would be safe. She began to sob with relief.

He swung down from the saddle and gestured to a tumble of rocks that led through a small pass in the cliff face. Alayna scurried to obey, clambering up the slick rock with the last of her strength. Lucien was behind her, following after a brief struggle with his horse. The path was too treacherous for the skittish animal, so after a few attempts, he abandoned it by the road.

They fled into the forest, slipping under the shelter of the thick canopy of trees. It came to her that it was not like Lucien to remain quiet for this long. She expected a tongue-lashing such as he had never given her before, and yet he continued to walk in silence. He must be furious, she thought, then an eerie feeling crept over her. She glanced sideways at him. He did not look at her, his hood still in place though hardly any rain fell on them now.

Alayna realized suddenly that she had never seen Lucien wear a hooded cloak.

A terrible suspicion took hold and she stopped. "Lucien?"

He stopped also, watching her from the anonymity of the cowl. Slowly he raised his hand and uncovered his head. A stranger with slitted eyes and a cruel slash for a mouth stood before her. She shrank away with a cry of alarm.

"Continue to cooperate so nicely as you were doing. You cannot overpower me and you cannot outrun me. I know these woods too well."

Alayna thought perhaps she would try to run all the same, then saw it for the useless gesture it was. He was right—she could not outrun him, and if she could, where would she go? She did not even know where she was.

"There is a hunter's cottage up yonder. We'll shelter there until the storm abates, then we'll continue on."

"Where?"

He only smirked back, an unattractive twisting of that overlong mouth. It made him look ghoulish. Carefully avoiding his outstretched hand, she pulled herself upright and walked calmly. There was no hope of escaping just yet, but she would look for the first opening, when his guard was down, and take it.

They came to a tiny one-room dwelling with a sagging thatched roof. The man gave Alayna a rough shove through the doorway. The place was filthy, overrun with cobwebs and dust, bare of any furnishings. It was, however, dry.

Once inside, he stripped off his sodden cloak. He did not speak, but watched her carefully as he heaped together some dry logs that had been set by the fireplace long ago. Alayna stood shivering in the middle of the room. She dared not move. The weight of her clothes, the chill of the wetness seeping into her flesh, her pure fatigue all went unfelt.

She was like a doe poised for flight as she watched the stranger go about his work. A cold dread crept into her veins, for she saw that he watched her covertly and there was undisguised lust in his eyes.

When at last the fire was lit, he undressed further, stripping off his overtunic and leaving only his coarse undershirt and leggings. He looked at her and smiled again in that hideous way he had. It was meant to be reassuring, but it set her blood curdling in her veins.

"Come sit by the fire, Lady Alayna," he said. He tried to sound polite, but his voice was simpering. She obeyed, knowing she had no choice but to wait for her chance.

"Take off your cloak to let the warmth in. Here, we will dry it on this peg."

She remained still and silent as he covetously took her cloak from her and hung it up.

"He did not lie when he said you were a beauty," he said conversationally as he sat down again at the fire.

"What is your name?" Alayna asked, ignoring the compliment.

"Call me John."

"John, who are you talking about when you say 'he'?"

John smirked. "You'll see. He likes to make his introductions himself."

They fell silent for a while, staring into the flames. She was thinking of how to win his trust, maneuver to the door, get a hold of a weapon—anything.

John dug into his pocket, pulling out a pouch of salted beef. He offered some of it to her, but she shook her head. He was biding his time, she could feel it. The tension in him was palpable, alerting her every sense.

Sliding closer, John smiled at her challenging look. "It will be better if we share our warmth."

Oh, God. Alayna closed her eyes, trying to summon strength or courage or wisdom, something with which to do battle, but all that came to her was numbing panic. She had to keep her wits about her if she had any chance of escape. His voice sounded close to her ear and she cringed. "You are incredibly beautiful. The girl told me you were plain and unpleasant, but I knew her to be mad."

"Girl?" Alayna's head snapped around. "Which girl? A servant, named Glenna?"

He nodded. "Aye. She answered my questions. Eager to help. I think my master will find her a useful ally. Her instructions were clear enough. I found you without any trouble." He looked over at her, his eyes narrowing. "God, you are the loveliest thing I have ever seen."

Cold, moist fingers closed around her arm. At her whimper, he pulled her roughly to him. Knowing there would be no clever escape, she began to struggle with abandon.

His grip tightened, making her cry out in pain. "Don't fight me, for he'll not like it if I mark you."

His kiss was putrid. Revulsion welled up inside her and she feared she would succumb to the heaving of her stomach. To her horror, she felt his hands grasping at her breast.

She swung at him, kicking and pummeling him with her fists, but he managed her struggles by pressing her back on the dirt floor and covering her with his body. She screamed. When she tried to bite him she was rewarded by a sharp slap that stunned her for a moment.

Her mind flew over the horrible realization of what was happening. What a fool she had been! She was a woman twice wed, yet a virgin. She had rejected her husband, a man whose touch set her blood racing through her veins, and refused a gentle, exciting initiation to be taken by a rough, repulsive brigand in a filthy hut.

She fought with all her strength, but she was no match for a man. He had his leggings untied and was trying to free himself, when suddenly, without warning, he was gone!

Alayna's eyes flew open in surprise. She had only a momentary glimpse of the man seemingly suspended in the air above her, his mouth open and his eyes round with shock.

Chapter Seventeen

Lucien stood over them, looking like some fabled giant with Alayna's attacker dangling from one hand. Giving a grunt, he hurled the blackguard against the cottage wall.

Dressed in black, soaked through, looking more blessedly evil than Alayna had ever seen him look, Lucien paused briefly, his eyes locking with hers for an instant before turning back to his foe. In a flash, he had the man by the throat and drew back his fist to bring it crashing down on the man's face.

John quickly recovered his equilibrium, hurling himself back at Lucien and connecting several heavy blows of his own. Alayna screamed when she saw her kidnapper had drawn blood with a powerful punch to Lucien's lip. Unfazed, Lucien remained merciless and focused, keeping up a relentless barrage.

In desperation, John drew a knife. Alayna gasped when she saw it, but Lucien's lip only curled as if he were pleased. She soon saw why, for at John's first lunge, Lucien deftly deflected the strike and felled the blade from his hand with a quick chopping motion to his wrist. Scooping it up in a flash, he clasped his adversary with one arm and, with a quick forward motion of his arm, he buried the man's own blade in his belly. Lucien held him thus, ignoring the weak clawing of his victim's hands as the life slowly seeped out of him. Another jerk, and John crumpled. Lucien supported him to the door, disappearing into the gray curtain of rain with his burden. He was back in a flash, closing the flimsy portal against the rain.

Lucien's chest heaved as he gulped in great lungfuls of air. His face looked dark and wild, his eyes full of pained worry when he spun to face Alayna.

"Did he harm you? Are you hurt?" he barked.

She could only shake her head, for she was still trembling and unable to speak.

Her mind spun with the dizzy realization that he had come for her and she was miraculously safe. How he had found her in this storm, she did not know. She forgot how much she was supposed to hate him, and felt an overwhelming need to have him hold her.

"I was coming back," she cried, trying to explain. "I was so afraid, I thought the floodwaters would drown me. It was raining so hard, I could not see. He came from Gastonbury, I thought it was you."

And then all at once she was where she wanted to be, enfolded in his arms, leaning on his great strength. She clutched him close, burying her face in his shoulder.

"He was touching me. Oh, God, Lucien! All I could think was how I had turned you away, and he was going to take what I never should have denied you."

"Shush," Lucien whispered.

She let herself surrender to all of it—the terror, the regret—venting freely with great, wrenching sobs that shook her slender frame to its roots. He soothed her, kissing her hair, stroking it gently as he spoke soft, incoherent words of comfort.

The smell of him, mingled with sweat and rain, was clean and sensuous, his arms strong, and it felt so natural to be there, his velvet voice telling her she was safe. She had never felt safer in her life.

It felt right, it felt instinctive, to turn her face toward his, to let him kiss her brow, to tilt her face upward and let his kiss fall on her eye, her cheek, her lips. It felt only natural to press against his mouth with hers, answering the unspoken question as his passion flared and the kiss deepened with the immediate response of her own ardor.

It was as if the bottom had fallen out of her heart and she was plummeting through leagues of space, soaring and out of control. She cared not a whit for her foolish pride any longer, for within her raged a hunger long denied. She did not wait for him to pull her to him, but molded her body against his, kissing him as fervently as he kissed her.

As his hands went to the fasteners of her clothing, she helped him shrug off her gown and lift her shift to bare her body to his gaze, his touch, his fire-hot kisses.

Her nerves skittered in anticipation of his intimate touch, those shocking caresses she had fought so hard not to crave. When he gathered her again to him, her hands would not keep still, alternately tangling in his damp hair or sliding voraciously over his body. She felt the rock-hard muscles move and shift under her palms. What madness had it been to deny him? Or was the madness this that consumed her now? She found she no longer cared, for she was marvelously afire, and it felt too wonderful to refuse, not now. If it cost her her last shred of pride, so be it.

Emboldened by her own need, she tugged at his tunic,

wanting it off him but not knowing how to pull away the intrusive cloth. He obliged her, quickly doffing the wet garment.

He took her again in his arms, pressing his naked chest to hers. Bending her back over his arm, he cupped her breast and captured the taut nipple in his mouth. She convulsed at the raw sensations that slammed through her as he gently nipped the sensitive peak. A sound, half cry, half moan, came from her as he closed his mouth full over it once more, drawing on it to send her to new heights of frantic, desperate arousal. Urgently she fisted her hands in his hair and pulled him closer, not wanting him to stop.

He straightened, pulling away. Alayna reached for him. "Nay, do not leave me like this. I do want you. I will tell you anything you command of me, anything you demand. But do not stop, not now."

His expression spoke of the effect of her words. For all of his normal fierceness, he looked as a boy in that unguarded moment. Wordlessly his hands touched her cheeks.

"I could not stop now," he answered huskily, taking her in his arms once more. "An entire army could not keep me from you. I will make you my wife in truth, Alayna, and nothing will stop us tonight."

Her insides leaped crazily as he shucked his boots and leggings, then kicked their clothing out around them. Drawing her down, they lay together atop the soft cushion.

"I am sorry about this place. Would that it was the comfort of our own chamber—"

"I care not, Lucien. I do not wish to wait any longer."

His mouth came down and covered hers, and she answered him. His hands were free to roam, sliding sensuously over her body, testing the feel of her, the languid curve of her hip, the sweet swell of the underside of her breast. She responded to his every touch, writhing under his tender ministrations with an abandon that would have frightened her had she any notion to consider it. But her senses were at his mercy, inflamed to a pitch that was almost beyond endurance.

He covered her body with his. He nipped her lips, kissing her mouth quickly, savagely, before easing himself into her.

"It may hurt, love," he whispered, and Alayna's eyes flew open at the endearment. The pain did indeed come, but it was faraway, for she knew only that he had called her his love. He kissed her gently this time, pausing to get her used to the feel of him inside her before starting his rhythm.

Whatever she had expected, it was nothing like this. She had heard that there would be pain, but the fleeting sting of his first thrust had given way to pleasure, then the burgeoning hunger had taken over, filling her mind and body with urgent need. His body pressed down on her, his hands claimed every inch while the gentle breath of his voice at her ear murmured soft, sweet words she had never expected to hear.

Something strange and wonderful began to build inside of her, a sensation like a great wave holding her aloft, making her arch and strain against him for some instinctive, unknown release.

His powerful arms held her in a crushing grip for a moment before his breath evened and he came to rest. Dazed, she clung to him as he rolled from her, bringing her with him so that they lay side by side, facing each other.

He stared at her, a smile curling lazily at the corners of

his mouth. He touched her face as if in wonder, making her shiver.

"Are you...all right?"

Alayna nodded, not yet trusting her voice.

"I did not hurt you?" he asked.

Alayna shook her head.

A twinge of the old, haunted look came into his eyes. "Do you regret it?"

She brought her hand up to brush aside a damp strand of hair clinging to his temple. "Nay, I do not." She paused, then added, "Husband."

"Nor I," he murmured, bringing his lips to hers once again. Alayna did not understand his meaning, but gave it no more thought when lost once again in the tender caress of his lips.

His hand slipped between them, gliding over her skin to rest just under her belly. She moaned when his thumb slid over her, finding the sensitive spot his lovemaking had stirred into aching need. His mouth covered hers as his strokes ignited the smoldering coals into exquisite sensation. She could not think a single coherent thought, though somewhere in a remote part of her she knew that she should be shocked at this new intimate touch. She could fathom nothing but the liquid feel of pleasure that ran through her limbs, gathering, tensing until it finally shattered into a million shards of brilliant fulfillment.

There was an acute awareness of everything at once—the feel of his lips, his well-muscled arm that cradled her, his hard body pressed against hers, their legs intertwined. It was a completeness of sensation such as she had never before experienced.

Coming back to herself, she felt stunned and weak. As she curled up to rest contentedly at her husband's side, he held her tight, kissing her brow while his hand played with a long curl.

"I fear our clothing will be the worse for our trampling," he commented. Alayna giggled into his shoulder, picturing the ridiculous sight they would surely make donned in the stained and wrinkled garments.

"I fear all will know what we were about," she whispered.

He chucked her chin up to tilt her face to his. "'Tis about time."

Alayna lowered her lashes. "Aye," she admitted.

"Do you play the maiden again with me?"

"'Tis not easy for a woman to accept, being intimate with a man. Men are raised knowing they will be the pursuers, encouraged always to seek the conquest of a woman. Yet women are taught to always deny these feelings and say nay to their suitors. Then, once wed, we are to then submit the very treasure of our maidenhead and allow things that, until the exchange of vows, were shocking and forbidden."

He considered her for a moment, a small smile playing on his lips. "You are a thoughtful wench, are you not?"

Knowing he was teasing, she let him draw her closer. It felt unbelievably wonderful to be with him like this, more wonderful than any dream of love she had ever known as a girl. His large hand sifted through her hair, grasping her neck to pull her to him to be kissed, a kiss that she responded to with enthusiasm.

Reluctantly he pulled away. There was a troubled look in his eye. "Why did you leave?" he asked.

Alayna stiffened. *Very well,* she thought, *I will put it to him and let him deny it if 'tis untrue.* "A young girl claimed to be your leman, and told me that you cared for her. She said you sought to make peace with me only to help your political standing. I—I felt the fool."

"So you left without a word to me?"

"I thought you a liar," she explained. "I left, to think. But I decided to come back when the storm worsened. When I saw John, I—"

"John? Did you know him?"

"Nay, 'tis what he told me to call him."

He rolled to lean down over her once again, suddenly impatient with the tale. "It does not matter. He is gone and will not trouble us again. Now, wife, understand this—I will always come for you."

He kissed her deeply, moving over her again, taking her this time without much preamble, for she was ready and eager and willing. When they lay together again afterward, Lucien reached up to the peg that hung over them and grabbed the cloaks, which had been hung to dry. They were still a bit damp but usable. He wrapped the two of them as they nestled together. They slept, sound and deep, still tight in each other's embrace.

Chapter Eighteen

Alayna woke to find herself alone.

She sat up quickly. The fire burned low, casting long shadows in the darkened room. Still groggy, she tried to piece together where Lucien could have gone.

The flimsy door swung open and he entered carrying a huge armload of wood. He was dressed in his cloak, with only his leggings and boots underneath. He gave her a warm perusal before crossing to the fireplace to dump the logs beside the small hearth.

He hung up his cloak and stoked the fire to life before coming to sit next to her. He toyed with a lock of her hair. "I found some dry wood under some spruce."

She shivered. Lucien's strong fingers moved to her forehead, smoothing away her hair from her brow. His touch was like a flame against her skin.

"Did you rest well?" he inquired.

The ripple of muscle in his shoulder and arm as his hand moved fascinated her. "Aye," she said in a whisper, shifting her gaze to his face. Some overwhelming need made her own hand rise up and run a finger along the line of his jaw, where the close-cropped beard ran in a thin line from chin to ear. Such a sinister look, she found it heart-stoppingly attractive. His eyes watched her, soft brown now. It was difficult, in these moments, to imagine them steeled to the narrow flints of coal black his anger could make them. His mouth curved sensuously, framed darkly by the mustache and beard. Soft, full lips—she suddenly realized they were lush and sensitive when not pulled tight into a grimace. Aye, he was a fine-looking man.

"What is it you see?"

Alayna caught his eyes, embarrassed at the course of her thoughts. And yet, he had not been shy in expressing his admiration of her, even when it was done grudgingly. She decided to speak honestly.

"I was looking at your face, husband. It is handsome when you are not being stern."

His grip tightened, and his face looked stricken. She could not imagine what she had said to cause this reaction.

"How is it you find me handsome? Do you not see this scar on my cheek?"

She blinked. "Aye."

"I must wonder what purpose you hope to gain with such false flattery, then, for no one can think this face handsome."

His eyes had that haunted look again, and though she should have been daunted by this sudden flare of temper, she was more annoyed that it was spoiling the moment. "Well, I hardly think that you should be an authority on your own handsomeness," she snapped. "If I say I find you handsome, then 'tis so, though now I myself am seeing why I never noticed before. Since you favor this churlish behavior, it does tend to mar one's perception."

He stared at her for a moment, then, unexpectedly, his face relaxed. His hand resumed its motion and he drew her close to be kissed, murmuring, "Why can you never simply agree with me?"

She was about to say something as to his never being in the right, but the retort died on her lips. She lost her breath as the fiery kisses trailed to her breast, and then her thoughts deserted her, too.

They rose some time later and Lucien left to hunt some game for their dinner.

The fire in the small room was warm, so she dressed only in her shift. She busied herself with trying to salvage her crushed and soiled clothing, brushing off each item and hanging it on pegs to air.

She had time to sweep a bit with a crude broom she found propped in a corner. The place seemed much cozier for her efforts.

Lucien came in carrying several animals, already skinned and ready for the fire. "Put these on the spit," he directed. "Do you have enough wood for the fire?"

"I think so. Maybe we could use a bit more. Is anything dry out there?"

"The storm is letting up, though it is hard to say what is happening with the forest being so thick. I'll fetch more wood."

Though no cook, she put herself to the task of roasting the meat. Lucien returned with fuel for their fire and several large boughs thick with leaves. He stripped the leaves into a large pile, covering the mound with John's cloak.

Delighted with his cleverness, Alayna laughed and clapped her hands together. "Bravo, my lord baron!" she exclaimed. "You are quite ingenious."

"Ingenuity is natural when one has a strong motivation," he teased. "I plan to made good use of this bed."

"You are indeed a lazy lout," she said, and giggled,

pretending to resist as he pulled her into his arms. "Is it that all you can think of doing is lying abed?"

He raised a brow. "Let me show you, madam, of what I am thinking of doing."

She melted against him as he kissed her, and she would have soon been lost had not the succulent smell of the game set her stomach to rolling. They had not eaten in a day.

"My lord, the game is done."

"Huh?" he grunted, applying himself to tasting the sweet curve of her neck.

"Our food," she insisted, followed immediately by a ragged gasp as he found a spot that sent shivers through her.

"It will burn," she said weakly.

Straightening reluctantly, he scolded, "Is that all you can think of, lady, your stomach?"

She giggled at his jest, a turnabout of her own. "'Twould seem foolish for us to die of starvation with this meat charring on its stick."

"Ah, but what sweet death."

She skirted away from him as he lunged for her again, and they laughed. They sat on their soft bed of leaves and ate the simple meal.

Watching her nibble the meat, Lucien was amazed, at her and at himself. Was that truly his timbered voice that had laughed so unabashedly a moment ago?

His life had been a series of events, some more painful than others, but none of them holding any happiness, not for a long time. He never smiled, without any mockery or ire. He never laughed unless it was a taunt. He had not, since he was a lad, been easy with another, allowing his guard to rest. It felt terrifying and exhilarating all at once.

Alayna caught his eye and smiled at him, and he felt a surge in his breast. She was lovely, more so with the flush of happiness. Aye, he believed she was as happy as he with this slice of time and space they had carved here in the wood. But could he trust that anything in this enchanted place could last? What of her desperate desire to return to London? Would she still leave him if given a chance?

He would be a fool to turn away from this woman for the sake of his fears. But he also knew that those old haunts would not release him this easily.

Seized by a sudden uncertainty, he held out his hand to her. She came into his arms and he lost himself again in the sweetness of his wife.

The following morning, they awoke to the silence of the forest.

"The rain has stopped," he said.

Alayna nodded. It meant that they would be returning to the castle as soon as the floodwaters receded. His grip tightened, drawing her closer. "Are you hungry?" he asked.

"A little."

"I should go find more game. I will not be long." He made to rise, but she tugged at him.

"Stay with me," she said, blushing with her own forwardness. His response, however, erased any hesitancy she had, for he immediately complied, lying back down and wrapping her in his arms again.

She wanted more, for she was also feeling the fragility of this wondrous alliance they had forged. He was like a different man, and she...she was able to speak and move without the stubbornness and pride that had dogged her since their first confrontation. Would these things remain once they were back at Gastonbury, or fade like a dream when the first rays of dawn split the night?

She needed him again, wanting his touch to banish the doubts and worries that all of a sudden seemed more real than the rock-hard feel of his body against hers. Urging him toward what she wanted, she slid her legs around his hips, moving against him provocatively. Her boldness inflamed him and she reveled in the impassioned response he gave her, coming into her all at once. She cried out, groaning softly. He answered her with another thrust and she moved with him, matching his movements against her so that they came together to their fulfillment in a wild, exhaustive end. Breathless, they lay together, reluctant to part.

After a time, he said, "Are you still hungry?"

She laughed into his shoulder. "Aye, famished."

"Good, so am I." He rose and pulled on his leggings. When he was dressed, he leaned down to kiss her and left.

After he had gone, she decided to do a bit of foraging herself, thinking that she could hunt for some berries, nuts or wild fruits the forest could provide. She dressed quickly and headed off in the opposite direction from Lucien, not wanting to inadvertently disturb his hunting.

She found some hazelnuts without too much trouble, and was excited to spy a thatch of blackberries, as well. She held her skirt out to cradle the foods, loading them in until she could fit no more.

She had started back to the hut when Lucien came barreling at a full run out of the brush. At the last moment, he captured her in his arms to keep from knocking her down.

She was whirled around, coming face-to-face with the

thunderous visage of her husband. "What are you doing?" he barked. "Is someone after you?"

Alayna stared at him in dismay. "No."

"What the devil are you doing out of the hut?"

"I went looking for nuts and berries," she stammered.

"I will provide the food!" he bellowed. "What could you have been thinking—wandering around the forest like this? Do you not realize the dangers?"

"Nothing happened!"

"What if you had come upon another like John? What if you had come upon some animal looking for its breakfast?"

"I hardly think I was in danger from the rabbits and squirrels about, or did you think that some crazed deer would find me?"

He gritted his teeth. "I never found your jests amusing, Alayna. Take yourself back to the hut and stay there."

Tilting her chin in that way he found infuriating, she said loftily, "Aye, I shall go back, but only after I have gotten what I came for."

"You will do as I say!" he roared.

"I told you, Lucien, I will not. Now you may help me or you can stand there and berate me, but I have my heart set on berries and nuts for breakfast, and so berries and nuts I shall have."

She was behaving like an insolent child, causing him to work his jaw in irritation. Good Lord, she could try him! While they were standing here out in the open, arguing about the damnable berries, they could very well be set upon if his enemies were about.

"It is not safe here, Alayna. Get back to the hut!"

Her eyes filled with tears, though Lucien knew it was

not over the ridiculous issue of the berries, but the hurt of his harsh manner. He groaned at the sight of her distress.

"Very well," he growled at last. "Gather your fill while you are here, for you will not be allowed to leave the hut again."

She gave him a sullen pout before stooping to pick up the scattered food. He stayed over her, keeping a steady eye on the darkness of the forest.

They walked back to the small dwelling in morose silence. Once inside, Lucien brooded, watching her as she unloaded her burden and began to pick the stems from the berries and eat them.

What could he say to her? Should he try to make her understand? Nay, he decided testily, he did not explain himself to anyone! She would have to learn that despite the fact they had reconciled in many ways, he was still her husband and must be obeyed without question or complaint.

Another glance showed her looking as miserable as he felt. With her eyes downcast and that lovely mouth turned down at the corners, she nibbled on her lonely breakfast, so deflated when only an hour ago she had been laughing and happy and loving.

All at once he felt the anger seep out of him. The whole incident suddenly seemed trivial.

As Alayna made to walk by him, he seized her without preamble and pinned her up against the wall. Struggling at first, she stopped to glare into his face. She raised her brows expectantly, as if awaiting some explanation.

He wished he had the words to tell her his regret. They stayed locked in silent challenge for a long moment.

Then, all at once, the tension dissolved and she relaxed against him, a slow smile spreading across her face. He was utterly amazed when she threw back her head and laughed. He laughed, too, his grasp becoming an embrace when she wound her arms around his neck. He brought his mouth down on hers, and she responded with full vigor.

He tumbled her down onto their bed, rolling her under him. He broke the kiss to look down at her. "Do not venture out alone again. If some harm came to you, I could not bear it."

She looked stunned at his vehement command.

"Promise!" he demanded.

Bringing her hand up to his cheek, she lovingly ran her thumb down, touching his lips. "Aye, my lord. I will do as you wish."

He grabbed her hand and pressed a kiss to the palm, his eyes closed. When he again looked at her, he saw a gleam in her eyes as if they were wet with unshed tears. She reached for him and he kissed her again, savoring the smooth feel of her lips, then nibbled on the fullness of that flesh. The need arose up within them both, fierce and pressing, and they melded together once more in the artful way of love.

They lay tangled in each other's arms afterward, listening to the dying fire, still fascinated with each other's bodies enough to keep their hands roaming lazily. Lucien watched her, noticing the way her heavy fringe of ebony lashes looked in contrast to the rosy flush of her cheeks. Her nose was straight, with a sensuous flare to the nostrils that he liked. And her mouth, so full and lush, curved with a pouting shape. Yet when her lips were spread into a smile, she looked youthful and guileless, and her green eyes danced like chips of emeralds in firelight. He suddenly knew he would never tire of kissing that mouth.

She laid her hand on his chest, running a finger down the shallow crevice that divided his breast. Her fingers splayed, and she tested how the light fringe of hair moved under her hand. Her touch felt feather light, innocent, sensuous.

She fingered a long strip of puckered flesh on his back. "A battle scar?" she queried.

Lucien only shrugged. "A battle scar."

She was silent for a while until her wandering hand brushed across another scar. "Another battle?" she asked. He nodded. Her brow creased in a frown as she contemplated the evidence of his life as a warrior.

"Aye, there were many. Many scars, many battles."

"It speaks of a hard life," Alayna said. Lucien shrugged. Giving him an assessing look, she ventured, "Would you tell me the tale and put an end to my curiosity?"

He was silent for a long time. Then he began, "When I was a slave, I was in the household of a Viking named Hendron. He was a jarl, which is like an earl here in England. He was very powerful and very rich, and he maintained his holdings by raiding his neighbors."

The memories were fading, but the hate he harbored for Hendron was still fresh. He could hear the heaviness of emotion in his own voice. "By the age of ten and six, I was well versed in the use of a sword, and I seemed to have some talent for it. It was at this age that I was taken to the Norselands and Hendron bought me. He saw my size and skill and so I was made a warrior for his cause and went a-Viking."

Lying very still, Alayna said nothing. He wondered remotely what she would think of his strange tale, and it occurred to him she might find it atrocious. But she had the right to hear it, he reasoned. And, surprisingly, he needed to tell it to her.

"The killing suited me, for I had a great deal of rage. I had been torn from my home, watched my father slain before my eyes. I barely survived the journey to the North Seas. And I hated Hendron, for he was a cruel and vicious barbarian. He despised the English and me most of all. I suppose it was because he needed me so badly. But all of that was good fuel for a warrior, and so I excelled. I fought many battles and won a king's ransom in booty that filled Hendron's coffers to near bursting. But I was always just a slave. No matter how well I did on the battlefield, I was hated."

Alayna dared not breathe. She could behold the emotion in his face and suddenly she could understand his bitterness, his distrust, even his unyielding selfishness at times. He had endured trials she could have never imagined. She could see it caused him pain to speak of it and it brought an ache to her own breast. Yet, she listened to it all, closely watching those dark features she was coming to cherish.

Because she loved him.

Should that thought surprise her? It did not, nor did it frighten her. She loved him, fiercely, protectively, and she wanted none of what he was telling her to be true. She wished she could tell him to hush and never speak of these scars again, as if doing so could take away the past. But, of course, nothing ever could. And now every time they made love and her hand came across the scars, she would know what inner wounds they represented.

"I killed him, of course," he continued. "In the end, I did it without a moment's remorse. I waited for years for the right opportunity, just the right time, though I would never have succeeded without Agravar. I was allowed more and more freedoms, and one day the situation was perfect, and I just did it. Most of his treasure was mine, since I never received my share, so I stole it back, bought a ship, weapons, men to fight for me. I had sworn to myself that I would return to England and seek my revenge on du Berg.''

''How did you know 'twas Edgar who killed your father?''

''I knew,'' he said simply, and she sensed that there was more here he was not ready to share.

She asked, ''Then Agravar was with you in the north?''

Lucien nodded. ''Agravar is a bastard, Hendron's bastard, gotten on an English noblewoman during one of his Viking raids to the English coast. Agravar's dame held no love for the issue of her rape, so he sought his fortune with his father when he was of an age. Hendron accepted him, but Agravar had no stomach for his father's savagery, and so he threw in his lot with me. We shared a bond, and as soon as we realized the kinship of like experiences, we became fast friends. If not for Agravar, I may never have made it out of Denmark.''

''I never knew any of this,'' she said in wonder. So many had tried to tell her that Lucien was a man of secrets, a man with reasons for what he did. Now that she knew what they were, her feelings for him deepened.

''I never speak of it.''

''But you have told me,'' she prompted, implying that she wished to know why.

She saw him hesitate, unwilling to meet her eye. ''I thought you should know. 'Tis not something that should wait, for these things have a way of coming up at an unexpected time and causing trouble.''

Suddenly Alayna understood. Taking his face in her

hands, she turned him to look at her. "So much pain," she whispered. She could feel the muscles move under her hand as he clenched his jaw. She brought her fingers to the scar on his cheek, lovingly tracing the length of it with her fingertips. "So much hurt."

He grasped her wrist, pulling her hand away from that wound. "Nay, 'tis not a remnant of some battle there, wife, but a token of another enemy."

Stubbornly she pulled her hand out of his grasp and brought him down to her so she could press a tender kiss to the marred flesh. She drew away to look at his face once again, hoping the love in her heart would show in her face, for she lacked the courage to speak the words.

"So now you see me for what I am," he said. "A barbarian, a savage. It fulfills your initial impression, does it not?"

"Aye, I agree, husband. I do see you for what you truly are. I see a man who is good and kind and gentle underneath a fierce mien. A man who would truly be different if fate had not decreed he endure trials undeserved and grievous. I see a face, open and clear and not at all bitter, that can look at me without the ugliness of resentment, and be the face of the man who would have been without the years of pain and misery."

She pressed small kisses on his shoulder and chest, nuzzling his neck as he had done to her. Instinctively she did these things to comfort him, as if loving the outside of him would seep in to heal the wounds in his soul.

With a growl, Lucien brought his mouth down onto hers. He gave her no recourse, taking her roughly, demandingly, needing to expel the pain his tale had evoked. He wanted to possess her, to bury himself inside of her and lose himself in tender passion. He craved the yawning vortex of oblivion, to be dead to all but sheer sensation.

This, the ultimate stoking of the external senses, would drown out the raging hell within him. Alayna could do that. She could quell the pain with her lush woman's body. He would find the only solace and peace he had ever known in the consuming rapture she alone could offer.

Chapter Nineteen

They set out at first light, walking silently through the woods, back under the deep cover of the trees to trace their steps to the road. When they came to the pass that cut through the cliff, Lucien whistled for his stallion. The great horse looked up and around at the signal, tugging impatiently at his reins.

"Is he all right? Has he been out here all this time?" Alayna asked, frowning at the idea of having to ride the oversize beast.

"I found a passage to lead him in and tended him each day. The lout has likely grown fat with the lack of exercise and all I've fed him."

As if understanding, the horse snorted arrogantly and tossed its head.

Alayna laughed. "I see he has the temper of his master."

She was rewarded by a sudden smile, one that died all too quickly when he turned away. She placed a hand on his arm, wishing there was some way she could tell him what lay in her heart. He stared at it for a minute, covering it with his own large one before lifting her onto the horse's back.

Their arrival created a tremendous fervor. People were running every which way, shouting the news that the master was home with his lady, safe and sound. Out of this chaos came Will, trotting toward them with an expression of relief. Lucien swung down to greet his knight. He was stunned when the man ignored him and went straight to Alayna's side.

"My lady," he called, reaching up his hand to help her down.

As he lifted her from the back of the large horse, Lucien made no move to intervene. He watched with an inner hardness when she smiled her thanks.

Good Lord, the man's feelings were written all over his face. The fool was in love with her!

And she? Was she susceptible to the charms of the handsome knight?

"Praise the good Lord, you are safely returned!" Eurice declared as she came rushing up to sweep Alayna into her arms. She fussed over her beloved charge, "Well, you do not look the worse for it, I see. Thank God, Lord Lucien found you in time! What were you thinking, running off like that?"

Alayna opened her mouth to answer, but Eurice waved a hand at her imperiously. "You had no reason—no good one, 'tis truth! Now, you are filthy, you need a bath. Come."

Glancing over her shoulder as Eurice propelled her toward the keep, Alayna gave Lucien a quick, exaggerated pout. He nodded back, his eyes sliding to study Will.

"I am glad you are well. We were all quite concerned

about you and Alayna," Will said, swinging around to grasp Lucien's forearm.

Lucien's eyes narrowed at the familiar use of her name. "Where is Agravar?" he inquired curtly.

"He rode out yesterday morning with Kenneth and Thomas. They were set to search the north woods for you."

"Good," Lucien said. "Have him fetched back here. When he returns, send him to me. I will be with the smithy. Gather Pelly and yourself and Lionel and join us there."

He looked at Will, who was staring back at him a bit perplexed. "We go to war," he explained simply.

Lucien's mind obsessed on his new knowledge. How far did Will's feeling for his wife go? And what of Alayna—did she know? Did she feel the same?

His old doubts began to churn again, warring with his reason. His wife was many things, but she had always shown herself to be forthright—when she had hated him she had said so without compunction, and when she had given herself to him, it had been completely. And Alayna was *not* like his mother. He must remember that.

But his father had been fooled, blind to his wife's treachery. And it had been a most deadly mistake.

Eurice flitted about the chamber, chattering incessantly about how worried she had been during Alayna's absence. Without warning, she was apt to grab her charge in a fierce hug or grasp her face in her palms and burst into tears. Alayna, for her part, felt numb to this display of emotion. In a detached way, she was touched by Eurice's warm affection but her mind was far too occupied with other thoughts.

Leda joined them, ushering in an army of servants bearing a giant tub and buckets of steaming water. When her bath was ready, Alayna allowed herself to be stripped of her filthy garments and submerged in the large basin.

"Now let the poor girl have a good soak," Eurice suggested to Leda, and the two found other chores to occupy them in the room. Alayna smiled. Eurice knew her so well; the nurse could sense she needed some privacy.

Lying in the tub, finally left to herself, her thoughts immediately reverted to Lucien. She wondered where he was now, and what he was doing. Did he think of her? Or did other matters weigh on his mind already?

She looked down at herself as she lay naked in the water. It had been just last night that his hands had slid over the flesh displayed before her. She saw her own breasts, high and firm, their pink tips hardened at the thought of her husband. She shivered at the remembrance of his mouth, hot and moist, closing over one tender nipple. And she remembered her own shameless response. A giddy tremor sprang to life in the pit of her belly and the dull ache of need asserted itself with sudden urgency.

She closed her eyes. Was she so afflicted with desire that she could not look at her own body without recalling Lucien's touch? Giving herself to him had done nothing to stem the wicked cravings, but seemed only to whet her appetite for his embrace. Nay, not just that, but him, all of him, for he fascinated her. She could think of nothing else. He was a man beyond comprehension or understanding, and she was obsessed with him.

Eurice came to wash her hair. "You seem distracted, my lady. How did you fare these last days?"

Alayna cast her eyes down, but could not keep the blush from staining her cheeks. "'Twas not onerous."

Eurice chuckled. "Indeed, child." She leaned forward,

whispering to Alayna as if imparting some great secret. "You are glowing."

Alayna rolled her eyes away, letting out a small groan of embarrassment. "Please, nurse, do not plague me with your curiosity."

Eurice sat back on her heels, laughing in glee. She rubbed her hands together with exaggerated mirth. "Oh, my proud and fine lady, all has worked out well, then, has it not? Your husband turns out to be a lusty fellow who sees well to your pleasure—"

"Eurice!" Alayna exclaimed, mortified. She felt like sinking under the bathwater.

Eurice only laughed the harder. "Oh, my dear girl. How often have you vexed me with your teasing and girlish pranks? And besides, child, 'tis a wondrous relief to this old woman's heart to see you finally contented with your lot."

"Not content—nay. Truly, our time together did much to span the breach between us. But now we are returned, and do we continue with that path, or return to the old ways? This is what troubles me."

Eurice smoothed her hair, her motion loving and soothing. "Aye, 'tis true you have much left to settle between you. But do not forget, Alayna, that it is not just up to Lord Lucien."

She understood. Yet, she did not know what she should do. Certainly she would try her best not to get drawn into another argument, and she must strive to acknowledge his sovereignty over her, no matter how much it galled her. In this way she could demonstrate to him what lay in her heart. But would that be enough?

One of the first things Lucien did upon his arrival home was to put out the order to have Glenna brought to him.

Perhaps it was just as well no one could find her, Lucien considered, for he feared he was capable of murder should he face the lying wench enraged as he was. When she did not turn up, he ordered she was not to be allowed back into the castle, and if she were seen on any of his lands she was to be immediately arrested.

The next thing he did was initiate preparations for war.

Wanting to tell Alayna himself of the impending battle, he looked for her that evening. She was in the hall, gathered with the other ladies around the hearth where it was their habit to converse over a lapful of sewing. He was glad to notice that she was no longer squirreled away in their chamber. She even looked as if she were passing a pleasant time. Her happiness, he suddenly found, was of consequence to him.

She looked up when he came to stand before her. A new feeling came over him, and he was surprised to realize that he felt decidedly awkward.

"My lady, a word," he said. He liked the way her eyes lit up and the corners of her mouth twitched ever so slightly, a distinct sign of pleasure. God's teeth, this was no good. Just that tiniest of movements quickened his pulse and the inconvenient response of his body was downright embarrassing.

"Yes, my lord husband?" He cupped her elbow and led her away from the ladies.

"I come to tell you that I will ride again today," he said. He hated how gruff he sounded, but it was hard for him to be gentle when his passions raged so furiously within him. And there was still the question of Will.

"I am going into the forest to rout any outlaws or spies that might be encamped there. The attempt to harm you is likely to have been the work of Garrick of Thalsbury. He was the one who sent the assassin for me. Other sources confirm he has been speaking openly of rebelling, and it is more than likely he who pesters Henry with a counter-claim to Gastonbury. I cannot ignore him, but I must be sure the castle is secure before we ride to Thalsbury.''

He saw her eyes widen in alarm and hastened to reassure her, ''I will leave a guard to protect you, and Pelly will be here with the rest of the army. He is a young lad, but able. Still, do not venture out unattended. Remember, we are at war.''

Alayna nodded. ''I will be safe. 'Tis you who must take care.''

He did not wish to mock her, but he could not suppress a smile at her earnest warning. ''I will return as quickly as I can,'' he said solemnly. He wanted to touch her, but he did not trust himself.

Giving her a nod by way of farewell, he quit the hall before he forgot himself and dragged her up to the master's chamber, much as he had on the occasion of their first meeting, but with a much more lecherous intention.

She missed him terribly through the following days. Determined to put good use to the time, however, she applied herself to the tasks of her station. It was under Alwin's patient tutelage she learned the workings of the castle and the duties expected of her.

The other women of the castle were thawing, and after her initial tentative overtures of friendship, she found a few whose company she enjoyed. Without Lucien, she was quite desolate, yet she thrived on her new role and the fullness of the relationships she was forging in this most unlikely of places.

Over a sennight passed before the watchman sounded the bell signaling that the master approached. Excitedly Alayna ordered some special dishes prepared for the evening meal, then quickly went to ready herself for Lucien's arrival.

In their chamber, she pulled out a gown of lavender brocade, sewn with seed pearls and silver thread. The trailing sleeves and train were generous, the latest style being copied from the French. It was one of her finest, and she was glad to be looking her best this evening.

She called for Leda to help her dress and her hair was brushed until it shone like polished wood. She requested a simple style that left most of the curls unfettered down her back, though it was a maidenly fashion. Lucien had told her he liked her hair loose. Selecting several pieces of jewelry from her chest, she surveyed the end result in the hand mirror and was for once well pleased.

When all was to her satisfaction, she visited the kitchens. By the time she arrived in the hall, Lucien was there, refreshed and dressed in a dark tunic and woolen hose. He must have bathed and changed while she was seeing to the meal. He still wore his boots, cleaned and shined, but had donned a silver brooch to clasp the cloak about his broad shoulders. This was quite frivolous for him, though it was unusual for any man to go without such adornment. He had trimmed his beard, but his hair, ever untamed, fell in its usual disarray.

He was talking to some men in the hall, standing taller than they, looking splendid in his arrogant stance and dark handsomeness. Alayna felt her heart lurch as she caught sight of him.

As if sensing her presence, he looked over. His eyes watched her move toward him, dark and hooded and intense. She felt speared by the piercing gaze. He seemed so aloof, so much the lord of the castle of old. Did any of her tender lover remain?

She trembled as she drew up to him. Dropping a small curtsy, she bowed her head. "My lord."

When she raised her eyes again to his, they were soft. She brightened and gave him a smile. His gaze swept over her, and she knew his approval. Inclining his head, he said, "My lady."

"Lady Alayna." Agravar stepped up. He took her hand in his. "You are looking particularly radiant this evening. I have been so occupied with my own duties that I have not yet had a chance to welcome you home from your sojourn into the wood." His eyes sparkled mischievously as he cast a sideways glance to Lucien. "I am very pleased that you fared so well. And grateful, too, for taking such good care of our baron. No doubt he would have faltered without your fortitude and resourcefulness to guide him. As I was not there, I am grateful he had you instead."

A roar of merriment went up from all within earshot. Lucien surprised everyone by flashing a good-natured smile instead of his usual scowl. Alayna laughed, her eyes only for her husband. He returned the look. It was as if time were suddenly suspended and there was just the two of them. Then someone broke in and he was forced to turn away.

They sat down to dine, Alayna at her usual place at Lucien's left, but he did not turn from her as was his habit of old. Instead, he attended to her, filling the trencher they shared with pheasant and mutton. When she was thirsting, it was he who proffered the chalice. His solicitousness was quite a departure from his mood of the past, and the drastic turnaround did not escape notice. They were the object of many a curious glance and a good many whispered comments buzzed about the room.

"The feast is well run, wife," Lucien commented. "My favorite dishes, I notice."

"'Tis not rabbit nor squirrel."

A slow smile curved on his lips at her allusion to the intimate meals shared in the hut. It made her heart lurch and the familiar flutter of pleasure tingled within her limbs as his eyes caressed her face. "Aye," he answered in a soft whisper. "Though I doubt any food served in this hall could match the delicious repast we enjoyed in the wood."

She flushed at his double meaning, darting a self-conscious look about to see if any had overheard. But she was pleased.

Lucien watched the color spread across her creamy complexion, and his heart quickened. He wondered if it would be seemly for him to sweep her up to their room yet. No, of course not. The celebration had only just begun.

Other matters pressed him, however. Even as he supped, men worked at the forge and in the smithy to make ready for the coming battle. He could not spare much time. After this meal, he and Agravar would meet to see how the preparations were progressing and begin the intense strategy sessions to analyze anticipated defenses and plan their assault.

With Alayna beside him, however, he did not feel the usual stirrings at the prospect of war. He was of a mind for a gentler sport tonight, and would have forgone those activities that up until recently had been his life's work. But one did not get to choose one's opportunities.

"Will, there you are," Agravar said as the knight entered the hall. "Have you word on the smithy?"

"Aye," Will nodded. "He said he and his lads will have

the swords ready, though there was some kind of delay. Apparently he had some problem with the forge. Nay, Lucien, do not look so, for we attended to it, and now all is well.''

Lucien had watched as Will had weaved his way among the trestle tables to the dais, had seen the ladies' heads turn to follow his passage through the hall. But the handsome knight had no time for these inviting looks, coming immediately to sit at his usual place on Alayna's other side, launching into his most charming demeanor. Lucien found himself sinking into a foul mood.

The evening drew to a close. Alayna rose to make her exit. Casting a demure look at Lucien, she excused herself and made her way to their chamber.

Lucien did not miss the glance. Despite his obligations, he was determined to follow as soon as he could extricate himself from his men. If only for a moment, he assured himself.

He watched her weave through the room, her back straight, head held high. He was struck again by her loveliness. The graceful way she moved exuded sensuality. Was it apparent to all, or were his perceptions heightened by lust?

Then he spied Will. He came up to Alayna, intercepting her, and she paused. As they conversed, Lucien's rival bent his blond head close to hers. They spoke for only a moment before Lucien saw Alayna lay her hand gently on the knight's arm. Such a tender scene, Lucien thought bitingly, feeling the bile rise in his throat. Impulsively he turned to Agravar. ''Let us get to work. All of this dallying has cost us precious time.''

He rose quickly and stormed out of the hall, leaving those behind in silence, thinking how unfortunate was the enemy of such a man.

Chapter Twenty

Alayna rushed to the chamber to make ready for Lucien. She had Eurice brush her hair until the cascading curls gleamed like burnished oak. She dressed carefully in a fine linen shift, thinking even as she slipped the delicate garment over her head that Lucien would more than likely damage it when undressing her. No matter, she had decided frivolously. She wanted to look her best, and this shift was one of her finest. It was worth the cost if it got ruined.

Her excitement flushed her cheeks, and her eyes sparkled in the roaring fire freshly built in the hearth. Eurice hummed and chuckled, but Alayna refused to be embarrassed. It was only her old nurse's teasing, and she could think of nothing but the thrill of her husband's imminent arrival. Dismissing Eurice, she settled comfortably into the great chair to await him.

Hours passed. The embers merely glowed and Alayna sat despondently staring into the dead fire. Eurice carefully opened the portal and crept into the room, coming to stand by Alayna. "The baron stays with his men," she murmured.

"'Tis war," Alayna said dully, her voice showing no conviction in her words. "I cannot expect him to linger with me when such vital matters are afoot. Of course, he is very busy with this nasty business with Lord Garrick."

"You speak the words, child, but your heart does not believe."

Alayna closed her eyes. With her excitement gone, she was bone weary. "Is it the battle? If not for that, would he be here with me?" She looked at her nurse. "Does he want me, truly, do you think?"

"Surely he has demonstrated that he does," Eurice assured her. Alayna blushed a little at her meaning.

"But he is my lord and husband," she protested stubbornly. "'Tis his duty."

"Duty! Is that how he did it?" the nurse exclaimed.

"Nay," Alayna admitted, coloring with memory. "Still, how do I know that 'twas not part of that terrible game we played? How can I know the gentleness 'twas real, or that what I felt was matched by him?"

"Surely, child, you do not still linger upon those doubts."

"He has never declared his heart, never told me of his feeling for me. He is a man who is beset by demons. Perhaps they are stronger than any caring for me. Aye, I do doubt a great deal. I am never sure when it comes to my husband, for there is so much I do not know."

There was a long silence before Eurice replied. "You do not know, of course, my dearling. No one ever knows for sure what lies in another's heart. You must *believe*."

Alayna sighed. "I do not know what to believe."

Smiling into the dim room, Eurice said, "Nay, child. 'Tis that you are afraid to believe." Brushing a shining lock from Alayna's forehead, she bent to kiss her good-night.

Alayna did not understand her nurse's words but was too tired to dwell on them. She closed her eyes, wishing for the healing oblivion of sleep.

Before it came, Eurice's words echoed in her brain. Be-lieve.

If she did dare to believe, then where was he tonight?

Lucien dozed in a corner of the stable while waiting for his horse to be reshod. He dreamed of soft chestnut curls swirling seductively in loose tendrils. He dreamed of pink lips, soft and lush, slightly parted and ready for his kiss. In sleep, he saw her emerge naked from a sparkling pool of water that was as clear and as emerald green as her eyes. She was lithe and lean, moving with the provocative gracefulness that was purely her own. Her arms reached out to him, and he stood on the bank of the lake, anxious to go to her, but he could not move. He could only watch her, Alayna, his wife, beckoning him.

He came awake at Agravar's voice calling for him. Croaking out an answer in a voice ragged with sleep, he winced at the aches his cramped quarters had caused. His mind flashed on the comfortable bed waiting close by with Alayna, ever soft and warm, curled up nicely in it. It deep-ened his already sour mood to think on it.

"Good, you are awake. Not a terribly restful sleep, eh? By the look of you, there must be spiny quills in that hay."

"Where is Will?" Lucien growled, running his hand through his hair.

"He and Pelly rode out to scout the road to Thalsbury. He should be returning sometime this afternoon."

Lucien nodded. He could not help but register relief that

Will was away from the castle. And Alayna. He must be careful to always know the knight's whereabouts.

Shaking off his preoccupation, he stood. "Very well. Then let us see to the supplies. I want the armory opened and the weapons dispensed to the foot soldiers. Have the mounted men make the last minute preparations for their own horses and their armor, then we will be ready. When Will returns with Pelly, send one or the other of them to me with their report, and then we will meet to put the final touches on our plan. If all goes well, we will be ready to ride on the morrow."

"What of the machines, do we bring them?" Agravar asked.

Lucien considered this for a moment. "Nay. The north road is still too treacherous with mire, and their heavy weights would get bogged down. Besides, we shall not need them."

At Agravar's raised brow, Lucien explained. "Garrick would expect us to attack the weakest side, and he is aware that I know the location of the secret gate near the cliffs, by the river. Yet, on the east side of the rampart wall there is a tower. The forest butts right up against it. 'Tis a spot I knew well as a boy. I would sneak in and out of the castle at night until my father discovered it and had the forest cut back. But the tree line is still close enough that we can send some men up into the branches and construct a walkway to the tower."

A slow smile spread over Agravar's face. "Send them over the wall and launch our attack from within? 'Tis lucky you were an incorrigible boy."

"It worked only for a while," Lucien said, remembering his final sojourn, when he had returned in the wee hours of the morning to find his father waiting for him. Raoul had never had to inspire fear in his son; Lucien's great respect for his father had been sufficient to insure his obedience. That night was the only time his father had laid a hand to him, and then only halfheartedly. As Lucien recalled the memory, he felt a warmth suffuse his heart. Strange that the pain was no more, though he still missed his father keenly.

He continued, "I'll lead the party up there. Will and Pelly shall stay on the ground to give them some problems in case we are foiled. Meanwhile, you wait with most of the army by the very gate at which they will be expecting us. When we have arrived inside the walls of Thalsbury, I will lead the men there and we will attack their assembled forces from both sides."

Agravar threw back his head in a hearty laugh. "A very fine plan, by far your best. I will gather the men, and we will lay it out to them."

"Call me when Will and Pelly are back. We can work out the details then."

The two men looked at each other, one fair, one dark. Both large, though the blonde hulked over his companion. They had been here before, caught in the excitement of impending battle. Lucien could feel the rush coming over him, his blood pulsing at the challenge. It was different than it had been before, for this time he looked forward not to the venting of his hate, but in the swift dispatching of his enemy. He had other things on his mind.

"A-Viking." Agravar smiled. It was a jest between them, the old Norse cry that their Danish comrades had used to whip themselves into fury for battle. For the two men, it was a reminder of the warrior in themselves, a call to bring the savage forward to serve the man in battle.

"A-Viking," Lucien agreed.

They parted. It was just before dawn. Lucien headed for his chamber.

Like many concerns after the space of a night, Lucien's jealousy had receded. He would see Alayna once more before he left.

He climbed the stairs silently, creeping carefully past the servants wrapped tightly in blankets on the floor. The guard he had posted outside the chamber door was awake, Lucien was pleased to see, and Lucien gave the man a nod. There would be no chances taken since Alayna's near-abduction. He eased the door open quietly.

He found her curled by the fire, in the great chair he favored. He paused a moment to study her face in repose. She was so incredibly beautiful that his heart faltered crazily at the sight of her. Heavy lashes fanning against the fair flush of her cheeks and her hair tumbled over her, covering her like a shawl of sable.

Coming closer, his shadow fell across her face. Her eyes fluttered open, resting on him and rounding slightly.

Neither one moved for a moment. Then he slowly bent down so that his lips were only inches from hers. Her eyes swept shut and she turned her face up for his kiss. Savoring the sight of that vision, he paused.

A racket behind him caused him to straighten bolt upright, his tortured back protesting the action after the abuses of the night spent on the stable floor.

The servant cried, "Oh, my lord, I—I did not know...'tis morn, I thought..."

Behind him, Alayna stood, unmindful of her provocative attire. The sheer shift strained against her breasts, revealing generous curves and taut pink tips that pressed against the fabric. Lucien's pulse thudded dully in his forehead.

"'Tis all right, Leda. My lord just arrived," she said

smoothly. She turned to Lucien, the picture of a solicitous wife. "Do you require a bath, husband? I could have one fetched for you."

He grunted his assent and turned away, all too aware that the evidence of his wife's heady effect on him was apparent to the casual glance.

Alayna hurriedly donned her dressing gown, sending Leda to fetch his bath. She watched him shyly from beneath her lashes as he stripped himself of his dusty garments, his body slowly revealed to her inquisitive eyes. She felt a heat spread like slow fire throughout her body, warming her and quickening her pulse. When he glanced over at her and caught her studying him, she looked away, blushing.

The men came in with the tub, then filled it with steaming buckets of water. Leda waved them out before closing the door behind her.

"Are you hungry, my lord?" Alayna asked. He had removed all of his clothing except the thick woolen hose. She was too aware of his near nakedness to think clearly.

"Aye," he rumbled, his eyes burning her. "Send one of the servants to fetch me a tray to be brought in here. I require you to attend me in my bath."

Her insides lurched at this, both with excitement and a twinge of resentment. Always the master.

"Aye," she answered, turning to carry out his instructions. She found a young boy in the hall and relayed Lucien's orders. When she returned to the room, he had eased himself into the bath, reclining with his head back, eyes closed. He made no move when she entered. She felt her heart sink, thinking he was asleep.

Opening one eye, he peered at her. "I am waiting, wife."

Coming to the side of the tub, she sank to her knees and took the soap in her hand. She sensed that he was aware of every move, like a cat who looks at ease except for the excited twitching of its tail.

Rubbing her hands together, she lathered them well and placed them on his breast. Slowly sliding across the broad expanse of his shoulders, her slick, exploring fingers moved down over the bulging muscles of his arms, then the flatness of his belly above the water line. Distractedly she returned her soapy caress to his chest, savoring the feel of the hardness under the warm flesh.

"I believe that area is quite clean, madam," he drawled softly. She blushed, glancing at his face to see both eyes open now, watching her from under heavy lids.

She rinsed her hands then splashed warm water on him. This done, she said, "If you will sit up, I can scrub your back."

A large hand emerged from the water, lifting to touch her cheek. Caught by his dark gaze, she froze as he slowly moved toward her, his grip tightening to hold her face in his hand. She closed her eyes in anticipation, feeling his breath against her lips just when a loud noise behind her made her jump back.

The portal swung open to admit several pages carrying freshly heated water. Leda was behind them. "Excuse me, my lord baron, but I thought perhaps your bathwater had cooled."

"Not likely," Lucien muttered, easing back in the water.

A bit wary of what her husband might do to the innocent intruder, Alayna hurried to thank her maid and usher her out the door with assurances of their comfort. Determined to do a good job, the young servant made her mistress promise that should she or the master need anything, she would call immediately. Alayna uttered the pledge, then shut the door with a sigh of relief.

"Enough!" Lucien exclaimed, rising out of the tub. Water sloughed off his magnificent body in sheets, leaving his skin glistening in the morning light. Alayna made to grab a linen towel, but he shot out an arm, and she found herself swept back against him. His mouth was next to her ear.

"Bolt that door, wife."

He released her abruptly, and she hurried to do as he bid. With the plank in place, she turned again to face him. He had fetched his towel and was hurriedly getting off the worst of the wetness. His eyes stayed on hers. A sensation leaped in her belly, alive and ravenous all of a sudden.

"Come," he commanded gruffly.

With a small cry, she ran to him, wrapping her arms around his neck. Her lips found his, and she was not shy in opening her mouth to his plundering tongue. She was afire, in a state of near desperate yearning, heedless of propriety or the nagging questions of his devotions. He wanted her. The hardness of his hunger pressed hotly against her hip, his mouth seeking hers with an urgent haste while his arms trapped her blissfully against him.

His hands tangled in her hair, holding her head as he rained kisses over her mouth, her eyes, then her ear, nipping the lobe with strong teeth. She shivered violently at the pleasure that tore through her, whispering his name and he answered with hers. Then he said it again, repeating it over and over like a prayer as he slid to one knee in front of her, impatiently unwrapping her gown and lifting her shift to bare her velvet skin until she stood as naked as he.

Lucien gazed at the perfect mound of her breast before him, reverently cupping his hand around it in gentle possession. It was so perfectly formed, tipped with a tight, raspberry-colored nipple that hardened under his gaze. With a growl, he lifted her with one motion and carried her to the bed. Laying her down, he paused a moment to gaze at her, his wife, his prize, yet more than any of that she was simply Alayna and he wanted her with a fierceness that could not be stemmed.

A loud knock sounded at the door, cutting through his drugged senses. Lucien's head snapped up. "Who is it?" he snarled.

"Lucien, 'tis Agravar."

Alayna moved as if to rise. Lucien dragged her back with a yank on her arm. "Go away," he shouted gruffly. He sank his mouth onto her neck, nibbling and nipping the tender flesh. Alayna squeaked nervously, only relaxing again when no more was heard from the Viking.

"And now, my lady wife, there is no one to save you," Lucien growled.

Alayna sighed, curling her arms about his neck. "What if I do not wish to be saved?" she whispered breathlessly as his mouth closed over a taut nipple. Groaning, she caught her hands up in his hair and squirmed. He played until her breath came in ragged gasps.

Once more, Lucien moved over her, slipping inside her in one easy motion. She mewled softly as she matched the rhythm of his deep thrusts. He ground himself into her over and over again, a primitive, guttural sound tearing involuntarily from his throat at the sheer physical ecstasy of their joining. Sensation swept them toward its inevitable, mind-shattering conclusion, exploding into a brilliant, shimmering climax that left her trembling, weak, depleted, yet not at all sated.

Restlessly Lucien's hands slid over her flesh. If he had

time, he would explore, build the tension until he was ready to take her again. He wanted to touch every inch of her, taste her, feel the texture of different parts of her body.

But he remembered the duties awaiting him and knew there would be no such dallying today.

"I must go," he murmured. He turned his head to look at her. Alayna kept her face averted, her hair shielding her features from view. Gently he nudged her chin up. Her lashes fluttered until he was confronted by that glorious emerald gaze. "I have a siege to see to." He tried a wry smile, but it did not alter her frown.

After a space, she nodded. Reluctantly he rolled away from her and started to dress.

Chapter Twenty-One

The bailey was teeming with horses and armored knights and servants running swiftly on last-minute errands. Lucien prowled through the throng, impatient with every small delay. He was in a black mood. He had no idea why. Alayna was not giving him any trouble, for a change. Quite the contrary. This morning in their chamber still burned in his memory. He was off to battle, an undertaking which had been his chief occupation for most of his life. One in which he excelled, and in which he had found no small amount of relief for the hate that raged within him.

Today, however, he wanted none of it.

"Mount up!" he yelled. At his soldiers' lack of immediate response, he roared, "Did you not hear me then, or must I shout it louder for your deaf ears!"

His men obeyed as their squires scrambled to see to their provisions. Lucien caught sight of Alayna, stumbling toward him as she struggled under the weight of several well-stuffed panniers. He dismounted, rushing to her side to take them from her.

"Some food, my lord," she explained breathlessly.

He smiled. "Alayna, I am perfectly capable of providing my own meals."

Although he had meant no reprimand, she frowned. "I thought it might help."

"It does," he reassured her, and strapped them to his mount. "My thanks, wife."

Agravar rode up. "All is ready, Lucien. We await your order." Lucien gave his friend a curt nod. Agravar rode away, leaving them once again to themselves.

Touching her cheek with his fingertips, he murmured, "When I return, my lady wife..."

"I will await you, my lord husband," she answered softly. "And may God be with you and bring you back safely."

Something pitched in his heart at such earnest sentiments. He nodded and swung onto his destrier. Waving his hand for the gates to be opened, he shouted out the order to proceed. The army surged forward, and Lucien waited until they were almost completely out of the lower bailey before kicking his steed into action. At full gallop, he followed his men out of the gatehouse archway, rode to the fore and led them onto the road due north.

They made camp on schedule, settling into a quiet vigil just outside of Thalsbury's wall as they waited for the call to arms to come just before dawn. Some men dozed, not wishing to get caught at less than their best. Lucien was surprised his fatigue got the best of him and he, too, slept.

She was there, as ever, in his dreams. The echo of the promise he had made to her before he had left resounded in his mind. When he returned...

He awoke, shaking off the remnants of the intoxicating vision and drew out his whetting stone to sharpen his weapons. As always, the mundane chore calmed him, focused his concentration. When he was finished, he buckled on the scabbards and sheaths and mounted his huge destrier.

Agravar, about to lead his troop to the hidden gate at the base of the cliffs, rode past with sword raised. Lucien struck it with his own weapon.

"A-Viking," the Viking whispered mischievously, then kicked his mount into action.

Lucien smiled darkly. He waved his men on and they rode to the east tower.

The invasion came off better than Lucien could have hoped. The watchmen had no warning of their approach. As he had done so often as a boy, Lucien swept up the trees, his men following. They quickly constructed the narrow walkway with flat planks, crossed to the ramparts and silently descended into the outer buildings. The guards at the postern gate were easily overcome and the portcullis was raised, allowing Lucien's full army to ride into his old home.

"Most of the place is still asleep," he hissed to his men. "Go to the stables and armory and secure them, then round up the soldiers quietly. You, gather the servants together in the hall. Agravar, come with me."

With the Viking at his side, he cut around to the solar where the master of the house slept. Pausing before the door, he was acutely aware that this had been his parents' room. He drew a deep breath to steel himself, then swung the door open wide.

Agravar shoved a lit torch inside the dark chamber. The master of Thalsbury was abed, entwined with a wench amidst the generous heaping of furs.

Garrick sat up, blinking into the light. As his bleary eyes registered the intruders, he lunged for the scabbard hanging on the post at the foot of the bed. He was on his feet in an instant, brandishing his weapon at his enemies.

"So, my lord baron," he snarled, "you sneak in like a thief in the night."

"It causes less bloodshed," Lucien explained patiently. "I am going to need these villeins after I kill you."

At his side, Agravar stood in a casual stance as he smirked at the naked man before them. "I believe you have forgotten your armor, sir," the Norseman said.

Garrick's gaze did not leave Lucien's face. "Your audacity is indeed amazing, de Montregnier. But your stupidity is even more so. Even with the surprise you have dealt me, do you think I would not have a defense planned?"

"I do not know. Do you?" Lucien sounded disinterested.

A slow smile spread across Garrick's face. "Look behind you."

Lucien would never have let his gaze be distracted from his enemy but for the light sound of steel touching metal from behind him. He looked to his companion, and Agravar's head snapped around. In one swift motion, the Viking whirled, drawing his sword up to face the men behind them.

Lucien did not move. He stayed as he was, watching Garrick with narrowed eyes. "You underestimated me, de Montregnier," the older man sneered.

"I never underestimate an enemy," Lucien answered.

"Ah, but here you have erred."

"Indeed?" Lucien raised a brow. "I see we have simply

evened out our game. Now Agravar will have someone to play with while you and I attend our business.''

With incredible swiftness, Lucien lunged at Garrick, who was hard-pressed to meet the swing. The clash of steel echoed in the room, and the poor girl who had been sleeping with her lord huddled fearfully under the furs.

Lucien pressed on, swinging his sword in rapid succession until he had Garrick against the outer wall. In desperation, Garrick struck out with a newfound ferocity, and Lucien was driven back a bit, but only for a moment.

"You were given Thalsbury as reward for helping du Berg kill my father. You were the one who ambushed us that day, were you not?"

Garrick sneered, a singularly ugly expression. "Well, you figured that much out. Aye, and I was happy to get rid of Raoul, for he was far too noble for my tastes and Edgar wanted Isobol. You had to be silenced."

"Now that we have settled the reasons for our feud, shall we get on with your death?"

With a quick flick of his sword, Lucien slashed a cut on Garrick's right shoulder, drawing a crimson line across the pale flesh. Stung by the injury, he winced and slapped his other hand over it to stem the flow of blood.

"Does that not ache, Lord Garrick?" Lucien inquired, his voice sounding deceptively polite. "When I was taken by your men, one of them wounded me there. I bear the scar to this day, along with many others. Such is the life of a man of war, eh? As I was saying, this one wound troubled me much. Indeed, I almost died of it, for it was deep and close to an artery. But I did survive it, as you can see. Shall I show you where else their swords found me?"

A lightning-quick slash brought another gash, then Lucien frowned. "Oh, how clumsy of me. 'Twas not there that the man did his damage. 'Twas more to the left, I think."

Another wound was opened so quickly that Garrick had no chance to deflect the blade. "Aye," Lucien said, satisfied. "That is where it was. Now, that one did not trouble me much, since—"

"Enough!" Garrick yelled. His voice cracked. He was becoming unnerved.

"We still have ten more years of various painful procedures to go. Do you tire of this game? I shall cut it short. Let us get right to it, then, though it does puzzle me that you wish so soon to die."

With that, his blade crashed down in a resounding strike. Garrick raised his sword to meet it, but staggered under the tremendous force. Lucien raised his weapon again, letting loose a barrage of blows that left his adversary stunned.

Garrick was beginning to panic, Lucien could see it in his eyes. Raising the tip of his sword, Lucien played out his cruel game to the end.

"It is justice then, that my father's sword shall see to your death."

Without warning, as if that last statement had driven any sanity or honor from the man, Garrick let out a blood-curdling yell. The sound echoed, then died, and with the madness that had fed that cry, Garrick ran full-tilt toward his tormentor. It took only one deft slice to end the man's charge. Impaled, Garrick stared at Lucien as they staggered backwards toward the window. Turning quickly, Lucien jerked his sword free, sending Garrick through the gaping opening, his eyes already closed in death as he was swallowed at once by the darkness.

In the ensuing silence, Lucien rushed to the side of the window and peered down. The chamber was along the western ramparts, the ones that perched atop the cliffs above the river.

He turned away after a moment. The rogue was gone and would trouble them no more.

Agravar was still busy with the last of Garrick's personal guard.

"Your lord is dead, cease this vain resistance," Lucien called, adding, "You will be treated fairly, for you are not to blame for your master's treachery."

The man faltered. A quick glance at the slumped forms of his companions helped him to decide. He threw down his sword.

The rest of the night was spent rounding up the last of the occupants, and once again Lucien issued his bargain of fealty or the dungeon. Apart from a few of Garrick's cronies, all readily acceded to their victor. Those few who refused were herded to the damp chambers under the castle.

That night, Lucien slept in his father's bed. He gave himself over to the bittersweet remembrances of his youth, finally making peace with the loss that had obsessed him for so long.

His last thoughts were comforting, for he thought of Alayna.

Over the next few days, Lucien found that he missed Alayna terribly. He would see a maid out of the corner of his eye and think for a moment that it was she. But when he would turn to look, he wondered how he could have been so mistaken, for the girl's hair would not be nearly as glorious, nor would she have the fine-boned features or the sensuous slimness of his wife. Or he would hear a voice and feel a quick thud in his chest at the thought that she would be there. But it would be some other, uninteresting and, upon closer inspection, not at all similar to Alayna.

On the sixth day, they fished Garrick's dead body out of the river, signaling the end of the seige. Lucien could stand it no longer. He left Will in charge, and he and Agravar took most of the soldiers back to Gastonbury.

Chapter Twenty-Two

Alayna was in the cellars inspecting the stores of wines and casks of ale with Alwin. Outside the circle of light of the seneschal's torch, she could hear the skitter and squeak of rats. The sound made her flesh crawl, but she pushed aside her squeamishness. Peering into the shadows, she pointed out a small wooden crate. "What are those strange flasks yonder? The ones with the distinctive shape."

"I do not know, my lady. I have never seen any like them before. They are stamped with an insignia, but I do not recognize it—a mountain and sun with a vine entwining both together."

Alayna gasped. "Those are wines from one of the finest vineyards in Bordeaux!"

"Wherever did Lord Edgar get those?" Alwin wondered, moving closer to inspect their find.

"Have them brought up and served at the master's table when he arrives home. I want the Bordeaux wine and no other."

Alwin smiled broadly. "Aye, my lady."

"Do you suppose there are more treasures as these?" she asked, peering into the dim recesses beyond the light.

"Please, my lady, let me get some pages with torches. They can drag those casks out for you."

Alayna nodded, finally conceding, for she had no taste to challenge her venturesome spirit further. The two of them climbed the timbered ladder up from the filthy cellar.

Smacking at her skirts, she tried to rid herself of some of the dust from the seedy caverns below. Cobwebs clung with sticky determination to her hair. As she detangled the offensive grime, hoping desperately that a resolute spider did not still linger on his old home, there was a flurry of activity as servants hurried about in some kind of excitement. She stopped one little girl she knew, a pretty lass of about eight years old, who was skipping by with the stale bread to set out for trenchers.

"What is going on, Clary?"

"The baron arrives home! The watchmen spotted him!" the child cried out with glee, then resumed her happy chore.

"The baron arrives home!" Alayna cried, alarmed. "Oh, nay! Look at me, I am a mess! Bess, start the preparations we discussed for my lord's arrival. Alert the cooks, and Alwin—have those flasks of Bordeaux brought up right away!"

"Aye, I will see to it. Go, I will take care of everything," her steward assured her.

Alayna flew up the stairs to her chamber. The water in the basin from her morning ablutions was cold, but she shivered through a thorough washing. She could hear the sound of horses in the lower bailey. The army was just arriving at the stables. Good, that should give her another ten minutes at least until Lucien could come into the castle.

She stood naked and chilled as she tossed open the lid to a trunk. Grabbing the first garment she found, a jade green silk, she held it up. It was far too fancy for daytime, but she had no time to hunt for something else. She slipped it on without any chemise underneath. When she realized her mistake, she cursed her forgetfulness, then shrugged. No time to right it now. Dashing to the table, she grabbed her ivory brush and began to rip it through her hair. How much time did she have left? Where were the green slippers that went with this gown? Was her gold circlet for her hair in the small trunk or—?

Her panicked thoughts were interrupted by the sound of the chamber door crashing open. Her hand froze in mid-stroke as she looked up to meet the coal black gaze of her husband as he stood framed in the doorway. He was dusty and disheveled from the journey, standing with his feet braced apart, his hand still on the catch of the door.

However did he get up to their chamber so quickly? she thought distantly.

The brush fell from her hand; her fingers were numb. His eyes, she kept looking into his eyes; the memory of their parting and the promise he had made her had her trembling.

He stepped inside the room, closed the door solidly behind him and slid the bar into place. In just a few long strides, she was in his arms.

He kissed her hard, pressing her full up against him in a crushing embrace. Her arms wound around his neck, pulling him closer and closer still until she could feel the full hardness of him against her entire body. Her hands slid hungrily over the muscles of his back, down the thickness of his arms. His mouth slashed over hers, twisting, opening it to plunder. The soft slide of the fabric against her breasts was like a caress, her nipples grazing against the roughness of the chain mail he still wore.

His hands moved quickly to slip the silken gown easily up over her hips. Quickly he untied his leggings and lifted her with her back against the stones of the hearth. Grasping her firmly, he slid inside with a sudden, exhilarating plunge. She cried out, a mingling of surprise and joy, then relaxed in the steely hold as he pinned her against the wall.

Moving against her, he covered her mouth to smother the sounds that tore from her throat. With each thrust, she strained to meet him, her pleasure beginning to take form from the elements of desire. She felt it building, and the need of it made her abandon herself to her senses, surrendering to the crystallization of pleasure and fulfillment that came in the end.

He leaned against her, his breath raging in her ear. Slowly he released his hold, and she slid her feet to the floor to stand on trembling legs, grateful that he still held her close. The sultry aftermath of their lovemaking still lingered in her veins, giving her a floating, drowsy sensation that made her feel like a feather drifting on the wind. But he was not finished. He kissed her with hot, demanding passion as if they had not just consummated their bodies' craving.

Grabbing some furs off the bed, he tossed them onto the floor in front of the fire, then pushed her down with him onto the plush bedding. He handled her roughly, laying her on her back, pulling the rumpled gown off over her head to reveal her completely to him.

His impatience was intoxicating, bringing to life once again the sensations he could so effortlessly command within her. His hands closed over her breasts, gathering them into his grasp, and he bent to kiss each one in turn, toying erotically until she arched against him and moaned a wordless plea. He lingered on the sweet mounds, testing and sampling the gentle curves while his fingers worked to unfasten his clothing and strip off the travel-stained garments until he was undressed. Then he lay down on her, covering her with the warmth of his fevered flesh.

His kisses, his caresses did not stop for a moment, exploring, touching, rousing until she writhed under him with desperate longing. With a growl of impatient desire, he came up over her again, taking her this time with gentleness, speaking soothing words that thrilled her to hear as she clutched him close to her heart.

"I missed you," he said much later.

They lay together in the big bed, the late afternoon sun spilling through the open shutters, creating long shadows across the room. His thumb moved over her cheek, then ran along her upper lip. She saw a small smile tug at the corners of his mouth as he considered her features.

Her heart gave one wild leap before lodging in her throat. He had missed her!

"So that pleases you, does it, my lady wife?" he teased wryly. "My men find it somehow less delightful, considering my temper this last sennight since you and I have been apart. And I drove half of them to near exhaustion in my hurry to return."

"I must offer my apologies to them, then," she quipped. "I would not like it if they blamed me for their trials at your hand."

"Do not worry overmuch. My mood will be much improved on the morrow."

"Ah." She nodded. "Then I have until the morn to cajole you into better spirits?"

Lucien raised a brow. "I would be most interested in this 'cajoling.'"

She laughed, unable to keep her eyes from sweeping over the broad expanse of chest, down to the tapered waist and flat abdomen. His body was magnificent, lean, corded with muscle—each movement a study in controlled power. In all of the times they had made love, he had always held the lead, boldly sampled her woman's body, touching and kissing and arousing her with an expert touch. She longed to explore his body in the same way.

Old inhibitions resurfaced briefly as she faltered in her courage. Determinedly she pushed them back. This was her husband. It was right to touch him intimately and offer him the same pleasures he had given to her.

"Then I had better get started," she whispered.

A sharp rap at the door brought Alayna awake. Lucien growled groggily, "Who the devil is that?"

Donning her dressing gown, she rushed to the door. Sliding back the bolt, she drew it open just a sliver and peered tentatively through the small crack to find Eurice standing in the corridor. Her nurse was wearing a remarkably pleased expression on her old face.

"Alayna, my dearling, do you and your husband care to join us in our victory feast?"

"Feast?"

"Aye. The feast you yourself ordered to be prepared. Did you forget?"

"The feast!"

"Ah, I see it slipped your mind. Well, then. I am glad I disturbed you. Your guests await their lord and lady. And some very special visitors have arrived to help in the celebration. You will not want to miss them."

"I cannot believe I had forgotten. We will be down immediately."

Eurice chuckled. "Aye, do not tarry."

Turning back to her husband, Alayna's look was contrite. "I had ordered a feast be prepared at your return, and then—"

"I heard," he groaned in mock grouchiness. "I suppose I must go down to the hall and make merry, when all I wish to do is to continue celebrating as we have been."

She smiled, seeing that he was not truly displeased. Picking up her rumpled gown from the floor, she saw the green silk, which would have been perfect for the occasion, was creased beyond use. Her maid would have quite a time setting the delicate fabric to rights. Alayna chose another, this one of deeper emerald, a perfect match to her eyes. She had no wish to call Leda, for it might drive Lucien away and she did not want to give him up just yet, so she shyly asked him to fasten her laces in the back.

His warm fingers brushed against her skin as he complied, a bit befuddled by the garment's workings but doing quite well in the end.

"I prefer to remove your clothing, wife," he rumbled in her ear when he was finished. "Somehow, it vexes me to perform this task for you."

"How are you with a brush?" she asked innocently, holding out the ivory-handled instrument. He looked surprised, raising his hands up in front of himself in denial.

"Nay, no lady's maid am I." His chuckle sounded deep and clear, mingling with the higher sound of her own laughter.

She attended to the duty herself while he stepped behind the curtain and made good use of the cold water left in the basin. He dressed in fresh clothes, black, of course. Alayna noticed that though he did not favor the colorful finery of the nobility, he did always wear clothing of impeccable quality. He spurned the soft shoes fashionable for court, favoring boots. Every bit the warrior, she mused proudly.

"Ready?" he asked. Taking his arm, she smiled. She couldn't help running a hand up and over his, appreciating the strength there. His eyes narrowed darkly at the caress.

"Take care, wife. We may never make it to the hall to feast with our companions."

Her laugh rang out as they swept from the chamber. In the hall, they were met with a rowdy welcome, the mood high and joyous at Lucien's recent victory.

Alayna received a great surprise when she spied Lady Mellyssand and Lord Hubert smiling warmly at her from a place of honor at the lord's table. She rushed to her friends, embracing both enthusiastically. "Why did you not send word that you were returning to Gastonbury? I had no idea that you planned to come!"

Mellyssand cast a look over her shoulder to where Lucien stood, and whispered, "I had Hubert bring me back to see how you had fared with the baron. I see by your entrance just now that all has worked out to your satisfaction?"

Alayna colored a bit, but smiled. "Aye, 'tis considerably more agreeable to me than 'twas before."

Mellyssand's smile deepened. "Hubert has a great admiration for him. He said that he remembers his father, Lord Raoul, and told me that he was as remarkable as his son. His mother, Lady Isobol, was a renowned beauty."

Immediately intrigued, Alayna said, "Lucien speaks highly of his father. I know he admired him a great deal. As for his mother...I believe he was not very fond of her."

"Yes, well, Isobol is something of a mystery. No one knows what became of her." Mellyssand's eyes shifted. "Here comes your husband now."

"Lady Mellyssand," Lucien said formally, joining the women. Hubert stepped up to grasp Lucien's arm in a warrior's greeting.

"My lord baron," Hubert rumbled as his wife dipped into a curtsy.

"Hubert, you look exceedingly well," Lucien said.

"Well, I am not, sir," the vassal grumped. "I was most displeased to learn of your recent campaign against Garrick of Thalsbury. I was disappointed to the extreme that I was not called upon to serve with you."

Alayna held her breath at the challenge. But Lucien, surprisingly, did not anger.

"'Twas simply not necessary, Hubert. Why disturb you from your recuperation when I still had my mercenaries? My resources were more than adequate."

Agravar came up just then. "Aye, when he has me to rescue him time and again." He punctuated his jest with a hearty slap on Lucien's back, to which his friend rolled his eyes heavenward.

Hubert, however, seemed somewhat mollified. "Well," he conceded, "then you must humor me with a detailed recounting of the battle. I will accept nothing less than every nuance of the battle, and I look forward to hearing how the late Lord Garrick received you."

"Come, Alayna, let us join the ladies," Mellyssand whispered, and the two women left the men to their tale.

The night was merry with the ebullient joy of the victorious. Alayna glowed under the gentle gaze of her husband and the good companionship of her friends.

They spoke of the future, and she was impressed by her husband's ambition, his insight. He talked in his soft voice of his ideas for improvements, his plans for the castle and desire to clear more land to expand the peasant farming. She had known him to be an accomplished man of war, but the ideas that he was expressing now showed him to have an equal talent as protector and governor of the burh. Others joined in as proposed reforms were bandied about. Lucien solemnly listened to their ideas, weighing each one with careful consideration.

The hour was not very late when Lucien's hand closed over hers and she glanced up to meet his warm gaze. "You look tired, my lady," he murmured. She smiled, knowing she did not look a bit tired, but it was an excellent excuse to retire early.

"Aye, I am very," she answered, breathless at how his eyes darkened so quickly to the languid look that could stop her heart.

They left more than a few knowing glances behind them as they slipped up the great stair. In the cloister of their chamber, they removed each other's clothing and made love again, slowly, gently, savoring each touch, each moment, giving themselves over to passion until they found ecstatic release and, afterward, restful sleep.

A fortnight passed like something snatched out of one of Alayna's girlhood dreams, filled with all of the love and passion and wild romanticism that she could have ever conjured up in her youthful imagination. Lucien remained attentive and kind by day and an amorous, nearly insatiable lover by night. What he felt for her, he never said. But she was content with all he gave.

Lucien, too, was content. He had Alyana, he had the friendship of Agravar, the loyalty of his villeins, and he was going to succeed in all his plans. He was, he realized with some surprise, perilously close to being *happy*. It was that elusive and most desirous of emotions that heralded the arousal of a long-supressed need.

His past would not rest until one final detail was resolved.

When he told Agravar his intention, the Viking tried to stop him. "Let it go," he urged.

Later, when Lucien informed Alayna of his plans, she was silent, but he could read fear in her eyes.

"I shall return within a sennight." His voice was stern. He didn't mean it to be so. He saw her flinch.

Alayna nodded, her emerald eyes locked on him.

He left without another word. He could think of nothing to say to comfort her, for he was afraid as well.

Chapter Twenty-Three

It took four days for Lucien to reach Erstentine Abbey. The nunnery was an ugly structure, an austere heaping of gray stone into stark, sharp spires that reached up to pierce the gray sky of dusk. The huge studded doors resounded with a dull, hollow thud as Lucien's fist struck the summons.

The small portal set at eye level was opened and he stated his purpose to the unseen answerer. He was duly admitted by a young nun who, despite her youth, was as gray and sharp as the building that cloistered her. He waited uncomfortably in the empty hall as she went to deliver his message to his mother.

He had discovered her whereabouts not long after he had arrived in England. It was the most incongruous place for the lofty Isobol of Thalsbury. As to why she had chosen it, he could venture no guess. But he would have the answer to that mystery soon enough.

If she would not see him, he would simply force his way in, Lucien decided grimly.

The young nun returned and indicated a small room where he could await his mother. It was a square chamber, sparsely furnished and smelling of grease from the candles burning in profusion along the wall.

She kept him waiting a long time in that tiny, uncomfortable room. The ordeal did little to improve his mood.

He felt rather than heard her enter. Taking a deep breath, he turned to face her, his mother, for the first time in over eleven years.

She was older, definitely older. Her face was lined, her skin sagging just a bit with the telltale signs of age. But she was still beautiful. Her hair, a pale copper shade that had no match, peeked demurely from beneath the wimple that bound her head. The eyes were still a startling blue, beautiful but cold, like bits of ice. The proud nose, a feature of hers he had inherited along with her strong chin, was still well-defined. Her legendary beauty had fared well through the years, he decided. But she still had the same frigid, haughty look.

He felt a tightening in his chest. He stood rigid.

Waiting for a moment on the threshold, Isobol only looked at her son. He was ready for her, bestowing upon her his most aloof perusal. Nothing about his appearance indicated the enormous inner tumult he was feeling at that moment.

"Lucien." It was a breath, a whisper. Tears sprang to her eyes and her full lips trembled. "My son."

He did not move. He could have handled a scene of the most vicious nature, but he was unprepared for this emotionalism. He watched her warily. Thank goodness, she made no move to embrace him.

"So you have come to confront me at last. I have been awaiting you. I had thought you dead these last eleven years. When I received the news you had returned, I prayed you would come to me."

"How have you been, Mother?" He was relieved to hear his voice sound so casually cool to his own ear.

"How do you think?" She smiled sadly.

"I would have no idea."

Silence. She moved gracefully forward to sink into a chair.

"I hear also that you have married."

Lucien stiffened, alert for any threat or innuendo against Alayna. "Aye," he said simply. He watched her carefully through narrowed eyes.

"I heard she is lovely."

"Who told you that?" he snapped.

"'Twas one of my servants. I still have some that are loyal to me. They brought me the news."

Considering her a moment, he tried to decide if she were lying. "Did they also tell you I just returned from war? I killed Garrick of Thalsbury. He was Edgar's man. Do you remember him? It was he who murdered Father." Unbelievably she flinched. "But I suppose you knew that."

He watched her as she rose slowly, as if laboring under an enormous burden. She went to the small window that was set high in the stone wall. He could only see her in profile, her beauty accentuated by the halo of daylight behind her. She said, "You will no doubt find it difficult to believe, but I did not conspire to have you and your father killed."

Lucien felt his heart pounding in his chest, half-fearing the sound of it would echo in the tiny chamber, that she would hear it and know his weakness.

"Though 'twas the same as if I had slain him myself." She turned her head, though still avoiding his eyes. "Raoul was a good man, an excellent man. He was a husband to be proud of, but I was not proud to be his wife. I was spoiled in my youth, conceited about my beauty and ambitious that it would fetch me an earl, perhaps even a prince. My father used to tell me stories of how my beauty would buy him a kingdom, and I was set aside from my sisters with special treatment. I was haughty and selfish. No one liked me, and I was terribly lonely. That only made me more spiteful. I told myself that everyone was jealous of me, my sisters and my own mother. It rotted my heart and turned them away from me even more.''

"Then why did you marry Father? He was no earl or prince," Lucien asked, amazed at his own curiosity. He found that he needed to know, now that he had the opportunity to learn the answers to the questions that had burned inside him for years.

"My father's hopes for a great marriage were dashed when he was unable to meet the dowry requirements for any marriage contract he deemed suitable. And any prospective grooms who were not interested in money were soon disillusioned by my shrewish ways. Until Raoul, your father. Despite my renowned beauty, he was the only man who ever asked for my hand.

"He had just inherited Thalsbury when we met. He was a spectacular man, and I admit even I admired him, though I thought him beneath me. I had been raised to be as a princess, you see, and now my father willingly gave me to a minor landholder. I think by that time, he was just glad to be rid of me.''

She turned to face him. Lucien looked back, outwardly calm, but his soul raged.

"I see it surprises you to see me talk so plainly. You do very well to hide it, but I am, after all, your mother. I see things that others do not.'' She considered him a moment. "You favor me, I think. I never noticed before.''

"You never looked at me," he said hoarsely.

She shook her head. "I did neglect you. I admit that, though it pains me to say it. I was proud of you, but you admired Raoul so, it made me feel rejected. You were my only child. If I could not have you all to myself, then I did not want you."

"You hated me," he said evenly.

Her eyes rounded. "Nay, Lucien, never that. I was mean-spirited, 'tis true. But I never hated you."

Lucien's hand came to his cheek in an involuntary gesture. He ran his fingers along the puckered flesh. He was unaware of the action until he saw the flare of her eyes.

"Aye, I see you remember that day. I used to look at your cheek after it happened, and even then, when I was so completely consumed with myself, even then, I would feel sick at what I had done."

Lucien felt himself trembling, a great sadness welling up inside of him. It could not be true. She had been a vicious harridan, plain and simple. He had never, in all of his youth and manhood, considered that she was ever in possession of a conscience.

"I discarded that ring. Threw it out of the window into the river. Do you know why I struck you that day?"

She did not wait for an answer. To his utter amazement, Lucien saw tears coursing unchecked down her cheeks. He froze, his pulse thudding painfully in his temple. She could not be crying. It was impossible. He had never seen his mother cry.

"The time you came upon Edgar and myself when we were at Gastonbury was not the first time you stumbled upon our liaison. It had been going on for years. I was so vain! I thought it exciting, I thought perhaps I could divorce Raoul if Edgar would marry me. He was young and handsome, and more powerful than your father.

"That day I struck you, and my ring cut you, I had received a message from Edgar to meet me. I left it, stupidly, on my table. You found it. You were always bright, and even at nine, you were a precocious child. You were learning your letters well. You read some of Edgar's message. I was enraged. I thought you would know what it meant." She closed her eyes at the memory. "I panicked, and I was angry. I struck you, though I realized later you did not know what it was you had read. I struck you out of my own guilt, and I scarred you."

"Not all of the scars are visible," he said bitterly.

"Aye, and well I know it. Why do you think I came to reside with the sisters? I do penance for the terrible sin of pride and vanity, and for betraying the trust of a good husband. And for my failure to you, my son."

"Failure," he rasped harshly. "Is that what you call it? 'Twas it not more like murder?"

"When you were sixteen and came upon us in the chamber, I was terrified that you would tell your father. But Edgar assured me no harm would come of it, and I believed him. I have thought of that so often all of these years. Had I but told Raoul myself, he would still be alive. And you..."

Isobol looked at her son with such a longing that he had to turn away.

"So, now, you see my guilt? I yearned for all that had been promised to me in my youth, then denied me. I felt myself wronged, abused, deprived. Yet, what I had was so much more. I had a fine, strong son and a husband who adored me. I could have had love, and learned love in return. But I threw it away for ruthless ambition."

She was sobbing now, stretching out her hands to him in supplication. "I begged God to bring you to me. I can only hope that He will answer one more prayer, for I am pleading with you to forgive me. You are my only kin. Please, Lucien, forgive me. Then, perhaps one day I can forgive myself."

Lucien stared at her. His hands fisted at his side and he had to fight the urge to strike her. He did not speak until he was sure his voice would not break.

"Some things cannot be forgiven," he stated. "This tender scene does nothing to bring my father back to life, or to take away from me eleven years of hell. You wallow in your sin within these cold walls. Well, that is as it should be. Had you been stretched on the rack for all of this time, it still would not have done justice for the suffering you caused. Now you know the evil that you were. Good. That is very, very good."

He brushed past her to the door, rushing out of the abbey to where Pelly waited with his destrier. He could hear the sound of his mother's wails echoing off the cold stones.

Agravar must have left word to be roused the instant of Lucien's arrival, for he was in the stables before Lucien had taken the saddle off his horse. The brooding warrior did not even acknowledge his friend when he felt the familiar presence at his side. He was in no mood for confidences.

"Lucien," Agravar began.

"I will not speak of it," Lucien interrupted curtly, not looking at his friend.

The Norseman watched him tend the great destrier. He did not press. Nodding, he stepped away. "The justiciar has arrived."

Lucien's head snapped around, his eyes wide with surprise. "So. We should greet him."

"You misunderstand. He has not just arrived. This is their third day."

Taking a moment to digest this news, Lucien said carefully, "And the Lady Veronica?"

"She is with Alayna." He paused, then added, "Veronica is very unhappy."

Lucien's jaw set, his temple flexing as he ground his teeth together. "No use in delaying the inevitable. Where are they?"

"The man is in the hall, and the women, as well."

As they walked together, Lucien prodded Agravar for information. "What manner of man is this justiciar?"

"He seems fair enough. He has been visibly impressed with the good and glowing reports of you that he has heard."

"Oh, really? And who is it who is glowing so much about me?"

"Your wife, for one. She has taken the lead with Wyndham, showing him all of the improvements your barony has gained for the shire and tempting him with the promise of prosperity Gastonbury can offer for our king." They paused outside the great doors of the hall. "Your old demons are on you, I can see. Shake it off, Lucien. Remember what is at stake."

Lucien nodded grudgingly and swept into the large room.

The justiciar was not there after all, but Lucien spotted Alayna where she sat with her ladies. Her back was to him, but he knew immediately it was her—that particular shade of chestnut hair, the erect posture, the graceful curve of her shoulders. His eyes slid to the woman next to her and he noticed the resemblance.

Petite, slim and comely of face, Veronica bore her years well, possessing a bearing that was almost regal. Alayna had most definitely inherited her grace and poise, though surpassed her mother in height, as well as beauty. All of this he noticed in one glance as he walked toward the group.

The chatter of the ladies fell to silence as he drew close. Veronica was the first to notice him, stopping in mid-sentence to stare. Alayna, Lucien saw, was smiling slightly at something her mother was saying, her full, lush mouth curved in precisely the way that set his heart thumping. She looked up at the interruption, and her eyes fell upon him. Her sewing dropped from her lap when she stood suddenly, and for one terrible moment he thought she was going to run to him. Inside him, his aching warred with the thrill of seeing her again.

Her face was alight with joy, but he felt no response within him. The rawness from his encounter with Isobol still throbbed painfully.

"Good day, wife," he said without warmth. He held himself stiffly, forcing himself to remote observance of the disappointment in her face. He could not move to touch her, as he had so easily done just days before.

"My lord," she breathed, instinctively treading carefully. Shooting an anxious glance at Veronica, she said, "May I present my mother, Lady Veronica of Avenford."

"My lord, 'tis a pleasure to meet you," Veronica said as she dropped into a curtsy, "but I must admit, there is much in the matter of the treatment of my daughter I wish to discuss with you."

He barely spared the woman a glance. He was watching Alayna, his mind racing.

He was thinking of his own mother.

And he was thinking that perhaps he had been as much a fool for his wife as his father had been for Isobol. Had he not always sworn to never let a woman touch his heart?

Watching his wife now, flushed and tense as she waited for him to respond, he felt something within him well up, something old and familiar and cold. Could any woman truly be trusted, or were they, as he had so long believed, all the same—treacherous, deceitful liars?

He sneered at himself and crushed the flitting surge of his heart.

Alayna's brow drew down in concern. "My lord, are you well?"

Everyone was looking at him oddly. He did not move, and she came toward him, resting a reassuring hand on his arm. "My lord?" she repeated.

He snatched himself away from her as if scalded. "Where is Henry's man?" he said unexpectedly. It was all he could think of to say.

"He has gone to the village to see to matters there. Will was summoned from Thalsbury, and he and Pelly escorted Sir Wyndham on the journey. He will return to sup with us, he has said."

Alayna watched the dark expression, knowing something was terribly wrong. She had seen it the moment she had greeted him. But with her mother watching, she tried to ignore it, for Veronica was not at all pleased with her new son-in-law, no matter how much Alayna pleaded her present contentment.

"Perhaps you are tired, husband. Come to our chamber and let me order you a bath. There you can rest and be refreshed to meet your guest when he returns from the village.''

She had no idea why he seemed so angry with her. Something was terribly wrong. Her solicitousness seemed to annoy him. "Do not coddle me," he snapped, and without another word, stalked off toward their chamber.

Turning around to the women, Alayna was embarrassed by the awkward looks she received. Lady Mellyssand came to put her arm around her lady.

"Do not fret over his temper," Mellyssand said smoothly. "No doubt he is tired and irritated from his trip. Alayna, why do you not seek your chamber and try to soothe his mood? It would do him no good to make a poor impression on Wyndham when he arrives this evening."

Alayna cast a glance at her mother, seeing Veronica's eyes were shadowed with doubt. Since her arrival, she had been adamant that Alayna return to London with her, where they would deal with the formalities of her daughter's unfortunate marriage from their seat of power at court.

"Nay," Alayna said quickly. She offered a tremulous smile and an unconvincing shrug. "He needs only some peace and rest. He will be restored by this eve."

Lucien's mood did not improve that evening, nor the next, nor for many nights after. Kept busy with the king's officials, he rarely was available.

Alayna was near mad with worry and fear. So far, she had given him a wide berth, hoping that time would restore him. But with each day's passage, his disposition grew worse, and with it deepened her despair.

Her mother's scrutiny was a constant concern as that one's sharp eyes caught every last detail of Lucien's outrageous behavior. Even with the glowing praises and sympathetic excuses from Mellyssand and Eurice, Veronica was growing more and more determined to take her daughter away. How ironic, Alayna thought, that the very deliverance for which she had so often prayed was now the thing she dreaded most.

It was late when he came to their chamber one night, in another sour mood. Swallowing hard at the look of him, scornful and brooding, she forced herself to sound pleasant. "How goes it with Wyndham?"

He cast her a baleful eye, grunting, "Wyndham will recommend in my favor to Henry."

"Excellent, husband!" she exclaimed, genuinely happy at the news.

"Aye, that should please you. Now you are officially the Lady of Gastonbury. 'Twas what you wanted from the start."

Her face fell, her body slumping in defeat. His eyes flickered for a moment as if he felt a twinge of regret.

"I am happy for you," she stated soberly.

"How touching."

It was their sparring of old, nothing new. Nothing had changed. Yet it was so much more difficult to take after the intimacy they had shared.

Deflated, she watched him undress, feeling the familiar effect that simply viewing that hard, muscular form had on her. His warrior's body was washed in golden firelight, and the spark of desire leaped to life within her belly, spreading quickly throughout her body.

His scowl caught her, but she did not look away. She couldn't know how she appeared at that moment, kneeling on the bed, watching him with her chestnut hair loose and falling around her like a curtain. But something in his eyes emboldened her. Rising from the bed, she came to stand before him, meeting his eyes boldly.

"I have missed you," she said. His eyes clouded immediately in response. He paused for a heartbeat as if struggling with something within him, then suddenly grabbed her shoulders and pulled her hard up against him.

"No need to lie. I will willingly see to your needs," he said cruelly, bringing his mouth down on hers in a savage kiss. Stung by the heartlessness of his words, she tried to pull away.

"What game are you playing, Alayna?" he growled at her ear. "First you make me think you want me, then you fight. Is this all part of some plan you and your mother have concocted?"

"You are a fool!" she raged, struggling against him, but he held her fast.

He chuckled. "You have come up with better names than that in your time. As for being a fool, I would be inclined to agree. It is exactly what I have been thinking. I have been quite the fool for you, have I not?"

His words cut, but the nearness of him, the feel of him pressed against her, and his soft, masculine smell was like a drug. She no longer fought him, welcoming even this angry embrace like one parched and thirsting would strain for a drop of water.

His mouth slashed down over hers, twisting and opening until she could barely catch her breath. She hated herself for her easy surrender. Unable to turn away from his loving, she let herself be swept away, and in those moments of tender giving, she could believe that they were as they had been, that nothing had changed and that the Lady Isobol had never risen up out of the past to strangle the fledgling love they had shared, like a weed choking a tender shoot. He was loving her again, inside of her now and they were moving as one, as if they truly were united once again without aged demons to torment them.

He held her tightly for a few quick moments after they calmed before rolling away and pretending to sleep.

Silently, in the dark, Alayna wept, surprised that she had any more tears to shed.

Alayna was fast running out of hope. Her mother observed with tight-lipped disapproval the worsening status of their relationship and Alayna had more and more difficulty finding convincing arguments why she should not leave him as Veronica so frequently, and persuasively, urged.

He came to her sometimes at night. In silence, he would hold her, their familiar bond sparking to life at his merest touch. Always, she would respond with genuine desire, melding with him for this short time. But these interludes did nothing to ease their rift. He would only turn away as soon as his passion was spent, leaving Alayna to stare at the ceiling long into the night, wondering which was the truth—his heartless dismissals or his wondrous, gentle loving of her body?

After some time, she grew despondent. She wished she could get angry, rail against him and prod him into at least a battle of wits, but somehow her strength would not come. She began to think of her mother's wishes with a new resignation. Perhaps it would be best to admit defeat and let her mother take her home to London.

Chapter Twenty-Four

It happened at one evening meal, when Lucien was feeling particularly cross, that Alayna found her anger again.

They were seated on the dais, lined along the head table in grim attendance to their dour lord, when Alayna made the unwitting mistake of speaking to Will.

She simply asked on the progress at Thalsbury. Instead of Will's reply, a low growl was heard from the direction of the master's chair. "Perhaps you would like to reside at that place with our good knight," Lucien spat. "There you could assure yourself of its condition, and Will's, at all times."

Will flushed, speechless at the viciously intoned barb.

Alayna whipped her head around and stared at him for a long moment, all too aware of the faces of those whom she loved and who loved her—her mother, Mellyssand, Hubert, and Eurice—staring aghast at the exchange.

As the harsh words died into silence, she was suddenly and completely overcome with feeling. Tingling spikes of rage began to dart through her body and her vision narrowed, tunneling onto that dark, damnably handsome face, and suddenly she felt shockingly, wonderfully alive after

the long weeks of dead numbness. She stood slowly, un-
steadily, on legs atremble with emotion.

Enough. She had finally had enough.

She had had enough of his insulting behavior. Enough,
as well, of his colossal pouts. It had broken her heart to
see him so haunted, so brought down by the pain of the
past. But no more. She had finally had *enough!*

She tilted her chin, bestowing her most arrogant and
shriveling look upon him. "You, my mean-spirited, vile-
tempered, boorish-mannered husband can promptly go to
hell!"

Agravar caught the choked laugh in his throat before it
escaped. When Lucien's livid gaze snapped up to glare at
him, he coughed profusely, covering his mouth but not
able to hide the telltale crinkles in the corners of his eyes.

Leveling a glower at his wife, Lucien rose slowly, towering over her. His bulk was daunting, but Alayna remained unfazed. Black eyes clashed with brilliant green.

"Take care, my wife," he warned. "I do not favor public displays of those things best kept private. But if you
push me, I will not stay my wrath for those who would
see your humiliation."

"Will you beat me then, Lucien?" she asked casually.

"I would not shirk the task should you prompt me."

She didn't believe him. Moreover, even if his threat was
good, she found amazingly that she did not care. It would
be a relief, actually, if he would do the one thing that
would decide their fate for good.

Notching her chin up further, she shrugged. "There is
nothing a buffoon such as yourself could do to embarrass
me."

She had gone too far, she knew it. She saw the look on
his face, and she thought, *this is it. He is going to strike*

me—he will *dare it. Finally he will take the last step to completely degrade me, here in front of everyone, and then he will lose me forever.*

He did not raise his hand to her, however. Agravar, who was watching carefully, silently came to his feet. He stood close to Lucien's elbow, and for the first time Alayna saw the threatening look of the Viking's anger. For a moment, she thought it was directed at her. But she saw his glare leveled at Lucien. The large, calloused hands curled reflexively, as if impatient to strike a blow.

"I am waiting, husband," she whispered. He did not move.

All of a sudden, he whirled and stalked out of the hall without another word.

Alayna stepped as if to follow.

"Alayna Eustacia." Lady Veronica sprang to her feet and grabbed Alayna's arms, whirling her daughter around.

Alayna yanked herself away. "Mother, please, not now!" Leaving the table, she ran after her husband. She was angry and she was afraid, and so utterly desperate. She needed to finish this, once and for all. This horrid limbo of lost hope and disappointment had gone on long enough. Before she reached the doors, her mother pulled at her again.

"Do not dare chase him like some simpering chit without any dignity!"

"Mother, stay out of this, I have got to settle this, one way or another. Please, move aside else I will lose sight of him."

"Let him go. He is a miscreant and a savage. Come home with me right now, we will see to this matter from London."

"Please listen to me. Even when we did not get on

well—at first when we quarreled and sparred at every turn—even then he never behaved this badly. I know that there is a something terrible inside of him that eats into his soul. He will not let me help him, but Mother—what we had was glorious! It was not something I will ever find again. I am going to fight for it, even if I have to battle you, him, and Henry's whole army.''

"Why do you persist in this infatuation with the man? He is a barbarian! It has been weeks since he returned, and I have been patient for your sake. I know you believe that you love him. But, sweet daughter, he does not merit the care you give him. He is not going to change, if he indeed ever did."

"I will hear no more against him!" Alayna cried, exasperated and angry. She was weary from fighting at every front all the time. Right now, her mind was on Lucien. "I know very well what you must be thinking. But I do not have time to soothe you just now. I must see Lucien."

She left her mother, hating to part on such terms, and raced in the direction where she had last seen her husband. Catching a glimpse of him disappearing up the curve of the tower stairs, she took the risers two at a time.

She found him up on the ramparts, standing braced against the battlements and staring out over the land stretched below him.

"That was a fine job, husband," she commented saucily. "How brilliant of you to so completely and utterly make a fool of yourself in front of everyone. Not to mention humiliating me in the bargain, but that is nothing new. You excel at that. Thank goodness my father does not live, else he surely would have drawn his sword and slain you on the spot for your insult to me."

He snorted. Clearly he did not believe that anyone could best him.

"I have spent near a fortnight trying to convince my mother not to have this marriage declared null by the church. She can do it easily, though—"

"Is that what you want?" he bellowed.

"Is it what you want, Lucien?" she countered. "Why do you punish me? Why do you not let me help you and together we—"

"Why do you persist in plaguing me with this idiotic prattle when I have made it quite clear I wish you to *leave me alone?*" He shouted these last three words, but Alayna remained steadfast.

"Leave you alone to what? Your misery? Aye, I would like to, for you try me sorely, and at times I would see you punished for the unparalleled stupidity you have shown of late. But, of course, nothing can do justice to your witlessness, for you are so impervious to all but your own private hell. Oh, my fine lord of vengeance, you shall always remain so untouchable to the perils of mere mortals. Therefore, it is fitting that your misery is of your own design, for only you—so singularly cruel—could conceive of an apt punishment for yourself."

"Do not try me, wife," he warned dangerously. He made to move past her, but she stepped in his way. She was surprised he didn't just push her aside.

"You are a fool," she flung at him. "You are so very, very stupid that I find it inconceivable you can find your way out of our chamber every morn. You give in to your hate and bitterness and throw all happiness away."

"That happiness is false. It is merely a figment of man's fantasy."

She considered him for a minute, the disgusted look on

her face betraying her feelings. "That is the most idiotic, senseless and asinine piece of refuse that I have ever heard!"

She continued, seeing his look of astonishment at her passionate rebuff. "You are angry with your mother? Is that what ails your spirit? Fine. I know not the cause, it might well be a good one. But I have done nothing to hurt you. I have been faithful and kind to you, no less!"

"Women—"

"Do not speak to me of women!" she shouted, stamping her foot. "You know nothing of women! They are much the same as men, husband—some good, some bad. We are speaking of *me*. I, Alayna, am no liar, and I have never deceived you. Have I ever given you cause to doubt me?"

Lucien said nothing.

"Nay, I have not!" she supplied. "Though judging from your comment in the hall just now, you have set your imagination to conjuring up some intrigue between Will and myself, but it is simply not true." She stopped, panting and shaking from her indignation. She forced herself to calm, taking a deep breath. Momentarily she began again, this time softly, pleadingly.

"I know you are in pain." He looked away as if unable to bear her words. "Whatever your dame did, it is over. She ruined your life once, do not let her do it again." Gentler now, encouraged by his silence, she approached him. "Lucien. Husband. Please do not put me aside. We had come so far."

His face remained closed, and he stepped away from her. When she moved toward him again, his head snapped around, showing his fierce expression. "Leave me," he demanded angrily.

Tears sprang to her eyes. Shaking her head as if to say no, that she would not leave him, she did nonetheless, too ashamed of her pitiful weeping in the face of such staunch and unfeeling anger. She whirled, running down the stairs at breakneck speed, choking back the sobs until she could get herself out of earshot.

To go where? She could not rejoin those in the hall. Though they were friends all, she could not return to them in such ignoble defeat.

She was sobbing uncontrollably now. Her feet carried her swiftly out through the inner gatehouse that led to the remote courtyards. Wanting to be away from everyone, she kept running. She had no destination, no thought other than finding solitude in which to indulge her grief.

It was the end. She had been defeated. She knew nothing she could do would unwind the stifling bonds around Lucien's heart. These shackles were too deeply entrenched. His heart had been bound with bitterness and rage years ago, and Alayna had no power to unfetter those huge and cumbersome chains.

Tired and out of breath, Alayna collapsed against a wall and gulped in great amounts of air. How she wished she could just keep running until the pain could no longer reach her. But no distance nor interval of time would lessen its grip on her heart.

Suddenly she felt strong arms close around her shoulders, pinning her arms to her sides. Her first thought was of Lucien—he had come after her! For a brief instant, a tremendous joy leaped to life in her chest. She cried out his name and spun around.

A dirty hand came down over her mouth. Her heart thumped in panic as she met the gray eyes of a foul and filthy stranger who held her captive in his grasp. He was smiling, revealing a mouthful of rotted teeth. The sight made him look macabre and sinister, causing Alayna's stomach to lurch in terror.

"Make no sound, 'ear?" he muttered. "Imagine this, the lady 'erself! Me lord is goin' ta be mos' pleased, mos' pleased, aye!"

She kicked him hard, landing a sharp blow to his shin.

"Stop it, ye lousy chit. I'll cuff ye!" the disgusting man warned. She did not stop, frantically trying to free herself. She sank her teeth deep into the calloused flesh of his palm.

"Aagh!" he cried, snatching his hand free. Alayna drew a breath to scream, but was stopped by the stunning force of her attacker's hand striking her face. "You bitch!" he snarled. "I came to spy and found me a prize. I'll not give it up easy."

With that declaration, he drew his fist back and suddenly her world exploded into a thousand stars, blinking and dancing for a brilliant moment before fading into a deep, dull void.

Lady Veronica was waiting for her daughter's husband when he reentered the hall. She had much to settle with the overbearing Lord of Gastonbury, her anger and tenacity showing in the determined set of her fragile features and the squaring of her shoulders. As he approached, she stepped up before he could pass her. "A word with you, please," she said curtly.

Lucien cast her a reluctant look, grudgingly nodding his assent. With serene poise, she moved over to the deserted hearth to insure some privacy.

"Please," she said, still calm, indicating that Lucien move closer. He complied.

"I have much that is pressing," Lucien stated stiffly.

"I will be brief," she countered, revealing a bit of her own hostility. She regarded him critically for a moment, eyeing him from head to toe. Never having been so thoroughly assessed by a woman, he felt inexplicably uncomfortable under the detached perusal.

"You are handsome, I suppose that is what she sees in you. Though your manner of command is also greatly appealing, or would be to the impressionable girl my daughter is."

Lucien frowned. Alayna an impressionable girl? She had been a hellcat full of fire and spite when he met her, impressed not in the least with him.

She continued, "But you are mean-spirited, and I cannot have this marriage."

His eyes narrowed at the attack. He opened his mouth to speak, but the small woman waived a dainty hand at him, dismissing his words before they were spoken.

"Oh, Alayna has begged me to reconsider. Eurice even agrees with her, and Mellysand, who I have come to trust and respect, speaks your praises. But I have seen none of these noble qualities they boast of. Moreover, your viciousness comes from your dame, I am given to believe. Aye, I have made it my business to learn about you and your family. It is regrettable that you do not emulate your father more, for I have heard naught but praise for him. But you favor the caustic ways of your mother."

The undeniable verity of her words settled over him like a slow, numbing frost. His mind careened and the truth hit him like a perfectly crystallized blade of ice, sharp and vivid and real.

He *was* behaving exactly like his mother.

Veronica continued, "I know that as a boy you were

misused, but you are a man now, and as such you make your own choices. I have no admiration for the kind of man you are—a brute.''

The man he was. His father, his noble and good sire, would be shocked and sickened by the man he was.

A tightness closed in his throat and he felt himself trembling.

Veronica did not notice his change. ''That bodes ill for Alayna, for a man who hates women is no man to place your love in. 'Tis unfortunate, is it not, that she has misplaced that tender emotion? 'Tis the only reason that I even considered her pitiable entreaties, because she told me she loved you. There is no hope for it, but she will recover, I pray, and with the blessings of the Lord, she will love again. I will make sure that her next husband will be suitable, for no doubt she will consider herself sorely abused by my interfering…''

Veronica's voice faded as Lucien felt his world narrow, converge and suddenly coalesce into one unbelievable thought.

She had begged her mother to remain with him. She had spoken of love. How could she still want him after all that had passed between them? And had that not been what he had secretly wanted, for her to leave him in safe, wretched loneliness?

But she loved him.

Why had he not known it? Though she had not said the words, she had patiently waited out the storm, and when he had snubbed her, striking out in his pain, never once had she turned away from him. She had chastised him, begged him even, to make peace while he had so stupidly clung to his dark humors, ignoring what was painfully clear and freely given.

He had wished never to be a fool for a woman. Yet, fool he had been.

Suddenly he was filled with the same contempt for himself that Veronica so openly displayed. He made a strangled sound, sinking down on one knee, half in sorrow, half in weakness from the gut-wrenching shock.

Taken aback, Lady Veronica stopped speaking as he grabbed her slender fingers and folded them in his large hands.

"My God, you are right to revile me," he said in a choked voice. "I did not see. I could only think of my past, of my family. I thought it was so simple." He lifted his head. "But it is not simple. And it is not easy. To hate, that is easy. To love…to love is the hardest thing I have ever done."

He saw her surprise in the rounding of her eyes, the drop of her jaw. "Aye, I do love her. It should be a joyous thing, to love somebody as I do your daughter. For a while it was. But you were right about my mother." How could he explain what it was that had happened when he had faced her, when he did not understand it himself? "Seeing her again terrified me. I feared what I feel for Alayna—I thought it would make me weak. If you know of my father, then you know that he was blind to my mother. In a way, I think I am as furious with him as I am with her. I swore that would never happen to me the same way."

"But Alayna would never hurt you," she said softly.

He nodded. "I know it. Aye, I know it. And I also know that weakness is not in loving but in fearing to love."

Kneeling, she placed a soothing hand on his cheek. She smiled, her eyes shining with unshed tears. Drawing him into her arms in a soothing embrace, she held him as a mother holds her child, be he boy or man, to ease his pain.

"You must make it up to her. You must go to her and tell her what lies in your heart. I have pushed her to put your marriage aside and return to London with me, and I believe she is coming to agree with that decision. Waste no time, Lucien, for you have caused her great hurt. You must make it right."

Together they rose, and Lucien drew her hand to his lips in the romantic Norman tradition. He caught her eyes, and Veronica nodded encouragingly.

"Thank you," he whispered.

When Alayna opened her eyes, she found herself staring into a pair of brown ones not more than a handsbreadth away. Her focus widened, and she took in the small up-turned nose, pretty, pouting mouth and dark hair. Glenna!

She tried to sit up, only to discover she was bound. The girl chuckled.

Glancing around, she saw that she lay on a cot against the wall of a sparsely furnished one-room dwelling with a dirt floor and mud walls and the high arch of the thatched roof stretching over her head.

Glenna bared her teeth in what was supposed to be a smile. Silently she brought up her hand, showing a small pile of powder cradled in her palm. Alayna looked at it curiously, instinctively fearful. Poison?

Glenna suddenly blew into her palm, causing the powder to scatter into Alayna's face. Gasping in surprise, she inhaled the dust and immediately felt the soothing effects of the drug as a languid numbness spread throughout her limbs. She fought the pull of it as it dragged her down into black oblivion. She heard Glenna's laughter from far away and a single word. "Sleep."

Then no more.

* * *

Lucien was growing alarmed at his failure to find his wife.

Immediately the thought she had run away again pressed foremost in his mind, but he dismissed the idea quickly. She would not run away when all she had to do was give in to her mother and she would be well rid of him.

She had been upset when last he had seen her—blast his own cursed pride!—and he thought it likely she had sought some solitude to ponder her wounded heart. In that case, he knew not where to look, for he had no idea where she found privacy when the need arose. So he simply looked everywhere.

Agravar joined the search, and Pelly, and Will, and eventually no one was idle as they scoured the innards of the castle for their mistress.

With growing dread, Lucien commanded a troop of men saddle up their mounts. The sentinels could report no notice of Alayna's having left, but on the chance that her exit was missed by the posted guards, and because there was nowhere else to look, they readied a party to ride into the forest.

No one thought to mention the cart that had left several hours earlier, laden with goods and drawn by a weary and aged donkey. It had been driven by a grizzled man, stooped and filthy, all alone and surely of no account to the whereabouts of Alayna of Gastonbury.

Just as they were preparing to leave, a village youth brought a message. He said a man, a stranger, had given it to him along with a shiny gold piece saying the lad was to deliver the missive only to the master of Gastonbury. It read simply, "I have her. Come alone to Silver Lake. Tomorrow at noon."

Lucien shook as he read the words. His hands fisted, crumpling the brittle piece of parchment as he barked out a quick order to have his stallion returned to the stables and the destrier brought out.

"What is it?" Agravar prodded.

"I am to go to Silver Lake. Alone."

"It may be a trap. Lucien, for God's sake, we do not know what we are up against here."

"We?" Lucien questioned. "This is for me to deal with, Agravar."

"You are certainly mad if you think I am going to let you go alone—"

"Do not question this, Agravar. Alayna's safety must come first. Know that if you disobey me, you will lose our friendship forever. I have got to meet this brigand on his own terms."

After a moment, the Viking nodded. "Aye, I swear I will not disobey your wishes. But if you do not return soon, I am coming after you."

"Give me until the next sundown, then pursue. I know not what to expect, I may need time."

"Not too much," Agravar conceded reluctantly.

Will came up behind them, his concern all too clearly written on his face. "You go alone?" he asked. He was silent at Lucien's curt nod.

Agravar walked away, too impatient and restless to converse any longer. He commenced pacing back and forth, leaving the two men standing across from each other. "I know you love her," Lucien said abruptly.

Will did not speak, nor did he move. Carefully he answered, "Her heart belongs to you."

Lucien nodded, wondering at his own daftness. Did everyone know of his wife's feelings but himself? A page came forward with his destrier. Lucien swung astride the mighty beast.

The horse pranced restlessly. Agravar came up to hold the reins briefly, just long enough to say his farewell, fiercely and fervently. "A-Viking."

Lucien answered the same, then kicked his steed into a full gallop and rode through the gate. To Silver Lake, to meet whatever and whoever had taken his beloved wife and to bring her home to reclaim the cherished love that he had so foolishly trifled with.

Chapter Twenty-Five

When Alayna regained consciousness again, she was alone in the hut, surrounded by deep silence. Her head ached. A sharp throb in her temples caused her to wince. She discovered she was no longer bound and immediately sat up.

She cried out as her limbs protested. How long had she lain in the same position? Her muscles felt impossibly heavy, making movement painful.

She remembered Glenna and froze in sudden fear. She glanced around frantically. She was terrified of the girl, for she believed Glenna was truly mad in her hatred. And here she was, at her mercy.

The room was empty save the cot she had been lying on and some cold ashes in the hearth. No chairs, no cupboard—nothing. A thick layer of dust covered the floor, showing a few footprints. There were no windows, but light filtered in through the cracks between the planks of the walls, so Alayna knew that it was daytime.

She was starved, but there was no food, nor was there any water. A quick inspection of the door and shutters showed them to be tightened fast. She shoved and pulled with her failing strength before admitting there was no way for her to flee.

Easing back down on the edge of the cot, she thought of Lucien and wondered if he was looking for her or if he counted himself well rid of her. She thought of her mother and the harsh words they had spoken last.

She had to believe that he would come for her. He had promised her that once, and she had believed him. But now, after his change of heart, could she still believe?

She had to.

She held onto that hope as darkness fell.

The scraping sound of a key in a lock woke her shortly after dawn. She sprang awake instantly, scurrying to wedge herself in the corner.

Glenna came in first, followed by an old man Alayna recognized as the one who had taken her from Gastonbury. Glenna gave Alayna a smug look as she assessed her captive cringing, terrified, in the corner.

"She is awake. Give her the food, Jasper."

The smelly old man came forward, and Alayna shrank away.

"She does not like you, Jasper," Glenna shrieked, a sharp, cutting sound.

"It don' matter, girl," he cackled. "Ye think she don' like me, jes' wait till she sees the master."

"Hush," Glenna snapped, truly angry. And a little afraid, Alayna saw. "He told us not to speak of him."

A stale loaf of bread was thrust at her. Though she was loath to take the food from his grimy hands, her stomach would not permit her to indulge her pride. She snatched it, tearing off handfuls immediately and stuffing them into her mouth, trying not to think about the filthy old man having handled it. "May I have water?" she whispered.

No one answered, but Jasper left, presumably to fetch her some. Glenna came closer as Alayna continued to tear ravenously into the loaf.

"How do you fare, my grand lady?" she sneered gleefully. "I can see our baron now as he rides off valiantly to your rescue. He has a surprise waiting for him. It is very touching, really it is. He goes off to save you, ready to risk all for true love."

"You are mistaken if you think he loves me. He will not come for me." She was not sure if she believed that or not, but apparently she was convincing enough for the girl to hesitate.

Alayna's mind had fastened onto something Glenna had said. A surprise? Had they set a trap for Lucien? "What surprise?" she asked.

Glenna was too shrewd not to pick up on her worry. "Oh, my master would not like it if I spoiled his fun, for it is a surprise for you as well." She leaned back, sighing. "I was so disappointed when John didn't get you out of the castle for good. He promised me he would. He said he would see you never returned. I was so happy, then, but Lord Lucien—he was so angry! I had thought that he would turn to me." She brightened, an evil gleam coming into her eyes. "And yet, I find I have another chance. John told me of someone who could help me. And I helped him. And this is much, much better."

She didn't seem to be making sense, but Alayna recognized important information was couched in her rambling thoughts. She mulled this over as she finished her bread. When Jasper returned with her water, she gulped it down and asked for more. He fetched it and she had just enough time to drink before Glenna hauled her up and bound her wrists behind her back.

Another puff of powder sent her back into slumber, dimly aware for a while of being slung over the back of a horse before the darkness consumed her completely.

Consciousness came again in the full sun of midday. Her headache was there, and so was her hunger. Both had gotten worse.

She was on the ground somewhere out in the open, her hands still bound behind her back and she was not alone. Voices floated on the air from behind her. Glenna and Jasper. And a third. Deep and authoritative and strangely, hauntingly familiar...

This was their master. He was here with them now, she realized.

She struggled to roll over. She wanted to see her enemy, the one whose orders held her captive. Something dreadful was forming inside her, a hideous suspicion. That voice.

"Ah, the good Lady Alayna is awake!"

Footsteps, then a boot wedged into her underside and prodded her onto her back so that she rolled and saw her kidnapper at last.

A shriek tore from her throat to take life in the trees and echo into the forest. It sounded in the quiet of the wood, and not far away, Lucien heard it and spurred his destrier to move faster.

Alayna's reaction won her a mirthless laugh from her kidnapper. Edgar du Berg, the presumed-to-be-dead Lord of Gastonbury, stood before her.

"What a greeting from my merry widow, would you not say, Jasper?"

The disgusting man cackled. Edgar looked terrible, bent and small, quite different from the blustering brute who had forced her into marriage. His face was thin, his frame near to emaciated. He noticed her horrified assessment and nodded.

"Yes, it is pathetic, is it not? My handsomeness is gone, and my health nearly, as well. Your new husband did this to me. Oh, I forgot, he is not your husband in truth." The ruined mouth stretched in what used to be a charming smile but what was now a grotesque twisting of the slack lips. "I am."

"You are dead," she said finally.

Edgar laughed again. "Oh, no, dear wife. Not dead. Your new baron did not kill me, as you see. He did run me through, to be sure, but fate decreed that near-fatal blow miss the vital organ that it had been aiming for. The physician who attended me could not explain it, saying that perhaps my innards are not properly arranged as they should be. That may very well be, as I am rumored to have no heart. Who is to say the rest of me is not similarly missing? I myself chose to believe it was divine providence."

His hard eyes studied her revulsion. "I may never regain all that blow cost me. But I could not wait my vengeance to find out. It is amusing, is it not, wife? De Montregnier returns from the dead to kill me out of his quest for revenge, and now I rise out of my grave for a vengeance of my own?"

Alayna could barely comprehend what she was hearing, what she was seeing before her very eyes.

This, then, was the trap they had set.

As if her thought had conjured him, her husband's voice suddenly sounded in the thick forest mist like a blade slicing through flesh.

"I am here," the deep timbre rang out. "I have come

alone. Show yourselves, and show me also that my wife is well.''

Edgar's mouth twisted, his eyes glowed. Reaching down, he grabbed a fistful of her clothing and pulled her roughly to her feet. With a shake, he brought her face only inches from his. "Keep yourself quiet, bitch, and do exactly what I say. Your life is worth nothing to me but the vengeance it will bring. Glenna tells me he loves you, and so you will serve me well. But dare defy me, and you will die.''

She would have spat at him, but he spun her around, shoving her ahead of him as they walked out of the shelter of the trees to the bank of the lake. Across the water, she saw Lucien waiting beside his great warhorse.

He looked calm, standing with his legs spread wide, his arms folded before him. When Alayna and Edgar stepped out from behind the cover of the trees, his casual facade dropped.

"Du Berg!''

Edgar smiled wickedly. "Aye, my lord baron,'' he called mockingly. "'Tis I and my lovely wife, Alayna.''

"I killed you!''

"Wrong, de Montregnier, though just barely did you fail. You foolishly entrusted my body to some men who were faithful to me. When they discovered I had survived, they saw me to a physician.''

Lucien stared mutely at his enemy, his confused thoughts whirling in undisciplined tumult. He tried to concentrate, but the look of terror on Alayna's face distracted him. "What is it you want?'' he called at last.

Edgar shrugged. "A simple bargain. I hold here our dear Alayna. I was once quite entranced by her beauty. But I tire of her spirited ways. So I seek a simple trade.''

"Let me guess."

"Oh, I am certain it is quite obvious. Her freedom for your life."

Lucien smiled.

"Du Berg, that is a ridiculous proposal. As my wife will tell you, I married her only for personal gain, to solidify my claim to your shire. There is nothing more between us, and I keep her benefit whether she lives or dies. You speak the truth when you say she has a wicked tongue. 'Twas a great relief to me when the message arrived of her being abducted, but Henry's justiciar was still in residence and it would look unseemly if I did not at least attempt the rescue."

"Liar!" Glenna's voice rang out. "He loves her, I tell you."

"Glenna," Lucien groaned, "you have persisted in that belief because you could not accept the fact that I did not desire you. It had naught to do with my wife, but that you simply did not interest me."

"Nay! Nay! I was to be your leman until you—"

"Never," Lucien snapped coldly.

"You were consumed by her before you wed. I sneaked upon you one night—you cried her name out when you slept."

"No doubt I was having a nightmare," he said, and shrugged.

"Enough!" Edgar roared. "De Montregnier, will you surrender in exchange for your lady's life?"

It was Lucien's turn to swagger. "Du Berg, you err. She is not my wife, she is yours. Therefore I will lose no honor if I fail in this rescue."

Stunned and mute in disbelief, Edgar and Alayna

watched as he mounted the destrier and kicked the great horse forward, calling over his shoulder, "Good luck!"

And with that he rode off.

In the silence that ensued, Alayna stood numb. Enough doubt existed in her heart to cause a single tear to roll down her cheek. She struggled not to succumb to despair. As Eurice would tell her, she had to believe.

But he had been very, very convincing.

She was not even aware that Edgar had released her and stalked away toward his small band of men, a group of five ragged miscreants. He was as confused and bewildered as she.

Glenna, devastated by Lucien's cruel admonishment, collapsed into a heap and began to rock back and forth, keening shrilly. Du Berg glared at her, then after a moment's consideration, he took a sword from one of his men and strode up behind her. With a flash of steel he brought the weapon down to bear with all the fury of his frustration, and the mad girl fell silent forever.

Stuffing her hands in her mouth to stem her scream, Alayna trembled at the thought she might be next. Edgar looked at her as if he were wondering the same thing, but he went back to commiserate with his cronies.

It was only a matter of time before he would dispatch her as remorselessly as he had Glenna. After all, if Lucien didn't want her back, she was of no use as an instrument of revenge.

Without any warning, a thunderously loud crash sounded and the ground trembled. From out of the trees, a horse and rider emerged in one clean leap to land squarely in the middle of the camp. With his sword already drawn, the rider skillfully maneuvered the steed over to several of the men. The trained warhorse reared up on its hind legs to trample three of the men while his rider wielded the great broadsword to bring down the others.

It was over in a minute. Then the rider turned to face Edgar, who stood alone.

Lucien smiled, offering a slight bow to du Berg. He dared risk not so much as a glance to Alayna, keeping his eyes on his enemy.

Edgar's look was bitter. "So you do have some interest in the lady?"

Lucien did not answer. He looked far different from the casual fellow he had appeared to be across the lake. His face was unreadable. His only response was to lift his sword to his old nemesis's chest.

"Would you kill an unarmed man?" Edgar said slyly.

Lucien's eyes narrowed. Dismounting, he unsheathed his dagger from his belt and tossed it to his opponent.

"Now do you consider us fairly matched?" Lucien snapped impatiently.

"Aye." Du Berg nodded craftily, obviously excited that his opponent had fallen so easily for his trick.

"Good," Lucien commented. Without further preamble and without error, he deftly sank his sword deep into the man's throat, slicing cleanly into the artery. The blood spurted out to drench Edgar's tunic, soaking him in an instant. As the realization of death dawned, his look turned from dismay into an expression of immeasurable terror as he contemplated the just rewards of his life.

Taking back his sword, Lucien observed the gaping hole left in its wake. He noted with satisfaction the torrential outflow of life's blood spilling forth from the fatal wound, watching until at last his adversary fell facedown in the dirt, there to die.

"Now, let us see if you can find a physician to heal you from that."

He stepped away, stooping momentarily to retrieve his dagger. Within a flash, he was before Alayna, crouching down to where she lay on the hard forest floor. Without a word, he passed his short blade over her bindings to free her hands. As soon as this was done, he swept her into his arms.

She pressed closer, savoring the steely embrace as his arms crushed her to him. She wanted to shout her relief, her joy, but her emotions had no voice. She merely clung to him, glad to be alive and safe in his embrace and giddy with the knowledge that he had, after all, come for her.

He pulled away, taking her face in his large hands to stare fiercely into her tear-filled eyes. They swam before him like pools of emerald.

"Did you believe my ploy that I did not want you?" he asked. She nodded, still unable to speak. "I told you, lady. I will always come for you."

She smiled, and the sob broke free from her at last. "You were rather convincing!"

Lucien nodded silently, drawing her up to stand with him. "Come away," he prodded gently, and they walked to his horse. Lifting her onto the destrier's back, he swung up behind her, and they left death behind them as they rode toward Gastonbury.

Sighing, she leaned her head against the hard chest while he cradled her fiercely in his arms. How she loved this man, her husband.

Nay, not husband. Her love, to be sure, but now there was nothing legal to bind them. She found that she could not banish her fears after all.

Just before they cleared the woods, Lucien stopped, dismounted and pulled her down to the ground with him. "Before we return, we must set things aright," he announced.

"Yes," she answered.

"There is something you must know," he said. He stood staring back at her, so unsure of himself that it showed. "Listen to me, Alayna. When I found you were taken, I cursed myself, and my damnable pride." Reaching out, he took her hands in his. "I punished you unfairly and I hurt you deeply, I know. I can never take those things away, except to beg your forgiveness and pray you will give it."

The tears slipped unchecked down her cheeks. He cocked his head to one side as he wiped the wetness away.

"I can see that this news comes somewhat unexpected. I can tell you, I was no less surprised to find out the truth of it myself. It was a difficult thing to come to terms with. Love has not been a part of my life for a very long time. I...it was hard for me to accept."

"You love me?" she asked incredulously.

"Hopelessly, I am afraid."

Aye, it was there in his eyes. If she had not known it before, it was here now, for he was saying it outright, and it was real and true and somehow wondrously and completely believable.

"Lucien, I love you, as well," she said. "I have for a time. I would have spoken of my heart, but I was afraid."

"Aye," he nodded. "I know I have behaved badly."

"Badly?" she cried. "More like an incredibly stupid, totally ignorant buffoon whose brain challenges the least—"

"I quite get the idea, madam."

"Well, you were horrid!" she declared, half teasing, half serious.

"Aye, my love, and I will make it up to you. We will have a lifetime to make amends." Lucien suddenly became tentative. "Unless you wish to return to London."

She met his gaze warily. She wanted him to forbid her to leave him, to beg her to stay.

"Do you wish me to leave?" she prodded, waiting breathlessly for his response.

"Of course I do not, what kind of idiot would I be to wish that? Nay—do not answer that." He cast her a self-deprecating look that won him a quick smile. "I just finished declaring my heart. Of course I want you to stay. I want you with me, always." Letting out a groan, he raked his hand through his hair. "Dear God, I am doing almost as terrible a job of this as I did the first time."

"On the contrary. You are doing quite well."

He took her face in his hands again, his eyes caressing her warmly as his voice spoke in a hoarse whisper. "Alayna, please marry me. Again. Because I love you, and I cherish you, and I do not wish to face a future without you."

Her smile was brilliant. "Aye, my love, I will indeed marry you however many times it takes to stick."

Epilogue

The anticipation of Alayna's third wedding day was very different from the previous two. It was filled with all the gaiety and excitement the joyous occasion warranted.

They began making arrangements the moment they returned to Gastonbury. To Alayna's shock, her mother was thoroughly pleased with the prospect of the marriage. She wondered at this drastic change of heart, but whenever she asked after it, her mother only pressed her lips together and refused to answer.

The only thing to mar their happiness was that Veronica insisted that they stay in separate chambers until after the wedding. Despite the months they had spent together as man and wife, Alayna was forced to lie alone in her chamber of old, restless and yearning for the feel of a long, hard body pressed close up against her, fiery kisses and hands, large and calloused, smoothing over her skin. The wait was nearly unbearable, making the days pass with leaden slowness.

Wyndham, Henry's justiciar, was favorably impressed with Lucien's barony, especially in contrast to the horrifying reports of abuse under his predecessor. He had passed his verdict, declaring that he would recommend to Henry that Lucien remain as the Lord of Gastonbury.

"I owe much of it to you," Lucien told Alayna. "Your efforts, I know, made a difference."

"What efforts?" Alayna wondered, pressing closer as she sat in the circle of his arms. They had ridden out together to picnic on the grassy banks of the river. Neither one was much interested in the basket stuffed with venison and pies, preferring to recline together in the shade of a tree and bask in the stolen moment alone.

"Wyndham was most impressed with my richly garbed peasants. That was your doing, as I recall, though the proponents of the sumptuary laws would be astonished at such finery on the lowly masses, no matter how well concealed. But I suppose there was only so much you could do to alter Edgar's clothes."

Alayna's jaw dropped. "How long have you known?" she gasped.

"For some time. It dawned on me that Edgar's chamber was much emptier that it had been when we were in there the first time. I admit, I did not suspect you at first, for my initial thought was of looters. But then there was this remarkable act of charity you seemed so enthusiastic about. And there was the question of where you had gotten the means to dispense this great treasure of clothing to the poor."

"Then you knew all the time!"

Lucien chuckled as he nodded, extremely interested in a lock of hair he had wound around a finger.

"And you were not angry?" she asked, amazed at this disclosure.

"I had no need for the garments. I probably would have done the same thing with them had it been up to me. Besides, I was interested in taming you, and I thought that the satisfaction from your game would occupy you."

"You cad!" Alayna laughed, pushing at his broad chest in mock indignation. "And to think of all of those times I quaked with fear that you would find me out. All of the plotting! You could have told me you approved!"

"And spoil all the fun of it—nay, madam, I would not have dared."

On the evening before the wedding, all were gathered in the hall when Agravar stood, his cup raised. "A toast to our lord, Lucien de Montregnier. And to his departed enemies, may they serve as warning to all who would challenge us in the future!"

Everyone drank, except Lucien, who considered his longtime friend. He accepted the toast, then rose and lifted his cup as the hall hushed to hear his words.

"To Agravar, a Viking, who we will all welcome as the new Lord of Thalsbury."

Agravar raised his hand against the shouts that sounded at the good news.

"Nay," he said seriously. "I decline."

A shocked silence fell. Lucien frowned darkly. "Explain," he demanded.

"I have no wish for the responsibilities of lord. I would be content to remain here as captain of the guard."

The crowd murmured a chorus of approval. The eased tension was no less evident on Lucien's face when he nodded his assent. After a moment of consideration, he swung around to Will, who sat at his usual spot on Alayna's other side.

"Then Sir Will, will you accept the offer and serve me as the lord of my old home?" he asked.

Will stood. "I would be honored," he stammered, then his eyes narrowed, a sure sign of his mischievous nature asserting itself. "But does this mean that I must call you 'lord?'"

Lucien laughed. "Aye, you must. And I will look forward with special anticipation to your yearly homage and term of service. Be assured, I will keep aside special tasks just for you."

The new castellan extended his hand to clasp his overlord's arm, laughing good-naturedly. "Then I accept."

"Good!" Lucien declared, and the hall erupted once again in a chorus of cheers. Cups were refilled and toast after toast was made.

Amidst these celebrations, a woman entered the hall. She wore a hooded cloak but stood rigid as she advanced toward the dais. She commanded the attention of those she passed, and when she stopped at the spot immediately in front of Lucien, the crowd quieted and glanced among themselves nervously to see if anyone knew the mysterious woman's identity.

The lord of the castle regarded the intruder calmly, awaiting her introduction.

She withdrew the hood, and those who were long in the shire gasped. Lucien stood, covering his shock. "Mother," he said tightly.

"Lucien," she breathed. "I have come to renew my plea for forgiveness. I beg you to do this if you have any pity in you. On this night, the eve of your wedding, when your heart is full of joy and goodwill, shall you not find it within yourself to grant me the peace I seek?"

Her words echoed in the silence of the lofty room. Alayna glanced anxiously at her beloved, her old fears bubbling up to threaten her once again. She held her breath as he regarded Isobol for an interminable amount of time. The woman stood under his fierce countenance bravely, unblinking against the daggers of his eyes.

"Lucien," Alayna said quietly, that one word a plea.

He looked at her, staring for a long moment. "Pelly!" he shouted.

The young knight leaped to his feet. "Aye, my lord."

Turning again to his mother, he said, "Have the stewards set a place for my mother at the end of my table."

Alayna breathed a sigh, exchanging a heavy look of relief with her own mother as Lucien resumed his seat. She reached for his hand, giving it a grateful squeeze.

The following morn, Lucien and Alayna spoke their solemn vows to each other for the second time in the grand chapel of Gastonbury. With joy and reverence, they promised themselves to each other until death and beyond.

Eurice was there, smiling her blessings, and Hubert and Mellyssand kissed her and congratulated her. Veronica watched her daughter's happiness with serene pride.

Afterward, Isobol was prompted to relay stories of Lucien as a boy. She reluctantly complied, all too conscious of Lucien's lingering resentment. Nevertheless, she was persuaded and eventually warmed to the task. Her eyes glowed with pride as she relayed how he learned to wield his sword at the tender age of seven on four groomsmen at once, setting them all fleeing for their lives. He had delighted, it was told, in terrifying the older lads who had, up to that point, teased him unmercifully.

"So you were a brute even then," Alayna whispered to Lucien, her beautiful eyes sparkling with merriment. The tickle of her breath against his ear made Lucien's eyes darken with desire.

"I fear if we are forced to await our marriage bed much

longer, all here will give witness to just what a brute I can be," he promised.

As soon as was decently possible, Lucien grabbed his wife's hand and bade farewell to their company. His look bespoke that he would bear none of the traditional games played on newlyweds.

He was hard-pressed to wait until they had closed the door behind them to sweep her up against him in a crushing embrace.

"Now you are mine," he said roughly. "Nothing will come between us again."

Smiling, she reached up to slip her arms about his neck. "I fear there is one thing that will come between us, my lord." Then she fell to giggling.

He looked down at her quizzically. "What are you talking about?"

"I was referring to my belly, of course. When it swells, it shall prevent you from holding me this close."

"Belly?" he repeated stupidly.

"Aye, from the babe."

"Babe?"

Alayna pretended to frown at him. "Aye, babe. Really, Lucien, you are going to have to learn to catch on more quickly if you are to teach our son. And quickly, too, for he will arrive in about six months' time."

A slow smile spread over his face and he shook his head. "Nay, no son yet. First I want a daughter with flashing eyes to rival the most priceless emeralds. And long hair of burnished chestnut like her mother's. We will have plenty of time to work on sons after that."

Cocking her head to one side, she said, "You who have such aversion to women now wish to add another to your life?"

He lowered his head to her neck, ignoring the gasp of delight as his lips brushed her ear. "Let us say that *aversion* is something I have gotten over. I find that the company of a woman with whom one shares certain…passions can be most rewarding."

"Most rewarding," she murmured. When he stopped his kisses, she looked at him, disappointed.

"Now, my lady wife, before we proceed with this night, are you quite sure that you want an addle-brained warhorse like myself? You have been telling me so long how much you want to be away from me, I want to be sure your recent change of heart is still in effect."

Reaching up for him, she sighed happily. "Though I may be daft to do it, I am quite sure that my decision is permanent."

"Forever?" he asked.

She answered his kiss, as always, with a hunger of her own. She recognized the feelings taking hold of her again and, just before reality dissolved, she whispered, "Forever."

* * * * *

Coming in March 1998
from *New York Times* bestselling author

Jennifer Blake

**The truth means everything to Kane Benedict.
Telling it could destroy Regina Dalton's son.**

Down in Louisiana, family comes first—that's the rule
the Benedicts live by. So when a beautiful redhead starts
paying a little bit too much attention to his grandfather,
Kane decides to find out what the woman really wants.

But Regina's not about to tell Kane the truth—that she's
being blackmailed and the extortionist wants Kane's
grandfather's business...or that the life of her son is
now at stake.

Available where books are sold.

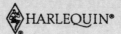

Not The Same Old Story!

 Exciting, glamorous romance stories that take readers around the world.

HARLEQUIN PRESENTS®

Harlequin Romance® Sparkling, fresh and tender love stories that bring you pure romance.

HARLEQUIN® *Temptation* Bold and adventurous—Temptation is strong women, bad boys, great sex!

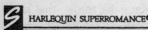 HARLEQUIN SUPERROMANCE® Provocative and realistic stories that celebrate life and love.

 Contemporary fairy tales—where anything is possible and where dreams come true.

HARLEQUIN® INTRIGUE® Heart-stopping, suspenseful adventures that combine the best of romance and mystery.

Love & Laughter™ Humorous and romantic stories that capture the lighter side of love.

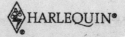